C000149073

PRAISE FOR DEAR HERO

"Put on the AC/DC soundtrack and grab your superhero cape! Hope Bolinger and Alyssa Roat deliver a hilarious, punchy, one-of-a-kind smash—the perfect read for Marvel and DC Comic fans. *Dear Hero* dazzles with its brilliant wit, irony, and loveable characters. Few other books have tugged at my heartstrings and made me laugh out loud, ranking *Dear Hero* as one of my favorite reads of 2020."

—Caroline George, author of *Dearest Josephine* (TNZ Fiction, HarperCollins)

"Playfully epic, adorably dark—a fun and witty ride."

—AJ Vanderhorst, author of *The Mostly Invisible Boy*

"A witty and compelling story, packaged in a delightfully unique form. I enjoyed it!"

—Kerry Nietz, award-winning author of *Amish Vampires in Space*

"*Dear Hero* is a fresh take on a modern superhero tale. It's complete with heroes, villains, romance, and epic humor. I thoroughly enjoyed every minute of this journey! If these ladies produce another book within this universe, it will be on my auto-buy list."

—Laura Zimmerman, award-winning author of *Keen*

"That was a delightful read. I laughed aloud so many times! Punchy, witty, fast paced, and unputdownable—*Dear Hero* is one of the best books I've read this year. Nicely done."

—Michele Israel Harper, award-winning editor and author of *Kill the Beast*

"*Dear Hero* begins with a hilarious concept—a dating-style website but with the goal of pairing up heroes with their perfect nemeses—and delivers in a big way! With a cleverly constructed narrative via text messages, Bolinger and Roat carry out a funny, fast-paced plot with authentically flawed and likeable characters. V and Cortex may struggle with what it means to be a hero, but their reader fans are sure to champion their story with superhero-level enthusiasm!"

—Kristiana Sfirlea, author of *The Stormatch Diaries: Legend of the Storm Sneezer*

"*Dear Hero* is a unique take on the superhero genre. Instead of explosions and fist fights, get to the behind-the-scenes of a hero and villain trying to match in an online service. Through their messages and texts, read about the up-and-coming Cortex and villainous Vortex. Will these two find a true nemesis in each other, or will their pairing be doomed? Enjoy a funny and romantic romp that turns superhero tropes on their heads."

—Jason C. Joyner, author of *Launch*

"*Dear Hero* is a witty, page-turning send-up of superheroes and social media and rom-coms. That last sentence was a fancy way of saying it's funny. And charming. And action-packed. If Rainbow Rowell wrote an Avengers screenplay, it might look an awful lot like this book."

—Patrick Hueller, author of *Kirsten Howard's Biggest Fan*

"A fun, fast-paced story, *Dear Hero* takes superhero tropes and tosses them to the sharks. This cast of flawed heroes includes an eighty-five-year-old henchmen, shark-serenading villains, and sidekicks who stink at brewing coffee, leap off the page, and stay with the reader long after 'the end.' Young love meets battles to the death in a quirky rom-com of heroic proportions."

—Jaimie Engle, award-winning author of *Dreadlands*

"*Dear Hero* is an imaginative, unique twist on the superhero genre that will leave readers of all ages reading deep into the night. Hope Bolinger and Alyssa Roat have flipped the genre on its head. *Dear Hero* offers the reader a peek into the backstage life of a hero trying to find the perfect villain. The characters, dialogue, and humor sizzle throughout the pages. As the old saying goes: It blew my mind!"

—J.J. Johnson, author of *Iggy and Oz: The Plastic Dinos of Doom*

"A clever, fantastic peek at what goes on behind the scenes between hero and villain, *Dear Hero* tells a great story while putting a unique spin on a number of tropes that ultimately keeps readers telling themselves, 'okay, just one more text.'"

—Galen Surlak-Ramsey, author of *The Gorgon Bride* and *Apocalypse How?*

"From the moment I opened *Dear Hero* I just knew I was in for a thrill-ride. It's laugh-out-loud funny, but criminally genius one-liners aside, this book had all the ingredients of a true hero story, with colourful characters that packed a punch—literally—and enough heart, soul, and delicious moral conflict to give me all the feels I crave. Seriously, a total must for any superhero-obsessed-fan who ever looked at their favourite and thought . . . what is going on inside their head?"

—CJ Campbell, award-winning writer and FanFic Favourite, CJCampbellOfficial.com

"*Dear Hero* is a wholly original novel that shakes up the classic storyline of 'hero versus villain' and delves into themes of 'good' and 'evil' in a fresh, fun way. I was immediately drawn in by the winsome voices of the characters, and the fast-paced plot kept me guessing right up until the satisfying conclusion. A must-read for superhero fans!"

—Dallas Woodburn, author of *The Best Week That Never Happened*

"What a creative idea! *Dear Hero* has engaging characters and a great story full of quips, twists, and a fresh look at superhero tropes. Loved it. Read this book!"

—Britt Mooney, author of *Say Yes: How God-Sized Dreams Take Flight*

"*Dear Hero* is an immensely clever take on the superhero genre. Funny, heartfelt, and enjoyable throughout."

—Michael Hilton, author of *Bobby Robot*

"Swipe Right for *Dear Hero*! A fun concept where Heroes and Villains are matched through a website. We get a behind the scenes look at the hero game, filled with humor, action, and wait . . . even a touch of romance! I look forward to whatever Bolinger and Roat do next!"

—Jonathan Rosen, author of *Night of the Living Cuddle Bunnies*

OTHER BOOKS IN THE DEAR HERO SERIES

Dear Hero

Dear Henchman

Coming Soon:

Dear Hades

DEAR HENCHMAN

HOPE BOLINGER
ALYSSA ROAT

Love2ReadLove2Write Publishing, LLC
Indianapolis, Indiana

Hope's Dedication:
To Linda Taylor, a positive and radiant gem.
Everyone often thinks of an editor as a sidekick to helping a book succeed.
We all know they're actually the hero.

Alyssa's Dedication:
To Stephanie, not my henchman,
but my partner in crime.
You've got the heart and strength of a hero.

Copyright © 2022 Hope Bolinger and Alyssa Roat

Published by Love2ReadLove2Write Publishing, LLC

Indianapolis, Indiana

www.love2readlove2writepublishing.com

All rights reserved. No part of this publication may be reproduced, stored in a retrieval system, or transmitted in any form or by any means—for example, electronic, photocopy, recording—without the prior written permission of the publisher. The only exception is brief quotations in printed reviews.

Library of Congress Cataloging-in-Publication Data is on file at the Library of Congress, Washington, DC.

Paperback ISBN: 978-1-943788-62-0

Ebook ISBN: 978-1-943788-63-7

LCCN: 2021948191

This is a work of fiction. Names, characters, incidents, and dialogues are products of the author's imagination and are not to be construed as real. Any resemblance to actual events or persons, living or dead, is entirely coincidental.

Cover Design by Kirk DouPonce of DogEared Design

META-MATCH

Every Hero Needs a Sidekick

———

Every Villain Needs a Henchman

PRIVATE MESSAGE
JUNE 6

6:47 PM
Himari: Kevin, you're friends with that pizza guy Billy, right?

> **Kevin:** If by friends you mean he cheats off my Calc home-work, and I steal his Red Bull from his dorm when he isn't looking, then yeah. Why?

6:48 PM
Himari: Well, V just kind of ... impaled him?

Himari: She feels awful.

> 6:49 PM
> **Kevin:** Is he ... in a better place now?

> **Kevin:** Like, is he lying in pain on Caleb's fabulous front porch? Or did he fall into the mildew-filled pool?

Himari: I thought cleaning the pool was part of your chores.

6:50 PM
Himari: Anyway, he's kind of on the grass right now. V was doing her target practice throwing knives in the backyard and he came around the corner and … yeah.

Kevin: I don't know why we went for pizza. I'm more of a taco person, anyway. So lemme guess, the sidekick's gotta go in and save the day?

Kevin: Where did V put that medical kit?

6:51 PM
Himari: I gave it to you to bring with you to chem lab. That's why I'm texting you.

Kevin: Oh, haha. Totally. Just gonna look in my bag for it. Lol. Silly me.

6:52 PM
Kevin: How would Billy feel about a Dora the Explorer Band-Aid I found on the floor? It's mostly sticky still.

Himari: Are you telling me that you lost my state-of-the-art fast-healing first aid kit? Because if you are …

Kevin: Haha. Um, nooooo. I'm just thinking that Billy is probably a villain anyways. Cheated off my Calc tests. Probably shouldn't get him healed anyway.

6:53 PM
Kevin: Hypothetically …

Kevin: If I were to lose it, what would you do?

Himari: …

Himari: You realize I work for a villain.

Himari: The very villain who just hit this guy in the back with a knife.

Himari: SIGH. Just get the regular kit then. Looks like we're going to the hospital. Again.

6:54 PM
Kevin: No problem-o. Want me to pick up some fast food on the way over?

Kevin: With my minimum wage sidekick budget I can go really fancy ... KFC. Boo-yah.

Himari: Billy is bleeding out and Caleb looks like he's going to vomit. Just get your butt down here. I see you watching through the window.

6:55 PM
Kevin: Got it. Colonel Sanders can wait for that sweeping romantic moment, I guess. Tacos are more of a romantic food anyway.

Kevin: ... Be down in one minute.

THE FABULOUS FOUR
JUNE 6

11:37 PM
Vicky: Kevin, I am so sorry. I didn't even see him come around the corner. He walked right in front of the target.

> **Kevin:** Yeah, well, Billy isn't the brightest bulb. And that's scary coming from me.

> **Kevin:** You guys still at the hospital? How's the ole cheater holding up?

Vicky: Pretty well—wait. Who changed my name to Vicky?!

> 11:38 PM
> **Caleb Ate the Last Popsicle and Stinks:** I don't know. I think it's kinda cute.

> *Vicky changed name to V*

V: Ha. Ha. Very cute. *rolls eyes* Anyway, Billy is doing okay. Not pressing charges, so that's a plus.

11:39 PM
Kevin: Probs because he doesn't like phone calls. Or lawyers.

Kevin: Sorry V, I know you were trying to keep a low profile. Especially with Caleb's parents tracking down those Shadow Assassin whack jobs. Those shady, shady villain bois.

Caleb Ate the Last Popsicle and Stinks changed name to Caleb

11:40 PM
Caleb: Speaking of shady …

Caleb: V wouldn't have hit him if SOMEONE remembered to set lights on over the target practice range. You know it's in a shady area, Kev.

   Kevin: Yeah, Himari!

11:41 PM
Hottttari: Excuse me, Caleb gave you that job like three weeks ago.

Hottttari: Kevin! Stop messing with the group chat names!

Hottttari changed name to Himari

11:42 PM
Kevin: Look, it's not my fault, guys. You keep giving me super lame jobs. You'd think being a sidekick/intern for a superhero would be more exciting than scraping scum out of the pool, turning on lights, and cleaning up Fluffy's litter box.

Kevin: V, that was a terrible name for a hairless cat.

11:43 PM
V: It's called irony, Kevin.

V: I kind of agree though, Caleb. You should give him a more exciting job. Himari gets to help me teach the sharks tricks.

11:44 PM
Kevin: WHAT?

Kevin: You don't let me near those things. In fact, you yelled at me last time I sang "Under the Sea" for them. I have to practice for those theater auditions somehow …

V: You were hurting their ears.

Kevin: …

11:45 PM
Caleb: Listen, I'd like to give you more responsibilities, Kev, but you can't even brew coffee right.

Kevin: Yes I can.

Caleb: Putting coffee beans in hot water and calling it "bean juice" does not count. I'm already on edge enough and need actual coffee in the mornings. I swear, sometimes my powers are the only things that keep me sane with a sidekick like you.

V: Himari makes frappuccinos sometimes. Those are awesome.

Himari: Best Google search ever.

11:46 PM
Kevin: Come on, Caleb, just give me something that actually gets me excited to get up in the morning and put on my Batman boxers. Not all of us have cool powers like you and need something more to get us out of bed in the mornings.

Caleb: Haven't you had those boxers since seventh grade?

Kevin: That's beside the point.

Caleb: Kevin, you're entering your final years of college.

11:47 PM
Caleb: Fine, I guess I can give you something else. The parents should still be in Canada a while tracking down the SA, so I'm sure we have plenty to do.

Caleb: V, any suggestions?

> **V:** Since I'm heading off to study great whites in Australia and taking Himari with me, maybe take him with you somewhere?

11:48 PM
Caleb: Oh, right. I almost forgot that was happening. You're the other thing keeping me sane, V. You going to leave your pet sharks all alone in the house?

> **V:** I hired a sitter.

Kevin: Is someone just going to sit on them?

11:49 PM
Kevin: Yeehaw folks, I'm a shark-boy. Yippee!! Y'all. Beer and

tractors. That's all I got. We don't speak cowboy up here in Indiana.

V: Omg, you done now, Kevin? You guys remember that villain Fishman?

11:50 PM
Caleb: The one who wore a lion costume? Yeah, he was ... different.

V: Well, he actually understands the sharks! He even knew what sort of songs to sing for Gonzo.

Kevin: Lemme guess. Muppets.

11:51 PM
V: Yeah ... this is why you're not babysitting, Kevin. I think he's going to do great. <3

Caleb: I don't like that < paired with the 3. Also, does anyone know why we can't do emojis in this chat?

Himari: Because I haven't gotten there yet. You can't have everything on a super-secure messaging server no one else is on.

V: That's fine, Himari. You're doing fantastic.

11:52 PM
Kevin: See that, Caleb? Positive reinforcement. Maybe it would do you well to sing me some Muppet songs from time to time.

Caleb: Sigh. Fine, Kevin.

Caleb: Since V and Himari are heading out, I guess we can head someplace.

> 11:53 PM
> **Kevin:** YASSS, BRO TRIP. I CALL DOING THE CAR TUNES.

Caleb: …

Caleb: Are you talking about that playlist full of theater and Disney songs?

Caleb: THAT'S 9 HOURS LONG?

> **Kevin:** Yeah, I've really been slacking on updating it.

11:54 PM
Caleb: I mean it could be a long drive to Silicon Valley. Lux and Aurumque are busy right now. Those are my parents' superhero names, Kevin. Since you've somehow not been able to remember those. Dad took the helicopter, and the jet got destroyed on their mission to Egypt last year, so it's either that or riding one of V's sharks.

> **Kevin:** You know my vote. ;) Yeehaw.

11:55 PM
V: Touch my babies and die.

> **Caleb:** People in the waiting room are looking a little concerned about that death glare she's giving the phone for you, Kevin.

> **Caleb:** I love it when you get that murderous gleam in your eye.

Caleb: Oh, sorry, did I mind-text that into the chat?

11:56 PM
Kevin: I wonder if Great Guy is hiring …

Kevin: Why Silicon Valley?

Caleb: There's a convention for techies out there. Been eyeing it for a while, and I forgot V was out during it. Timing works. Plus, I figure with the whole I can control technology with my mind thing, it could be cool to check out.

Caleb: And, I got wind that one of the members of SA might be there. Could be useful to spy on him.

11:57 PM
Kevin: Where'd you hear those rumors?

Caleb sent a screenshot

Kevin: Nice. The dude literally wrote, "I'm heading to the TechieCon Event on June 10." Although he doesn't have a user-name. Just OpE84672. Probs forgot to customize it on Meta-Match.

Kevin: Whoa, wait, Meta-Match. That old hero and villain pairing app? Throwback!

V: I feel like it's mostly used by cosplayers as a dating app now. So two years ago, bro.

Kevin: Haha, yeeeeeah. Definitely don't use that app to access the Sidekick/Henchman Support Forums at all.

11:58 PM
Caleb: True, but it never hurts to try to find him (or her) at TechieCon. I guess we should pack our bags tomorrow when we get back from the hospital, eh? Also, Billy's healing remarkably fast. It's almost like the knife barely went in at all.

Himari: V and I are all packed. Note for the two males in this chat who seem to forget everything: we're literally leaving tomorrow morning.

Caleb: Wow. That fast?

Caleb: All right, I guess we can head out after I catch some sleep too. Get to packing, Kevin.

11:59 PM
Kevin: Got it! Already packed. I don't need anything but you, bro.

Caleb: Bro.

Caleb: Please pack clothing.

Kevin: No promises. ;)

PRIVATE MESSAGE

JUNE 7

1:07 AM
Kevin: UGH, with your parents not home …

Himari: Are V and Caleb making out on the couch again?

Kevin: Hence the text to you. I'm too scared to leave my room. V might send Fluffy after me for interrupting.

1:08 AM
Himari: You did literally interrupt their first kiss that night by listening to EVERYTHING. She's still a little salty.

Kevin: It was hilarious, okay?

1:09 AM
Kevin: Speaking of hilarious things, your brother and I on a road trip together … we're going to kill each other. Wish I were going with you instead.

Himari: Just try not to hit on him too much or he might hit you.

Kevin: Violently in love with me … I see.

1:10 AM
Kevin: I mean, first you go off to MIT a year early. It's like I've barely been able to see you, and now you're heading to Aussie to hang with the Crocodiles and Giant Spiders.

Kevin: It's like the most romantic place on earth. Totally unfair.

Himari: Don't worry, we'll be too busy chasing sharks to chase any menfolk.

1:11 AM
Kevin: I know, but they'll get you with that accent. I have a feeling my high-pitched yodel just doesn't quite measure up.

Himari: I've been at one of the country's top tech schools for the past year. Your yodel is … better than a lot of things you see with a whole bunch of geeks.

1:12 AM
Kevin: Well, promise you'll text when you can?

Kevin: And feed one of the Aussies to the sharks. You know. For educational purposes.

Himari: Omg, Kevin. You're supposed to be a sidekick, not a henchman, and here you are advocating murder.

Himari: I'll keep in touch, but just to make sure you don't do anything stupid and get my brother killed. I know he's a super-hero, but … you gotta watch out for him, okay? It makes me nervous when V isn't there to be scary for him.

HOPE BOLINGER & ALYSSA ROAT

1:13 AM
Kevin: Yeah, well, it doesn't help that he likes to throw himself into situations that are likely going to kill him. Lucky duck lets his powers save him all the time. Show off.

Himari: That does not comfort me.

Kevin: I'll try my darndest. Yeehaw. Y'all. Rhubarb.

Himari: Thanks, Kevin. I'm counting on you.

1:14 AM
Kevin: Lol, who isn't? ;)

KEVIN'S STICKY NOTES
JUNE 7

1:14 AM

Kevin: Oh gosh, she's counting on me. I hope I remember. I'm bad at remembering.

SIDEKICK SUPPORT GROUP FORUM

TOPIC: WHAT DO I DO IF I DEVELOP A CRUSH ON A HENCHMAN / VILLAIN?

Vega: Hey, guys, long time no post. I have a problem that I thought you all would understand. Crushes. Huge ones. I have one on my villain's henchman. It's sort of awkward because the villain can read body heat signatures, so she can tell my temperature changes when I'm around her henchman, but if she noticed, she isn't letting on. Maybe for leverage or something to use against my hero and me.

Anyways, I really like this guy. He's one of those henchmen who doesn't have any powers, but he makes up for it in smarts, and maybe I'm wrong, but I think I caught him flirting back with me.

Makes me wish I could also read body heat signatures ...

Should I go for it or hang back?

Everyone knows that an internship with a hero can mean everything. Making it big in the business, opens a lot of doors, and don't we all wish we can become heroes ourselves after paying dues? I remember all the hero wannabes at my college practically about killing each other for an internship with an A-list hero. Doesn't help that our Hero U required us to do 160 hours of a practicum with a hero.

Anyway, I always pictured myself fighting crime, but I also never meant to envision myself doing that and being with the henchman.

Help a helpless girl out?

ANSWER THREAD

Syracuse: Yeesh, you're starting to sound like a love interest. Don't become a DID (Damsel in Distress, for those new to the forums). Sorry, I know, rules state that I shouldn't use Henchmanese in here, so it seems more inclusive to the newbies. #Sorrynotsorry

Syracuse: Anyways, girl, you sound desperate. Everyone knows heroes try to avoid falling in love, especially with villains. Besides that one incident with Cortex and that V chick, it doesn't work out all that often. I say swipe left and get a cat. It's the only way heroes can cope.

> **Vega:** Yikes. Not quite the feedback I was hoping for, but sorry to hear if some villain hurt you.

Hera: Totally disagree with Syracuse. I say you stick it to your hero and go out with the henchman. If they cry foul, then dump their sorry butt. (Yes, read the rules, I know there's no swearing in here—see, Syracuse? Some of us actually follow the rules.) You can always find another hero. Everyone knows there's plenty of them. And if the henchman can't be man enough, dump his sorry butt too. Just dump a bunch of butts. That's my policy.

> **Vega:** Thanks, Hera. Although, question: Why's Syracuse in your profile pic?

Hera: Whoops, forgot to change it. Thought I would after I dumped his sorry butt, huh?

Vega: Oh, ummm, never mind.

Thiva: I won $3,000 from playing games on my apps, and you can too. Click this link to learn more about how to get these amazing prizes: www.gammercentrl.urg/7939500348

Vega: Thiva, I think you got hacked by some spambot or something.

Thiva: No spam. Glad you have good day, Veega.

Vega: You too, Mr. Spambot.

Chad: If you ask me, that henchman ain't worth your time, sweetheart. Now, if you would stop playing coy and ignoring our private messages, I'd love to tell you about how much we'd be a great pair. I'd take you to brunch and tell you about how pretty your blue eyes are. I'd buy you three dozen roses and take you on a boat ride in Venice. Say the word, and I'm yours, amore. <3 <3 <3

Vega: Chad, don't make me report you to the Admin again. I've told you, you're not my type.

Chad: I'm everyone's type, baby. That's literally my superpower. I get everyone to like me. Great Guy wishes he was me. Just let me take you on one coffee date, and you'll see that this loser you have goo-goo eyes for pales in comparison with a REAL hero.

Vega has reported this thread as potential spam

Kevin: Listen here, sidekicks and henchfolks, because here's the gouda cheese. I'm absolutely head over heels for my villain's henchwoman. We haven't run into any snags since our villain/hero started fighting over two years ago, and if a girl like her can fall for a guy in a fish costume like me, well, then I don't see why Vega doesn't have a chance.

Vega: Wow, that's great, Kevin! When did you two start dating?

Kevin: Dating?

Vega: You know, coffee dates, movies, running away from men who have chainsaws, that sort of thing.

Kevin: Oh, we haven't started dating. I don't even know if she actually likes me. But she hasn't tried to kill me whenever I've flirted. That's a good start.

Vega: Oh, um, thanks for your input, I guess.

KEVIN'S STICKY NOTES
JUNE 7

2:36 AM
Kevin: Yeah, maybe that answer thread could've gone a little better. Dang it, I was hoping to use a Gouda-related pickup line on Himari later ... better delete this sticky note before Caleb sees it with his mind. Although I do like this Sticky Notes app on my phone. It's like a Captain's Journal, but more sticky. That sounded weird. Aaaaand now we're deleting this.

Sticky Note has been moved to trash

KEVIN'S STICKY NOTES

Kevin changed "Kevin's Sticky Notes" to "Captain's Log"

Kevin: No, I can do better than that.

Kevin changed "Captain's Log" to "Kevin's Log"

11:04 AM
Kevin: Kevin's log at 1100 hours and twenty-one songs into the Break a Leg Playlist. I think Caleb really does want to break my leg, owing to the fact I've made him stop for the bathroom three times already, and we're only four hours into the trip. I don't know how he made the hotel arrangements and all that so fast, but with his ability to control technology, I'm sure he did it in his sleep. Probably the only thing giving him sleep, his powers. He says only three things keep him sane: driving, powers, and V. And apparently I do a horrible impression of his girlfriend, so he'll just have to cope with two out of three.

Kevin: Oh no, that can't be good. What kind of hotel did he book us in his sleep?

11:05 AM
Kevin: Anyway, according to him, we have a 35-hour drive to Silicon, so he wants to split it up into three days. We're taking turns driving, with me starting in command of the wheel.

Kevin: When I accidentally took a right-hand turn and set us back about half an hour, he took the wheel.

Kevin: I have a feeling the loser won't give it to me again.

11:06 AM
Kevin: But honestly, that's A-OK. We're approaching Chicago right now, and traffic doesn't look all that fun at this time.

Kevin: Although, hopefully we're stopping for lunch soon. Chicago pizza sounds nice. Tacos are always better, but hey, when in Illinois.

11:07 AM
Kevin: Caleb gave me a weird look when I asked if we could put honey on it.

Kevin: What? It's a thing.

Kevin: Plus his family is half-Japanese, so they have some odd dishes from time to time.

Kevin: I could be worse.

11:08 AM
Kevin: I could put candy corn on my pizza.

Kevin: Or worse … pineapple.

11:11 AM
Kevin: Apparently it's not a good idea to belt out a catchy song when he's trying to merge lanes.

11:14 AM
Kevin: He's shut off the music.

11:16 AM
Kevin: I don't know if I can last much longer.

KEVIN'S LOG

JUNE 7

1:11 PM
Kevin: Huh, I guess the time difference doesn't work on this thing. It's stuck in Indiana time. I guess Himari hasn't worked out all the kinks.

1:12 PM
Kevin: Anyway, stopped for lunch (no honey on the pizza, but lucky for us, Cortex likes some good ole pepperoni) and looked at a big silver bean. It's reflective and we could barely find a spot to look at it with all the tourists. Was gonna take a pic with it until Caleb got annoyed.

Kevin: Apparently naming the bean "Sean" and asking why it dies in every movie is "embarrassing" to Mr. Too Cool for Sidekicks Who Yell in Public.

Kevin: Like, I'm not even the weirdest thing we saw.

1:13 PM
Kevin: Some dude dressed up like Yoda was trying to sell tickets to something.

Kevin: And I don't think it was a Star Wars movie.

Kevin: *shudders*

1:14 PM
Kevin: Anyways, so here we are rolling along to the lovely silence that is suffocating the car. Caleb just stopped for gas, so I might make a break for the bathroom inside.

Caleb has entered Kevin's Log

Kevin: What the heck, man? This is a private Sticky Notes log of my adventures.

   Caleb: Did you forget the whole "I can control technology with my mind" thing?

Kevin: …

1:15 PM
Kevin: Do you mind?

   Caleb: What is this anyway? A diary?

Kevin: No.

   Caleb: What then?

1:16 PM
Kevin: It just happens to be a daily record of events and experiences in the life of Kevin whose last name is sadly not linked with any breakfast meats.

   Caleb: So … a diary.

Kevin: A manly one.

1:17 PM
Kevin: Don't you roll your eyes at me, mister!

   Caleb: Why are you writing in this anyway?

Kevin: Because SOMEONE vetoed the idea of me adding anything superhero related to my social media stories, since the press swarms you anytime we so much as put out a Yelp review. So I have to keep all the escapades somewhere.

Kevin: I can't even tell friends back at school about the cool stuff we did these past two years.

1:18 PM
Kevin: They all think I work at a movie theater.

   Caleb: I know, man, but we gotta keep things low profile.

Kevin: Yes, I know, I know, because the SA is going to come in dark clothing and start monologuing all over the place. I'll be right at home with the theatrefolk.

   1:19 PM
   Caleb: Okay, I know you're joking now, but I don't know if you're recalling the little detail that I almost died two years ago because of them.

   Caleb: And they got a hold of V. Plus, they had originally turned her into a villain in the first place. She's told me horror stories about their initiations.

   Caleb: We can't let that happen again.

1:20 PM
Kevin: Yeah, yeah, fine. Whatevs. I get it.

Kevin: Obviously I don't want to lose my hero and all that.

1:21 PM
Kevin: Because then I'd have to work at a movie theater.

   Caleb: OH, I get the Kevin and breakfast meats joke now.

Kevin: Took you a while.

1:22 PM
Kevin: What say you that we listen to "Something Rotten"?

   Caleb: What do you think we've been listening to this whole time with that playlist of yours?

Kevin: Hardy har har.

   Caleb: Heading into the station to grab some snacks.

1:23 PM
Kevin: Hey, why won't songs play?

Kevin: How are you doing this from inside the store??

Kevin: CALEB! YOU CONTROL FREAK, LET ME TURN ON MY MUSIC.

   1:27 PM
   Caleb: I'm checking out. Grabbed you some Snickers. They seemed like a fitting food for you.

Kevin: …

Caleb: Now how about we let me play some of my own playlists for a couple hours?

Kevin: Can I drive?

1:28 PM
Kevin: You're going to say, "Sure, you're driving me crazy, aren't you?"

Caleb: We know each other so well.

VORTIE AND CORTIE

JUNE 7

12:01 PM
Caleb: How many movies did Sean Bean die in?

Caleb changed V's name to Vortie

1:47 PM
Vortie: Very cute, dork. Um ... at least Lord of the Rings, I think? You know I don't pay attention to actors. Why?

1:48 PM
Caleb: Does Himari ever drive you crazy in public? Like, is it normal to be embarrassed by your sidekick/henchman?

Vortie: Ha! What did Kevin do now?

Vortie: And no, Himari is great.

1:49 PM
Caleb: Well, only as great as a younger sister can be. She takes way too long showers and leaves only cold water behind.

Caleb: Anyway, you don't want to know.

    Vortie: You know he tries … I think.

1:50 PM
Caleb: Yeah, I know. It's just, with getting that Rookie Award for Superheroes in New York last year, everyone's been eyeing my website, Insta, everything to make sure I don't screw up. Even though we've been lying low on social media, I still hired that one social media manager to make it look like I'm still active.

Caleb: He just posts the same pictures from all the things we've done these past two years, but I don't think anyone's really noticed.

1:51 PM
Caleb: Anyway, Kev's great. It's just, I have to be a little more careful now with how I am in public.

Caleb: It was so much easier when we just threw punches at each other behind coffee shops, you know?

1:52 PM
Caleb: I mean, I'm still hogging the chat all these years later.

    Vortie: If you need some stress relief, we can fight when I get home. I know there's been a lot of pressure. You've had a saving scheduled like every week for a year.

Caleb: I know! Now I'm starting to understand why that hero Dimension I used to idolize got all jaded. And that's not even the savings that come up super last minute. Do ladies really book heroes in advance for putting cats in their trees? How does that even work?

1:53 PM
Caleb: Back in the day I could've sworn heroes just saved people because people actually needed saving. Not any of these weird publicity stunts. I think Dimension was at the beginning of when all this craziness started. No wonder he wanted to retire so bad.

Vortie: You know ... you could get out of the scene.

Caleb: Well, but what would my parents say? They've been wanting me to take up the mantle since the first time I made their lights flicker with my mind.

Vortie: Hey, babe, I'm hopping on the next leg of our flight and I gotta switch over to in-flight Wi-Fi, but I'm having issues. Can you log me in?

1:54 PM
Caleb: Anything for the world's best villain.

1:55 PM
Caleb: Looks like you have a nice tailwind. Lucky.

Caleb: No Kevins to veer your drive off course.

Vortie: Neat, Wi-Fi is all set. Anyway, back to the topic at hand. I think you should do whatever you want to do. You know I'll support you whatever you decide, right?

Vortie: Kind of like you did when I took up marine biology and decided to do villainy as a side gig?

1:56 PM
Caleb: Yeah, but I still think you could take whatever these posers on TikTok are doing. I swear, every villain wears red contacts now. It's like they can't even be original. You started that trend.

Vortie: UGH, that's MY thing. Makes me want to maybe off a few of them.

1:57 PM
Caleb: Well let me know if you ever want to get back into it full time. I get about twenty emails a day from people wanting to do interviews with the two of us.

Vortie: Yeah, I'm going to show up at some interview and half the world's villains are going to want to kill me for "betraying our kind."

Vortie: Whoops, flight attendant saw me, and she's looking a little skeptical. I think she might recognize me. I'm going to put away my phone so I can hide in my hood and pretend to be asleep. Love you, babe. You've got this.

1:58 PM
Caleb: Love you too. Don't make the plane crash by taking down anyone who makes you mad: pilot, attendants, etc.

Caleb: Please.

Caleb: Remember Albuquerque.

Vortie: That was not my fault! Bye!

KEVIN'S LOG
JUNE 8

6:03 AM
Kevin: Curse morning people.

Kevin: Looking at you, Caleb.

6:04 AM
Kevin: Lucky for us, Caleb and I had a chat last night. Asked him if I could have this log to myself, even though he has the ability to access it.

Kevin: He agreed.

6:05 AM
Kevin: Said he used to have a private chat with a villain V killed. I guess that's where he'd get stuff off his chest. Since he couldn't really confide in anyone, he figured a dead dude worked out pretty good. So after he mentioned that, he said it was fine for me to have my own "Manly Diary."

6:06 AM
Kevin: We'll see how long that lasts.

6:07 AM
Kevin: I want to trust him. Really, I do. But how can I when he doesn't trust me?

Kevin: Probs should say something funny because "That's what Kevin does."

Kevin: Patience, my precious. The Kevin Maester will have his moment.

6:08 AM
Kevin: But I've been his sidekick for two years. Got to go with him to all these awesome destinations.

Kevin: Like the time he almost found an SA hideout at the Grand Canyon. They'd all disappeared by that point, but man, what a view.

Kevin: I couldn't even think of anything funny to say.

6:09 AM
Kevin: Or the time when we visited Israel to learn about some ancient heroes. Dudes who could run really fast and teleport through walls and into other locations. I always thought heroes became a thing in, like, the 1900s, but I guess they went back way earlier.

6:10 AM
Kevin: And who could forget when Cortex (Caleb) got to go to New York for the Annual Hero Awards last year. He won "Most Promising Rookie." Bet he could get tons of sponsorships and put his face on cereal boxes.

Kevin: Or on movie popcorn buckets ...

6:11 AM
Kevin: We've been through all that together, but he can't trust me with simple tasks.

Kevin: Won't even let me drive.

6:12 AM
Kevin: I've thought about quitting. Which is why I'm glad Caleb isn't reading this.

Kevin: Because maybe I'm not cut out for this thing. I still puke anytime things get too violent.

Kevin: I don't even have superpowers. Himari often gets down on herself because she doesn't have powers, but at least she has smarts. I have "forgets." The power to literally forget everything. My sidekick name should be Amnesia.

6:13 AM
Kevin: Maybe I should read another Sidekick Support Group Thread. Those always seem to perk me up.

Kevin: It'll distract me from these weird purple lights Caleb has inside his car.

Kevin: They're starting to give me a headache.

6:37 AM
Kevin: California can't get here soon enough.

6:39 AM
Kevin: This purple light in the car is driving me crazy.

SIDEKICK SUPPORT GROUP FORUM

TOPIC: SHOULD I QUIT BEING A SIDEKICK?

Andromache: Hi, y'all. Been with my hero for about 18 months, and all she does is make me get coffee. She doesn't even have good taste in coffee. It's mostly oat milk. Anyway, I know most people can't have an "in" into the superhero business without working your way up the Skyscraper (or unless your parents happened to be supers). Still, I'm wondering if I can just start freelance. Any tips for how I can make it on my own?

ANSWER THREAD

Syracuse: Sweetheart, it's an underdog eat underdog world. If you can't "handle" the difficulties of being a sidekick, get out of the game. There's plenty of bright-eyed Henchies and Kickies who'd love to take your spot.

Syracuse: Want my advice? Go ahead and quit so your hero has an actual sidekick she can rely on.

There are no more answers to this thread. Have a question? Post a thread below!

PRIVATE MESSAGE
JUNE 8

7:24 AM
Himari: Hey, how's it going? Keeping my brother alive so far?

Kevin: Well, I don't know if he's going to be alive if he keeps insisting on driving all the 12-hour days, but he is a superhero. I'm sure his powers will save him.

Kevin: Dang, you're up early.

7:25 AM
Himari: It's 11:25 here in Sydney.

Kevin: Nice! You gonna get lunch soon? Bet they don't have honey on pizza down there. G'day, yeehaw!

Himari: 11 PM. Think about it. We're on the other side of the world.

7:26 AM
Kevin: Ohhhhhhh. Yeah I'm all discombobulated. Doesn't

help that the time thing in this app is Eastern when we're in a different time zone than that.

Himari: That's one of the downsides of a private, secure network. I didn't hook it to outside systems that would do that automatically. Hmmm. I'll have to look into that when we get home.

Kevin: So whatcha doing at the hotel? Wrestling kangaroos and naming crocodiles Steve?

Himari: Well, V's in the shower, but we just had a conversation, and ... I don't know what to think.

7:27 AM
Kevin: Just do what I do. Don't. Forget everything.

Himari: So we both signed up as sidekicks/henchmen because we want to be heroes/villains someday, right?

Kevin: Eee-yeah, sort of. I just needed an internship for college credit. I don't go to Hero U, so I didn't have to work in the hero business, but the Teach was cool with me interning for a hero. Beats working at a movie theater.

Kevin: But I mean, after everything, being a hero sounds amazing. Obviously the Broadway thing ain't kicking off any time soon, so I figured superhero is not a bad gig at all.

Kevin: Why?

7:28 AM
Himari: Well, I've wanted to be a villain ever since Caleb started being a hero. And I thought, when V came along, it would be perfect. I could be a villain by the time I was in college. But we never really do anything, like, evil. Sinister, maybe, but not evil.

Himari: I asked her today if we were going to steal something or fight anyone while we're down here and she said no. She said we're just studying sharks. Which is great, but, how am I ever going to become a villain?

7:29 AM
Himari: I keep asking if we can do villain things and she says no. She's the coolest villain I've ever met. Why doesn't she want to do anything?

    Kevin: Probs because you out-cool her.

    Kevin: Even if you take up chats like your brother, lol. Dang, you guys are talkers.

7:30 AM
Himari: Sorry. We both tend to have a lot to say. Be glad you don't see our PMs to each other.

    Kevin: And I thought I had to read a lot for class.

    7:31 AM
    Kevin: I wish I could help, but honestly, Caleb wouldn't let me do anything heroic if I tried. Maybe it's just a thing villains and heroes do now. Sidekicks/henchies are just there to hand them a ray gun or spill coffee all over their skin-tight clothing to spare them from ever putting on those monstrosities. Hypothetically.

Himari: V has never actually said she's given up being a villain, but … I'm starting to get that vibe. She hasn't fought anyone in at least six months. I'm worried about job security.

    7:32 AM
    Kevin: Huh, I hadn't realized that she hadn't battled

anyone in a while. Then again, I probably wouldn't remember if she had. Too bad she couldn't off Billy. She's starting to get henchman numbers in body count. Gotta pump those things up. Kidding, of course. Killings make me get flashbacks.

Kevin: I don't know. Maybe once they crack the SA, she'll get back to it?

Himari: I sure hope so. Is she scared or something? It's so frustrating! I feel like you and I would be more effective against the SA.

Kevin: I would be offended, but come on. I'm too beautiful to be effective.

7:33 AM
Kevin: Let's wait it out and see what Caleb finds at Techie-Con. Maybe one of the kangaroos can knock her in the head and she'll remember her villainy ways.

Himari: Maybe. Thanks, Kevin.

Kevin: What are sidekicks for?

7:34 AM
Kevin: I mean, actually. What are they for?

Kevin: I'm dying here. Help.

Kevin: Everything is fine. *everything catches on fire*

Himari: Just don't catch my stupid brother on fire. We'll chat later. V's finally out of the shower. FINALLY my turn. I'm exhausted.

7:35 AM
Kevin: Have fun!

Kevin: Good night. Or morning. It's so confusing.

PRIVATE MESSAGE
JUNE 9

3:43 PM
Unknown Number: Hey, Himari! What's up?

    3:44 PM
    Himari: Hi! Sorry, who is this?

Unknown Number: Lol, it's Scott, from physics class, remember?

    Himari: Oh yeah, I think so. Sorry, there were a lot of
    people in that class.

3:45 PM
Unknown Number: Well, I definitely remembered you! Always
the one the prof called on. We were in the same study group. I've
missed you since the semester let out.

    Himari: So ... I'm guessing you want homework help?

Unknown Number: I mean, I am taking a class over the summer.
I'd love it if you came over to my place. Not far from campus. My
roommates are gone this week.

3:46 PM
Himari: Sorry, I'm not really in the area. But you could email me your questions if you want.

Unknown Number: lol

3:48 PM
Unknown Number: Oh. So … is that a no, then?

Himari: … No? Like I said, you can email them to me, but I'm not in the country at the moment.

Unknown Number: Huh. Guess I should've listened to Carlos when he said you were savage.

Himari: What? You mean that guy who was always asking for homework help for English?

Himari: I tried to be nice, but he never sent complete essays. They were always more along the lines of love poems, which I didn't think really fit 20,000 Leagues Under the Sea. I didn't realize I was too critical. Tell him sorry for me?

3:49 PM
Unknown Number: … Right. "Homework help."

Unknown Number: You could've just told me no. You don't have to play dumb, you freaking nerd. That's just insulting.

Himari: Um, okay. Sorry? Good luck on the homework!

You have been blocked by this number

Himari: What is it with guys only wanting homework help in person?

Message undelivered

KEVIN'S LOG
JUNE 10

12:25 PM
Kevin: At the TechieCon conference. They opened the doors
twenty-something minutes ago, and the line's still out the door.
Caleb looks like a zombie. That's what he gets for making us get up
at 5 AM every morning and insisting he drive the whole way here.

12:27 PM
Kevin: So while we're waiting, let me fill you in on the fun scenery.
And by "you" I mean future historians who find this note when
they unveil the past of the greatest sidekick of all time. It's already
hot as heck outside and it's morning here. Inside there's a whole lot
of huge TVs plastered everywhere and a bunch of booths.

12:28 PM
Kevin: Good ole Cal just shuddered because someone brought in a
granite countertop for some display. I keep forgetting granite is his
weakness. Can't use any of his powers when he's near it. He hasn't
had a villain use the ole granite maneuver on him since two years
back when one had his house full of it, when Caleb had to go
rescue his ex-girlfriend. Guess it's a good thing we don't publicize

that stuff on social media. Reporters would eat him alive. That girl-friend turned out to be a villain anyway.

12:29 PM
Kevin: And not a villain like V. Like a villain who throws knives at you and doesn't give you a Dora the Explorer Band-Aid afterward.

12:30 PM
Kevin: Line's moved. We're officially inside. No more sunburned Kev!!

Kevin: Listen, when you're as pasty as me, the indoors are your best friend, okay? Wow, I really should do this as voice to text and not texting. Hurts my thumbs. But I can't risk someone dastardly overhearing any of this. So hurty thumbs it is.

12:31 PM
Kevin: Oh, wait, some dude in flannel just spotted Caleb. *eyeroll* Even when Caleb isn't wearing his Cortex mask, some fans have theories about his secret identity.

12:33 PM
Kevin: Flannel guy says he's a family friend and that we can go ahead and skip the line. Guess the dude knows Caleb's dad. Or at least, he mentioned knowing Aurumque. Caleb's dad has gold powers or something. Never saw the powers in action. Makes sense with Caleb's house, to be honest. Didn't see a name or name tag, but he mentioned them by name, so sounds legit. I asked him if he wanted to take a selfie with *gestures to my beautiful self* but he gave me a weird yet strangely polite look. Starstruck, I guess.

12:40 PM
Kevin: Just got our name badges and heading toward the booths.

12:53 PM
Kevin: Caleb wants to split up.

12:54 PM
Kevin: It's weird. We started looking at booths together, and there was this one station with a bunch of robotic toys and stuff. I saw one that looked like an anime-style cat and thought of Himari.

Kevin: Himari really likes cats.

12:55 PM
Kevin: So I said, "Yo, Caleb, I should get that suuuper cute cat for your seester."

Kevin: Something about the way I said it or the way I looked made him go all red. Got really interested in looking at a booth.

12:56 PM
Kevin: With an SA member buried in one of these booths somewhere too. Things might get a little messy.

12:57 PM
Kevin: So right after the whole cat thing, he suggested splitting up. "We can cover more ground that way."

Kevin: Something tells me he's afraid of plush cats. Another granite kryptonite, if you ask me.

12:58 PM
Kevin: I don't know why he trusts me with looking for an SA person anyway. Besides the ones we encountered two years ago, I don't know what they look like.

Kevin: Do they wear black cloaks? Fear garlic? Sparkle?

12:59 PM
Kevin: But by splitting up, I think I know exactly what Caleb was trying to say.

Kevin: "I trust you, bro, to help me with this mission and hunt down the SA member."

Kevin: Finally, he trusts me! I think we're bonding!

Liam has entered Kevin's Log

1:00 PM
Kevin: Ummm, what the heck, dude?

    Liam: Ope! So sorry. Was trying to hack into the Wi-Fi. Can't get a signal with all these people.

Kevin: Oh, feel you, man. There's gotta be thousands of people here. And did I mistake that Midwestern "ope," or did we just become best friend-os?

    1:01 PM
    Liam: From Indiana. Born and raised.

Kevin: No way, dude. Same! Where at?

    Liam: Indy, you?

1:02 PM
Kevin: An hour and a half away, man. We're basically in each other's backyards.

    Liam: *cries tears of joy, and anguish, and confusion* Everything in Indiana is so spaced out.

Liam: Anyways, I can try to find another network. Don't wanna waste your time and steal your precious Wi-Fi.

1:03 PM
Kevin: Waste my time? Bro, I've been sitting in a mostly silent car for three days straight. If I wasn't head over heels for an amazing girl in Australia, I'd take you to coffee right now.

Liam: Ah, man, I'm blushing.

Liam: You sure I'm not encroaching on this chat thingy? I don't mean to be a bother. Is this a Sticky Notes app?

1:04 PM
Kevin: Nah, just a bunch of intern lingo. You probably can't make any heads or tails of it.

Liam: You got me, man.

1:06 PM
Liam: Not to overstep, but I couldn't help but notice you might need help finding something? I don't know anyone named SA, but are they a conference head or something? Maybe I can help you find them.

1:07 PM
Kevin: Well, I don't know how exactly to explain this to a civilian.

Liam: A what?

1:08 PM
Kevin: Is there maybe a section of dark tech? Where some shady stuff goes down?

Liam: Hmmm. I did see a booth covered in blacklights.

1:09 PM
Liam: They were playing some sinister movie mix and huddled around in black cloaks chanting.

Liam: I don't want to judge based on appearances, but it was weird, bro.

1:10 PM
Liam: I think there's some EvilleCon next door. Maybe they set up their booth in the wrong spot?

Kevin: Mayyybe, but I think you just helped me uncover my lead. Where are they located?

1:11 PM
Liam: The booth at the very back of the room, on the right. Can't miss it.

Kevin: Oh, Liam, I could kiss you.

Liam: Haha, thanks, man, but I have a special someone too. I do like hugs, though. Maybe next time.

Liam: Gonna squeeze on out of here so I'm not any more of a bother.

1:12 PM
Kevin: You shall be missed, good sir.

Liam has left Kevin's log

Kevin: Okay, Caleb, now to find the SA person and prove I'm a good sidekick.

GIRLS RULE, CALEB DROOLS
JUNE 10

1:10 PM
Himari: V? Where did you go?

Himari: I just woke up and looked over and you were gone.

1:12 PM
Himari: It's five in the morning. Usually you only go to bed a few hours before this.

Himari: V? Are you doing villainous nighttime activities without me?

> 1:13 PM
> **V:** Sorry, didn't want to wake you. I'm on my way to the beach.

Himari: At five in the morning? Why on earth?

> **V:** Sunrise is at six. Besides, it's, like, afternoon back home.

Himari: I don't think you've ever seen a sunrise in your life.

1:14 PM
V: First time for everything. I have an idea for a children's book about sharks set in Sydney. I thought the beach would be … inspirational.

Himari: That's nice. Um …

Himari: This might be a weird question.

Himari: Do you often cry in your sleep?

1:15 PM
V: Yup, that's a weird question.

1:17 PM
Himari: So … you good?

V: Fine. Just some bad dreams lately.

Himari: Girl, you haven't been sleeping at ALL these past few days. I see your phone light up at three in the morning.

V: Eh, time difference. Makes things weird.

1:18 PM
Himari: Okay. If you say so. You know you can tell me things, right?

V: Yeah. It's just some … old stuff, I guess. It's fine. I'll get over it.

1:19 PM
Himari: Hey, that's fine. Mom's been cancer-free for like a year, and I still get weepy sometimes thinking about when all that was

going down. You're allowed to process. But we don't have to talk about it right now if you don't want to.

1:23 PM
Himari: So, um, you at the beach?

1:25 PM
Himari: You need anything?

1:30 PM
Himari: Okay, well, just message me back to let me know you're okay? I mean, I know you're probably fine. You're a super awesome villain and all that. But just check in?

1:35 PM
Himari: V?

PRIVATE MESSAGE
JUNE 10

1:15 PM
Macy: Ugh, I can't believe the line for the bathroom is that long. I might have to sneak into EvilleCon to use their restrooms.

Kevin: Ummm, Macy, did you just hack into mine and Caleb's PM?

Santiago: Shoot, the Pella booth is swamped. We'll have to check it later this afternoon when the crowd dies down.

Kevin: … ?

1:16 PM
Scarlett: $52 for a cat plushie? What a rip-off.

Caleb: Oh, nice, they're selling pretzels. Ooooh, and they have the cinnamon ones with sweet glaze. Mmm. Maybe after I track down the SA dude.

1:17 PM
Kevin: Caleb?

Caleb: Huh? Oh, shoot, man, sorry. Didn't realize I was mind-texting.

> **Kevin:** Not to freak you out, bro, but I think a bunch of people just hacked into our private message. We might want to talk to Himari about working out the bugs.

1:18 PM
Caleb: What?

1:19 PM
Caleb: Oh, sorry, just scrolled up to read. No, that was when I was mind-reading. I guess I'm so tired I accidentally transferred all the minds I was reading into this chat.

> **Kevin:** I sometimes forget you can read minds. You don't really use that one as much as the tech thing. Hasn't it been two years since you last used that power?

1:20 PM
Caleb: Ummm, yeah, sure. V says when I use it, it feels like I don't trust people. I haven't used it on any villains I've fought in the past years, because for most of them, if you take down their tech, you take them down.

> **Kevin:** True. Villains have become a little too dependent on their precious gadgets.
>
> **Kevin:** And I guess that makes sense with the tired, out-of-it thing. That's what you get for not letting *gestures once again to beautiful self* this bad boy take the wheel.

1:21 PM
Kevin: So I guess you were reading the mind of some guy named Liam earlier too, huh?

Caleb: Um, what?

Kevin: WAIT A MINUTE.

1:22 PM
Kevin: Your veins glow purple when you read people's minds, right?

Caleb: Oh, shoot, I forgot about that. I guess I should get a hoodie at one of these vendor booths before continuing, eh? Otherwise, the SA person might spot me in this crowd.

1:23 PM
Kevin: I mean, a bunch of these booths are glowing, so maybe no one noticed.

Kevin: But that's not the reason for the all caps, dude.

Caleb: I just figured your keyboard is always stuck on that setting.

1:24 PM
Caleb: Ah, there's someone selling hoodies.

Kevin: Bro, you totally were glowing purple in the car. At first I thought it was your car, since you installed those sick interior lights. But I was wondering why I could see them during the day.

1:25 PM
Kevin: Why were you reading my mind?

1:28 PM
Kevin: Caleb!

1:29 PM
Caleb: Sorry, just bought the hoodie.

1:30 PM
Kevin: Look, I know you don't trust me to brew your coffee and all, but you can't even trust me to my own thoughts, man? You don't even use the mind-reading things on villains. You saying I'm worse than a villain, bro?

Kevin: Even after we had the talk in the hotel about how you'd leave Kevin's Log alone.

Kevin: I don't want you in my head.

1:31 PM
Caleb: Look, I'm sorry, okay? You just kept messaging your phone, and I got curious. But your phone picks up whenever anyone enters the app. Figured I could get a glimpse if I read your mind.

Caleb: Stupid Himari. Why do you have to be so darn smart?

1:32 PM
Kevin: Bro, I'm at a loss for words. Well, I'm actually thinking of quite a few I hear a lot back at the frat house at Ball State.

Kevin: Guess you'll just have to read my mind to find out what they are, huh?

Kevin: After our two years together, I thought you'd trust me enough to let me think on my own.

1:33 PM
Logan: Sweet! They're giving away a free electric pencil sharpener at that booth. Gotta grab me one of those.

> **Kevin:** Dang, how is the chat picking up people's names? Unless …

> **Kevin:** Caleb, seriously? You're just gonna read people's minds and ignore this conversation?

Genesis: Was that Sonya Dazzlepants? Omg, I swear I just saw her behind that balloon float.

> **Kevin:** You know what? I don't need you, man. I'm almost toward the back where Liam spotted some dudes in cloaks. Gonna track down the lead from there.

> **1:34 PM**
> **Kevin:** Because I'm trustworthy. Trustworthy as a bank, I tell you!

Antonio: Ay, demasiada gente.

> **Kevin:** Gesundheit.

> **Kevin:** Wait a second. There's no booth with black lights and people in cloaks chanting.

> **1:35 PM**
> **Kevin:** Did I go the right way? Maybe Liam meant the other right.

Mariana: Someone please tell me they're selling coffee somewhere on this floor. I don't want to head downstairs and end up with nothing.

Kevin: No, I can see it from this end of the room. No cloaks on the other side either. Weird. Maybe Liam got confused, or maybe HE accidentally walked into EvilleCon.

1:36 PM
Liam: Ope, I see him. Get ready to shove him under the granite countertop. Everyone ready? Hydrated? Okay, excellent.

Kevin: Liam?

1:37 PM
Liam: Now, now, now. Please?

Caleb: Ugh, get off me!

Kevin: Shoot, all the lights just went out. Caleb, are you okay?

Caleb: Crap, there's too many of them!

1:38 PM
Caleb: Oh, Lordy, one of them has a taser.

Kevin: Can you turn it off with your mind powers?

Caleb: No, I think it's using some weird energy source. Solar power?

1:39 PM
Kevin: How can you tell it's a taser? It's dark in here except for the glow of people's phones.

Caleb: Tasers make noises, Kev—unnng. He just missed me.

Caleb: Stop distracting me.

1:40 PM
Kevin: I'll try to find you.

> **Caleb:** Do me a favor and—unnng—just keep the line dead for a few minutes, okay?

> **Caleb:** Okay?

> **Caleb:** Crap, they formed a wall around me.

> **Caleb:** AUGH!

1:41 PM
Kevin: Caleb, the lights just came back on.

1:42 PM
Kevin: Are you okay? Please message back if you're okay.

1:45 PM
Kevin: Crap.

SIDEKICK SUPPORT GROUP FORUM

TOPIC: MY HERO'S BEEN KIDNAPPED, HELP!!!

Lumos: Hey, Kickies, 'fraid I'm going to have to limit this thread to just sidekicks. Henchfolks, I know your villains occasionally get kidnapped by other villains, vigilantes, or heroes who want to play it rogue, but I think I want the advice of some fellow comrades at the moment.

So my hero is not the type to get kidnapped. He can turn himself into a shadow and often slinks away without people noticing. Think Peter Pan. I know that seems more like a villain type of power, but he sees himself as more of a dark, gritty kind of hero.

Getting off topic.

Anyway, his villain discovered his weakness.

Soooo they took him away and now I don't know what to do.

The villain doesn't seem like the kill-you-immediately type, but we can't rule out torture quite yet. Even though he's never shown an inclination toward that stuff, you never know. And even if they don't go that route, now I have no hero to call my own. Everyone knows that if you lose your hero, you can kiss your sidekick career goodbye.

After all, you couldn't even keep your eye on them long enough to prevent their capture.

TLDR: My hero got hero-napped. Help a sidekick cope.

ANSWER THREAD

Syracuse: Woooow. *slow clap* Way to go, rookie. I can see from your profile that you've only done sidekick work for THREE WHOLE MONTHS. Incredible. Really. Even if you do manage to get your hero back, I hope he drops you and picks up a more deserving sidekick. Be glad you don't work for a villain. They would've killed you for your poor, shoddy job.

> **Lumos:** Syracuse, don't you have something better to do
> than troll these threads? And from what I can tell from
> your profile, you've hopped from one hero to the next.
> Can't even keep a steady gig for four months, man. My
> advice: start following your own. And stop ruining the lives
> of everyone here.

> *Syracuse has reported this thread as potential spam*

Crios: :'(Sorry. Lost my hero three years ago and still :'(I can't :'(even. Or odd :'(really. You never :'(get over the pain of :'(losing someone who feels like :'(family. You try to remember :'(the good moments and keep :'(moving on, since everyone :'(seems to have moved on without you :'(deep condolences :'(for your loss :'""""""(

> **Lumos:** Crios, I appreciate the heart, but I don't even know
> if I've lost, lost my hero. The most threatening thing the
> villain has done is create a ray that gave him shin splints.
> Sure, he can't run 5Ks anymore, but he sucked at running
> in the first place. But I'm sorry to hear you lost someone
> you loved.

64

Lumos: Wait a minute. Crios, your profile shows that you're a cosplayer. You haven't even worked for a hero.

Crios: :'(

Lumos has reported this thread as potential spam

Nyx: I say you get back at the villain. You stab him with a poisoned blade and make him regret the day of his birth. Don't stop until you've only spared him an inch of his life and take your hero back, gosh dang it. Flay him alive; feel the verve pulse through your bones as you make each slice. I've included some links about some fun torture practices from the Huns, Vikings, and Assyrians. You might want to take some tips from these websites or create your own. We can always use more innovation in torture: www.funtorturemethods/fun-torture-methods-throughout-the-ages-2.0/37870458321

> **Lumos:** Well, that seems a little too hardcore for the villain. He really seems like a mostly harmless guy. TBH, I think he just kidnapped my hero so he can monologue for a while. Really gets things off his chest. Torture seems too extreme. Honestly, after he gets the whole monologue bit done, I bet he'll have my hero back in no time.

> **Lumos:** Wait, Nyx, it says on your profile that you're a henchman. I said above I wanted only sidekicks to answer this thread.

Nyx has reported this thread as potential spam

PRIVATE MESSAGE
JUNE 10

1:50 PM
Himari: Has Caleb heard from V? She's not responding to my messages, and I can't find her on the beach.

> 1:52 PM
> **Kevin:** Heyyyyyy, so Hi-Ma-Ri. Do you have a map, because I keep getting lost in your beautiful brown eyes.
>
> 1:53 PM
> **Kevin:** Speaking of lost things.
>
> **Kevin:** And things with the same shade of brown eyes as you ...
>
> **Kevin:** On a scale of one to that neat-o health kit you made, just how angry would you be if Caleb happened to have gone missing all of a sudden?

Himari: You've got to be freaking kidding me. You had one job.

1:54 PM
Himari: What happened?

> **Kevin:** Look, he wanted us to split up at the convention. I think I embarrassed him or something. I know, right? Craaaaazy.

> **Kevin:** Anyways, so he may or may not have found the SA member there who he tracked down on the Meta-Match app.

1:55 PM
Kevin: And by found, I mean they found him.

Kevin: And tased him.

Kevin: … And stuffed him under a granite countertop until he either passed out or they knocked him out. Idk, the chat gets all fuzzy from there.

Kevin: Here are some screenshots of the conversation.

Kevin sent multiple screenshots

1:56 PM
Himari: Holy … okay. Do you know where they're taking him? Where they are? Are you tracking them?

> **Kevin:** See, these are all great suggestions.

> **Kevin:** If Caleb had actually taught me how to do any of those things, I'd be down. I swear he just keeps me around to take pics of him for Insta. I AM good at that.

Kevin: Any chance if I put it on my Insta story people will come to our aid?

Himari: Don't you dare put it on Insta—you'll just broadcast his weakness to all the villains who follow you hoping you'll leak something.

1:57 PM
Kevin: Haha, one sec. Just gotta hop into an app. Not to delete an Instagram story I posted or anything ...

Himari: Does he still have his earbud in?

1:58 PM
Kevin: Oh, huh, maybe? We didn't really use the speech-to-text thing at the conference center, but I don't think he took it out. Plus, even if SA took him in, it's buried pretty good. Can't really find it unless you're looking for it. Why?

Himari: Maybe I can track his location. But all my tech for that is at home. Argh!

Kevin: Yay? Road trip?

1:59 PM
Kevin: Look, I know you're probably a tad bit the slightest bit upset and thinking that this may be possibly ever-so-slightly my fault. But maybe seeing my beautiful face back home will help all that go away?

2:00 PM
Himari: Wow, great observational skills. I mean, I guess I won't actually kill you, since I know how stupid my brother is, but I definitely don't want to see your ugly mug.

Himari: V and I need to get home ASAP. If only I could FIND HER.

Kevin: Okay, first of all, "mug"? What is this? Some 50s movie? "Put up your mitts, Lucy!" And second of all, MISS I'M ALL MAD AT KEVIN FOR LOSING THINGS, you lost your villain?

2:01 PM
Kevin: Oooooooooh.

Himari: Listen, she didn't get KIDNAPPED, she just probably got distracted by sharks or something ... or eaten by a saltwater crocodile. Argghhhhhh, fine, we're slightly even, but yours is worse.

Himari: Where would V go?

2:02 PM
Kevin: Beats me, Mari. Maybe she got embarrassed too? Kind of like Caleb did at the conference center? Maybe our villain/heroes want new sidekicks or something.

Himari: Oh gosh, finally, I see her. She doesn't look good. Hold on.

Kevin: I'm holding on to some stranger's bag at the conference.

2:03 PM
Kevin: He's giving me a weird look.

2:04 PM
Kevin: Oh, shoot, now he's calling over the security guards.

2:05 PM
Kevin: Message me on our Fab Four chat when V gets back. And I'm going to hide at EvilleCon.

2:06 PM
Himari: No good, Kevin. If Caleb is compromised, we don't want the villains seeing the Fab Four chat on his phone and seeing what we're up to.

2:10 PM
Kevin: Whatever floats your float, or whatever that saying is. Just snuck into EvilleCon. Going to look menacing and wait for our group chat between the three of us.

Himari: You have any experience with panic attacks? I suck at this, apparently.

2:13 PM
Kevin: Hold on, had to shake loose some dude in a blue cloak who was handing out pamphlets. I get one before every show on stage. Panic attacks, I mean. Not pamphlets.

Kevin: V having one?

Himari: Don't tell her I told you. I sure as heck don't want to tell her what's going on with Caleb right now. I think she's actually breathing now? Kind of?

2:14 PM
Kevin: Yeah, breathing's going to be abnormal. Right now what she's experiencing feels like a heart attack. It's not, but that's what it feels like.

Kevin: Are you familiar with the term grounding?

Himari: Like when you prevent a plane from taking off? I do tech, not people.

2:15 PM
Kevin: Get her to focus on her five senses. Have her touch the sand, smell the beachy air, and count breaths. Let me know if this is working.

2:19 PM
Himari: I think it is. She's calming down.

Himari: Oh, gosh, do I tell her? No, I'm going to bring her back to the hotel first.

2:20 PM
Kevin: Yeah, probs a good idea. Give her some time until she's back in sorts, and then we can lay on the news. I guess I have a 36-hour drive to look forward to … alone.

Kevin: That speech-to-text function still work on the super private network? I need some peeps to chat with.

Himari: Yes, it does. I'm going to go get V settled, then I'll book some flights before breaking the news. Want me to book you one too?

2:21 PM
Kevin: Nah, walking home sounds like a great option.

2:22 PM
Kevin: Book me a flight, please. And fast. There's some dude who is pulling knives out of his body, and I don't feel comfortable saying where.

Kevin: EvilleCon is weird, man.

Himari: Let me know if you have any updates. Gonna go now.

2:23 PM
Kevin: Update: He also pulled out a sword.

Himari sent a screenshot

2:45 PM
Himari: That's your flight info. V wants to hop in a group chat, so … be prepared.

Kevin: Too late to turn in my resignation?

KEVIN'S INSTAGRAM STORY

[Blank black screen with text]
Hey, guys, so remember that hero Cortex I sometimes hang around?
[Blank black screen with text]
So I was chilling with him at TechieCon.
[Blank black screen with text]
Welllll, he may or may not have just gotten kidnapped.
[Blank black screen with text]
And by may or may not have, I mean he actually did.
[Blank black screen with text]
Sorry, don't mean to post so many stories in one day. Can only fit so much text in here.
[Blank black screen with text]
If you see my friend-o, let me know.

Views of Story: 549

This story is no longer available. The user may have deleted it.

GROUP CHAT
JUNE 10

Victoria added Himari to the group

Victoria added Kevin to the group

2:47 PM
Victoria: Kevin. How.

Victoria: Have you looked around? Tried to find them? Asked if anyone saw anything questionable?

> **Kevin:** If you saw the crowd here, you'd understand how Kevin-stupid these questions are. And besides, at this point, the security guards will recognize me. Also, apparently EvilleCon decided to make all their booths look like the Labyrinth. Even saw a guy dressed up like a Minotaur.

> 2:48 PM
> **Kevin:** No wait ... I think that's actually a Minotaur.

Victoria: That's beside the point. Himari got us booked on a plane leaving in an hour and a half. (Nice skills there, girl.) Your flight will get in before ours, I think, but it leaves in two hours. Did you get the screenshot?

2:49 PM
Kevin: Yeah, but I don't even know if I can get out of here. Also, pretty sure I passed the henchman of one of the villains Caleb put in prison. I need a disguise or something. My red hair's sticking out like a hot tamale.

2:50 PM
Himari: You have my brother's stupidly flashy car, right? You realize you can remote access that thing? Get it to pick you up? Some of my finest work, even though I would have made the exterior design more subtle.

Kevin: Yeah, the vibrant blind-your-eyes purple fits right in.

Victoria: I thought it was sexy.

Kevin: But wait, it'll just crash in here?

2:51 PM
Kevin: Guys, these booths are made out of solid rock. Like, the Tower of London–type bricks we saw in England.

Kevin: You sure the car can navigate through all of this?

2:52 PM
Himari: It has sensors. Just press the remote-access button and the distress button and the button that looks like a superhero mask on the key fob.

Himari: Just don't hit the button that looks like a tank.

2:54 PM
Kevin: Hypothetically …

Kevin: If a sexy little redhead, while hiding in a booth full of "Evil Puppets for Sale" hit the tank button …

Kevin: And the keys started flashing purple …

Kevin: Just what would happen?

2:55 PM
Kevin: Welp, I had my question answered.

Kevin: Himari, does this thing work like a car?

2:56 PM
Himari: UGH, there is nothing subtle about the tank transformation. But yes, mostly. It just goes slower and destroys things. Do NOT touch the gun turret.

Kevin: Don't even know what a turret is.

Kevin: Just gonna slide into this tank nice and easy.

Kevin: With all these villains and henchfolks giving me the stink eye.

2:57 PM
Kevin: I shouted "Cortex stinks!" and put one of the puppets on my head as a makeshift mask. They've accepted me as one of their own.

2:58 PM
Kevin: Rolling right on out of here.

Kevin: Nice, it drives automatically!

Kevin: WAIT! CALEB AND I DIDN'T EVEN HAVE TO DRIVE MANUALLY HERE. WE COULD'VE JUST SAT IN THE BACK SEAT.

Himari: He's a frickin' control freak.

2:59 PM
Victoria: Let us know when you get to the airport, Kevin. We're on our way now.

3:31 PM
Kevin: Dis airport about to be stupified by the Kevin Maester. And sorry for the large time gap. There was an accident on the highway.

Himari: Omg, Kevin, they're gonna kill you if you come to an airport in a tank. Get out and press the button that looks like a car.

Kevin: Fine, fine, gosh. You're no fun.

3:32 PM
Kevin: Mari, why didn't you put a plane or helicopter function on this fancy car of his?

Himari: Anything that flies is harder. That part's in beta mode.

Kevin: It's me. I've been distracting you from fixing the bugs in the app and decking out this car. So sorry. I know the effect I have.

Himari: You're right, it was definitely you and not all my classes at MIT.

Kevin: Blah, blah. I'm going to check in, but see you guys on the other side.

3:33 PM
Kevin: Himari, any way you can make this car drive home?

Kevin: I don't think I have enough to pay for the parking ticket.

3:34 PM
Kevin: Never mind, I hit the button that had a little flame on it, and that seemed to incinerate it.

Kevin: Glad I was out of the car for that.

   Himari: I am going to kill you.

3:35 PM
Kevin: Well, get in line. Talk soon!

VORTIE AND CORTIE
JUNE 10

4:27 PM
Vortie: Hey, babe. If you can, message me, okay?

Vortie: Doesn't have to be here. Just some sort of technology?

4:28 PM
Vortie: I'll even take pigeon.

4:31 PM
Vortie: And if whoever kidnapped my boyfriend is reading this, I have a message for you.

Vortie: This is Vortex. I was trained under the Shadow Assassins from the time I was a child by none other than Stroke. And then I killed her. My body count is higher than most people's IQ. I'm the daughter of Dustdevil and Firewhirl and trained under the late Bernard the dragon. I have no known kryptonite and literally suck the superpowers of any other superhumans I touch, and I can and will use them against you.

4:32 PM
Vortie: I WILL find you, I WILL kill you, and it WILL be horrific. So make the smart move and let my boyfriend go. Or I will bring all the wrath of both heroes and villains against you.

4:33 PM
Vortie: And if there aren't any kidnappers reading this, I know you're at least going to find that super hot, babe.

Vortie: Message me, okay? I'll rip out those mean kidnappers' innards and make sausages for the sharks. They haven't tried human sausage yet. Not good for their tummies, but I might make an exception.

4:34 PM
Vortie: And then we'll order vegan pizza? I know you and Kevin like the stuff with all the meat, but you owe me for making me worry like this.

Vortie: Of course, I have full faith in you to get out of there. You're a hero, after all. My hero.

4:35 PM
Vortie: And ... I think we need to talk about some things.

4:38 PM
Vortie: Looks like it's almost airplane mode time. But you know how to get through that. Message me.

Vortie: I love you, Cortex.

VORTIE AND CORTIE
JUNE 11

10:01 AM
Liam: Oh, morning. Didn't see you were awake. Goodness, I could go for some cinnamon pancakes right now. You thirsty? Hungry? Sore from being tied to that chair?

Caleb: I'm good. Thanks for asking.

Liam: That's a neat-o thing you got going there with the glowing veins. Can't let you read my mind, which I'm guessing is what you're tryna do. Also, you can't control the tech in this house. Everything else runs on —

10:02 AM
Caleb: Solar power. Yeah. I discovered that. Too bad this thing isn't hooked up to some speech-to-text chat app where I could let my friends know what I was doing. And where it picked up your voice.

Liam: What was that last part? You were whispering, sort of hard to hear ya from the other end of the room, ya know?

Caleb: I said, "Who wears flannel in the middle of summer in Indiana?"

Caleb: Nice helmet, by the way. Lined it with granite? Must be heavy.

> **Liam:** Oh yeah, thanks for noticing, man. Get all embarrassed because I get really bad helmet hair. Doesn't do these golden locks no justice, ya know? But figured don't want ya snooping in my head and reading my thoughts and all that.

10:03 AM
Caleb: No worries. Still planning to tell me what you're thinking anyway via monologue?

> **Liam:** Oh, you hero types are so direct.

> **Liam:** Still no to the pancakes?

Caleb: You know, I would normally say yes, but you've sort of tied down my arms. Also, nice room arrangement, by the way. I like the jukebox and all the old superhero posters. Feels all retro. How old are you anyway? Twenty? Twenty-five?

> **Liam:** Oh thanks, man, and I don't mind feeding you. I might have just kidnapped you and all, but mustn't forget what Mama always said: "When you kidnap someone, at least offer them refreshments."

10:04 AM
Caleb: Wait a minute, flannel. You were the guy who met us at TechieCon.

> **Liam:** There you go. Was wondering if I should start giving

hints, but figured you might get a headache being knocked out with a nasty sedative. Super sorry about that, by the way.

Caleb: You know, you spared me and my sidekick from another three-day drive, so you might be doing me more favors.

> **Liam:** Speaking of sidekicks ... eh, Billy. How are those cinnamon pancakes coming along? They smell delicious, man.

Caleb: Funny, my girlfriend accidentally impaled a dude named —

> **Billy:** Heya, boss, shouldn't be long. The bacon on the stove's taking a little longer. Want to wait for the whole entourage?

Liam: Oh, you made bacon? Billy, you're the best sidekick a villain could ask for. Have a raise, man.

> **Billy:** Yes sir! I'll bring out the pancakes and bacon all together. Back in a jiffy!

Caleb: B-Billy? You hired the dude V—er, I mean, the pizza guy?

10:05 AM
Liam: Oh, no need to be bashful, man, I did my research all about you and all your friends. You got a great résumé and everything. Follow you on social media and all that good stuff. You have some A-list villains following you. And at your age, maaan.

Liam: And yeah, poor Bill Meiser. Could use a pick-me-up after losing his job to getting impaled and all. Gotta love those first minimum wage jobs we had to pay for college.

Liam: Figured since Ball State wan't too far from Indy, he wouldn't mind all that much staying at the Liam Lodge.

Caleb: Yeah, I wondered if you were going to talk about the fact you have a name tag on your flannel with "Liam" on it.

Liam: Oh, you have one on too. Figured we can avoid that embarrassment that comes when you can't remember people's names. Really isolating, you know? We like everyone to feel welcome at the Liam Lodge.

Caleb: ...

Caleb: Isn't it just you, me, and Billy? Or am I missing something here?

10:06 AM
Liam: Oh no, just the three of us, but figured we could beta test the name-tag thing in case we wanna throw a party here later or something. Made yours in Bodoni, your favorite font. Heard you liked graphic design and all, considering you're majoring in that in college.

Caleb: How, um, thoughtful?

Caleb: ...

Caleb: So are you going to monologue, or ... ?

Liam: Oh no, not before breakfast. Some villains can be so rude, ya know, making their heroes all hungry before they finish ranting. At least give the poor dude some breadsticks, ya know?

Caleb: Again, I'm really not in the mood for any —

10:07 AM
Billy: Who wants some cinnamon pancakes?

Liam: Oh, Billy, you've done it again. I could give you a big hug.

Caleb: Huh, Billy does have a name tag on too.

Billy: I could give you a hug too, boss.

Liam: Let's hug then. But let's not make Caleb here feel excluded.

Billy: Yessir! Let me just put this plate down.

Caleb: No, really, I'm good. I don't need to get in on this act—oof.

Liam: That's right. Big squeeze. Feel the love, man. Okay, that's good, thank you, Billy. You give the best hugs, my dude.

Billy: Ah, boss, I'm blushing.

Liam: Do me a favor, man, and give yourself the rest of the day off. You more than earned it.

Billy: Yes, sir. Call me if you need me.

10:08 AM
Liam: Oh, don't you worry about me. Now buh-bye for now.

Caleb: I have. No words.

Liam: And you haven't even tried these delicious pancakes yet. These bad boys'll leave you speechless. I must insist that you have a few bites.

Caleb: No, really, man, you can keep those to yourself.

Liam: Here comes the superhero fighter jet. Neeeeeeeee ...

Caleb: Isn't it supposed to be a train—ung. Oh. Oh, wow. Those are actually good.

Liam: Billy's a gem. Okay, here comes the villain's supersonic helicopter. Vroooo ...

Caleb: Uh, uh, mmm, okay, Liam. I'm full. I'm full.

10:09 AM
Caleb: You poison these or something?

Liam: The audacity. No, man, we don't poison our fellow prisoners. Mama always said, "If you poison a hero, you are just a zero." And no one likes to be a zero, my dude.

Caleb: You had a weird mom.

Liam: Who said she was my mom?

Liam: Anyways, now that you've had some sustenance, you don't mind if I monologue a bit? I don't want to overstep or make you uncomfortable.

Caleb: Oh, um, sure. Most villains don't ask me for permission.

Liam: I can keep it real short. I promise.

Caleb: Clearly, I'm not going anywhere.

Liam: Okay, cool. You comfy? Does the pillow on the chair give you some nice back support? Dang it, should've listened to Billy and gotten the one with extra down.

Caleb: Nice and cozy.

10:10 AM
Liam: Great, okay, whew. Practiced this. All right. Here we go … Caleb, how would you define a hero?

Caleb: A hero? Like a superhero? Are you about to go into a monologue or not?

Liam: Yeah, sure, man. A superhero.

Caleb: Well, that definition has changed a lot, I guess. What it used to mean was people who risked their lives to save others, usually without any reward. Now it's more about how many views you get on social and saving A-list influencers with high followings.

Caleb: Did you just giggle?

Liam: Sorry, got a little giddy on you there. Sorta hoped you would say something like that. Now, how would you define a villain?

10:11 AM
Caleb: Same as heroes, I guess. It's changed. Villains used to hatch diabolical schemes and do things just for the sake of evil. But now it's more about if you look the part: red contacts, black capes, the whole shebang.

Caleb: Okay, how did you just squeal, but like, in a manly way?

Liam: I swear you've been listening to my monologue when I shower, bro. You're hitting all the major points I wanted to cover. I think this calls for another hug.

Caleb: I think not. Please continue with the monologue.

Liam: All right. Well, why do you think the definitions of heroes and villains have changed so much?

Caleb: Not sure ... because the market's gotten saturated. Too many of them.

10:12 AM
Liam: Eh, sort of. Close to what I'd practiced in the shower, at least. At this point, I'm rubbing the conditioner in my hair during the practice speech. The conditioner smells like the woods. Smell it, Caleb?

Caleb: What?

Liam: Anyway, I can give you one word for the reason why we have so many fake heroes and villains in the world.

Caleb: Capitalism?

Liam: Powers.

Caleb: Oh.

Liam: Think about it. Since so many people have these supernatural abilities, it not only clogs the market, since everyone now needs someone to save, but people don't try as hard anymore. Back in the day, heroes and villains would save or destroy the day with or without powers. Without social media followings and podcast interviews.

10:13 AM

Liam: So now the true heroes and villains, those without supernatural abilities, have to fight for survival. Most heroes will turn them down for even sidekick positions because they have too many résumés of "gifted" folks to filter through.

Liam: People have gone as far as to get radioactive bugs to bite them and buy gifted DNA on the market in hopes they, too, can achieve stardom by getting powers.

Liam: It's like ... these pancakes Billy made.

   Caleb: You're losing me.

Liam: Hang on, buckaroo. We'll round the corner soon.

Liam: Billy doesn't have any powers, but he tried his darndest to make these pancakes. He saved my stomach from hunger. But people with powers. Nah, man, they get the job done, but it's shoddy. Lazy. It's like those breakfasts they feed you on airlines. Like plastic.

10:14 AM

Liam: So I figure, we get all this plastic food out of the mix and bring back the pancakes.

Liam: Okay, whew, sorry man, that was like four minutes of a monologue. Really hope I didn't waste your time and all of that. Try to be conscientious, you know?

   Caleb: Uh-huh. So let me get this straight. Heroes like me, who have powers, make plastic food.

Liam: Bingo.

Caleb: And we don't want plastic food.

Liam: Hence why I ban straws at Liam's Lodge, my dude.

Caleb: So you want to get rid of these plastic heroes by killing them all.

Liam: Whoa, whoa! Killing? Why would I spend twenty-five dollars on a pillow if I wanted to kill you?

10:15 AM
Caleb: Well, because you work for the SA. I did my research too. Not enough to know what you looked like, obviously, but I do know SA. Two years ago, they'd talked about wiping out all heroes and villains. To even the playing field, you know?

Liam: Eee-yeah, but you remember what happened when they tried that route with V. Huge cleanup in Las Vegas, and not to mention, that plan backfired.

Liam: SA found me and liked a concoction I was brewing. They want to even the playing field in a different way, or so I've heard.

Liam: …

Liam: Don't you want to ask me, "In what way?"

Caleb: No thanks.

Liam: Glad you asked. Figured I should do what my writing teacher back in school said. Show don't tell. Which was weird because we also did show-and-tell presentations in that class, so she confused us a lot.

Caleb: Uh-huh?

Liam: Caleb, you see this syringe full of this fiiiiine translucent liquid?

10:16 AM
Caleb: Yeah, looks like the bottle we used in the car for when Kevin kept asking to stop for bathroom breaks.

Liam: Right-o. Now, you see those plump veins on your neck that you're making glow right now, making it really easy to know where to put this needle?

Caleb: …

Liam: Before I proceed, I need to make sure you aren't afraid of needles. Because I can blindfold you and all if you don't want to watch it go in.

Caleb: I'm good.

Liam: Great, now let me put this antiseptic cloth on your veins. It'll be a little cold. Rub, rub, rub-a-dub. Okay, great. You ready?

Caleb: You're being weirdly considerate for a villain.

10:17 AM
Liam: Want me to count to three?

Caleb: Just do it already.

Liam: You might feel a pinch. And then a slight sensation that everything is on fire.

Caleb: Whatever man, just … augh! Au—

GROUP CHAT

JUNE 11

11:45 AM
Victoria: Oh my gosh, guys, check out these screenshots ASAP.

Victoria sent several screenshots

11:46 AM
Kevin: Anyone else craving cinnamon pancakes right now?

Himari: Why can't you ever be serious, Kevin?

Kevin: My therapist says I joke as a "coping mechanism."

Victoria: I don't know what happened after that. It went to transcribed screaming and then just went blank. I tried messaging, but no response.

Kevin: Huh, that's weird. Maybe he's just asleep again? So Liam can take him to an actual evil lair instead of a knockoff fifties diner?

11:47 AM
Himari: That aside, anyone know of a "Liam's Lodge"? Also, sorry we're late getting back — the checkout line at Walmart was way too long. Only one lane open.

Kevin: I feel so betrayed by Liam.

11:48 AM
Kevin: And Billy.

Kevin: Told y'all he'd turn evil!!

Himari: All right, all right, I'll admit he did turn out to be a villain.

Victoria: So when are you guys going to be back? That was the longest "fifteen-minute grocery run" ever.

11:49 AM
Kevin: Probs fifteen minutes.

Kevin: So in the meantime, what's the game plan? How we gonna get Cortie and Vortie back together so they can make out and make things awkward for us third wheels again?

Victoria: Dang it, I forgot you could read the group chat name.

Victoria: Anyway, I Googled "Liam's Lodge." Only thing I'm seeing is some nonprofit in Ireland, so I'm thinking he's not super public about this lodge. I mean, it is only two people.

11:50 AM
Kevin: You mean we have a hipster villain? That explains the flannel. And the weird niceness.

Victoria: He sounds pretty Midwestern too.

Kevin: Well he did say Indy. That's only an hour and a half away. Any other clues to figure out the location?

Kevin: Wait, solar panels. Most of the stuff in Indiana runs on electricity or wind power. That has to narrow it down, right? A whole lodge running on that stuff ... you could probs see the panels from outer space.

11:51 AM
Himari: That's a great idea, Kevin. Pulling up satellite feeds on my phone right now.

Kevin: Whoops, didn't mean to have a good idea. Don't tell Cortie, though. Can't ruin my unhelpfulness streak.

Himari: Maybe he'll want to kill you less. Argh, it's so much smaller on the phone screen than the monitors in my room.

Himari: Okay, searching the Indy area ... this could take a while, guys.

11:52 AM
Kevin: While we're waiting, let's play a round of FUN FACTS ABOUT KEVIN YOU DIDN'T WANT TO KNOW.

Kevin: Fun fact numero uno: Kevin is allergic to mayonnaise.

11:53 AM
Kevin: Fun fact number two: Kevin is also allergic to latex bandages, so the Dora the Explorer thing could send him to

the hospital. Vamonos! Okay, want to know what else I'm allergic to?

Victoria: I've got a fun Kevin fact. Fun fact about Kevin number three: he's about to die in five minutes if he doesn't shut up. How's it going, Himari?

Himari: Yeah, when I said a while, I meant like, give me a solid half hour at least. Kevin drives like an old lady. This will be a lot easier at home.

Kevin: Precious cargo in the car. Also, thanks for turning on speech to text for me. Was getting dangerous there with me texting and driving.

Victoria: You're capable of turning it on yourself, you know. I didn't know you were driving. Keep my favorite henchwoman safe.

11:54 AM
Kevin: We'll bring her home in one piece, ma'am. As for Kevin, let's hope we don't crash into a pile of Dora the Explorer Band-Aids. Should be home in a jiffy.

GROUP CHAT
JUNE 11

Kevin changed group name to "SquadGoals"

12:25 PM
Kevin: So how we gonna get our homeboy back? I'm starting to miss him throwing stuffed animals at me when I sing. Where is the justice? Where is the order in this world?

Kevin: Also, remind me why we're doing this on speech to text when we're literally in the same room?

Himari: Because, Kevin, sometimes you forget everything. No offense. Just precautions. Like that time you forgot which airport to pick us up from. Or the time you forgot Caleb at the potential SA lair because you got distracted by the Grand Canyon gift shop. Or the time you —

Kevin: Okay, okay, I get it. I don't have the memory of a flash drive. All righty, so y'all want this on a chat so I don't screw things up and can refer back to this if my mind goes all blank.

12:26 PM
Himari: Hold up! I think I found something. Zooming in.

Kevin: Wowza, look at that cute little chimney. It looks like a house from a fairy tale.

Kevin: If that fairy tale had a bunch of men with guns stationed at the front of it. I don't know if I remember Disney doing something on that.

    Victoria: That's got to be it. We have coordinates?

12:27 PM
Himari: Already ahead of you. Sending them to all of our devices, in case we get split up.

    Kevin: And because you said that, it definitely won't happen. Lol, LOVE FORESHADOWING, Y'ALL.

    Kevin: So I call not going against the dudes with guns. What's the game plan to get past them?

Victoria: I'm just … not going to respond to your first weird comment. I think the game plan is pretty simple. We go in. We kill them. We get Caleb. We leave.

    Himari: So I finally get to actually stab someone?

12:28 PM
Kevin: I don't know, Himari. It would be kind of weird seeing you kill someone. You've never really done it before. And I don't know. Could just be dumb Kevin talk, but I don't know if I can see you doing it.

    Himari: You don't think I could kill somebody? Wow.

Kevin: Nah, I believe you can. Could've sworn you'd stab me when you found out I incinerated the car, but I don't know. V, yeah. Stab, stab, stabby. But you?

Kevin: I guess I'm being weird, though. Henchfolks have to do some killing at one point, right? Like sidekicks do some saving.

12:29 PM
Himari: You know what … I'm just going to move on. V, I think killing everybody is great. But we gotta do it with finesse.

Victoria: Of course. I always stab people with finesse. So, here's the plan. Split up, and … gosh dang it, Kevin.

Kevin: I KNEW WE'D SPLIT UP!

Victoria: Kevin, you'll be our getaway driver, at the road right here. I'm going to attack the guard from the south, here. I'll take down as many as I can and cause a distraction. Himari, you'll come in from the north. You'll go in and get Caleb. We'll meet up at the car and hightail it.

12:30 PM
Caleb's Mom: Knock, knock!

Victoria: Wha—Mrs. Takahashi?

Himari: Mom?

Kevin: Why's she only labeled as Caleb's Mom in this thing? She's Himari's mom too.

Caleb's Mom: Came home early from Canada and brought

back souvenirs. Himari, here's some maple syrup for you. Give me a hug!

Caleb's Mom: Ooof, I wasn't gone that long. Okay, and some syrup for you, Kevin.

Kevin: This is going on pizza.

Caleb's Mom: Pretending to ignore that. And some maple syrup for you, V. There really weren't many other souvenirs. Dad wanted to bring a pet moose home, but we reminded him the sharks are already pretty messy.

Caleb's Mom: Where's Caleb? I have a souvenir for him. Take a wild guess at what it is.

Kevin: A moose!

12:31 PM
Caleb's Mom: It's a good thing you're pretty, Kevin.

Victoria: Wow. Um, so, did you find what you were looking for up there? We weren't expecting you for another week.

Caleb's Mom: Yeah, well, the trek was pretty much a bust. Didn't find the SA members we thought we would, and only basically confirmed some of our suspicions about the weapons already being sold. But I did get a sweater for the hubby with a maple leaf on it, so I say it wasn't a complete waste.

Caleb's Mom: Anyway, this bag's starting to weigh down my arm. A liter of maple syrup is a lot heavier than it looks. Any chance Caleb's gonna swing by soon?

Victoria: Oh, um, I think he had a saving or something scheduled today.

Caleb's Dad: Oh hey, kids.

12:32 PM
Caleb's Mom: Doesn't he look like such a catch in that sweater of his?

Himari: He looks like … something. Morose?

Caleb's Mom: Oh fine, sweetie, you don't have to wear it. Go back to our room and change.

Caleb's Mom: Another saving, huh? That's … nice.

Victoria: Yup. Um, this is kind of awkward, but Kevin and Himari and I were about to head out to, ah, go bowling. With college friends.

12:33 PM
Caleb's Mom: Oh? Oh! That's a great idea. If you get a chance, go ahead and invite Caleb. I'm proud of him and all for all these savings, but I feel like he could use a bowling getaway.

Caleb's Mom: You know, I don't ever remember hero work being that taxing in my early years. Seems like with all the social media and publicity, you kids have way more to deal with than I did at your age.

Caleb's Mom: Well, anyways, I should unload the luggage and start putting away clothes. And hope your father hasn't burned that sweater.

Caleb's Mom: Have fun, kiddos!

12:34 PM
Himari: Bye, Mom!

12:35 PM
Victoria: I just have to say I'm glad Caleb inherited at least a little bit of his dad's quiet side. That was ... a lot.

Himari: We could both be a lot worse.

Kevin: Yeah, some people just don't know when to shut up.

Victoria: It's good you're self-aware, Kevin. Anyway, we better get going. Let's turn our speech to text off until we get there so we don't clog it up with things that aren't important for Kevin to remember.

12:36 PM
Himari: Speaking of, Kevin, can you bring the fast-healing med kit? I hope we don't have to use it, but just in case? I found it buried in your room under a bunch of pizza boxes.

Kevin: What were you doing in my room?

Himari: Just remember, okay?

Kevin: On it! Gotta go use the little sidekick's room first, and then I'll meet you guys in the car.

Himari: Great. V and I will talk about some fun ways to stab people in the meantime.

SQUADGOALS

JUNE 11

2:43 PM
Victoria: Okay, Himari, you in position?

Himari: Roger that.

Victoria: Kevin?

Kevin: Parked right on this random street here. Also, there's a dog peeing on a fire hydrant right by me. Let me know if you want to hear of any excitement on my end.

Kevin: Trying not to be bitter and all. It's just clearly you gave me the most important part of the job. Everyone knows that the less action you see the more important you are.

2:44 PM
Victoria: Sorry, Kevin. You just don't have any weapons or martial arts training.

Kevin: Not my fault my hero didn't train me in that stuff like you did with your henchie. Himari can stab someone in her sleep if she wanted to.

Himari: Kevin, please be quiet. I'm nervous enough as it is. We ready, V?

Victoria: I'm going in.

2:45 PM
Victoria: Hey, there, buddy, it's sleepy time.

Unknown Source: What the — ungh!

Victoria: Okay, one down, guys. Closing in on number two, and ... wow, okay, he's actually asleep. Moving on.

2:46 PM
Victoria: *thunk*

Kevin: What was that noise? Besides the past tense of think.

Victoria: Found this neat PVC pipe. It's really fun to knock people out with it, and it makes funny noises.

Kevin: Is it good to be back, V?

2:47 PM
Victoria: *thunk, thunk* ... Gotta say ... missed this a little.

Kevin: OMG, guys, I see something adorable outside of my car. And by adorable, I mean completely threatening to the mission. Gonna swoop out and investigate.

Himari: Nice. Keep our spot safe.

Victoria: Whoops. That was harder than intended. My bad. I hope you have good insurance. Oh, look, a friend.

Unknown Source: What's going on—augh!

Victoria: Well now there's blood on my new costume. Three more of these outside dudes. Don't know how many inside.

2:48 PM
Kevin: Come here! Come here, I won't bite. You're not a pizza with honey on top, don't worry.

Kevin: Errr, that's how I threaten people? He looks really intimidated now.

Victoria: I'd definitely be weirded out. Okay, Himari, I'm about to do some explosions. You ready?

Himari: Poised and ready.

2:49 PM
Victoria: *BOOM! BOOM! Crackle Crackle Crackle BOOM!*

Kevin: Who's a good boy? Who's a good boy? You—

Kevin: Obviously not you! Be prepared to meet your maker, villain!

2:50 PM
Himari: I'm over the outer wall, V.

Victoria: Great. *THUD.* I've got—*schwink*—a good crowd of goons here that just ran out. Stupid. Explosions literally ALWAYS mean a distraction from the real threat.

Himari: Oh, look, the door's unlocked. There's even a welcome mat.

Victoria: Is it booby trapped? *thwunk*

Himari: Nope, just a cute little chickadee and bunny being friends. Okay, I'm inside.

2:51 PM
Kevin: I think I'm going to call you Mr. Fluffers and you're going to be my best friend forever.

Kevin: Errr, that would be if you hadn't betrayed humankind and turned to the dark side. You are NO best friend of mine.

Kevin: Sorry for yelling at you, pal. Have to make this convincing, you know?

Himari: It's hard to concentrate with your weird mind-trick stuff you're doing to that villain.

2:52 PM
Kevin: Mind trick? Right, yeeeeeah. Well that's what he gets for messing with the Kevin Maester. But I'll try to keep it quiet. Going to intimidate him nonverbally. Get ready for one heck of an interpretive dance, buddy.

Unknown Source: Heh, heh, heh, heh, *lick, lick*

Victoria: Omg, is it eating him?

2:53 PM
Himari: V, this place is nuts. Super cozy, but a lot of vintage stuff? No stupid older brother yet, though ...

Victoria: Really? Come on, you could've fallen the other way and not bled all over me. Oh, sorry, Himari. Yeah, keep looking.

2:54 PM
Himari: OMG, V, I think I see him.

Victoria: How does he look? Can he talk? Where is he?

Caleb: Eh? Wha-washapen — ?

Himari: Hey, bro, you look awful. We gotta go.

Caleb: Himari? That you? Everything feels so heavy. You put lead in my veins or somming?

2:55 PM
Himari: Did they drug you? All right, let's untie you.

Victoria: At least he's talking. Does he look hurt? DIE! Not him, this dude. I SAID DIE! I just stabbed you three times!

Caleb: Why my amazing girlfriend in my ear? Hunnn. Feet don't work.

Himari: Turned on his earbud to our chat frequency so you two can talk.

Victoria: *thunk* You're a gem, Himari. Hey, babe. Himari's breaking you out while I distract the guards. Just follow her lead, okay?

2:56 PM
Caleb: 'Sit a problem that I'm seeing three Himaris? I try to

follow the one in middle. Okay, maybe if I stand now. Whooop. Too fast. Heeheehee.

Himari: Ooookay, hold on to me, I'll get my arm under here … you're heavier than you look. Also, you smell weird. All right, V, we're evacuating.

Victoria: Nice. These guys are pretty much all—oh shoot.

Unknown Source: *TAKATAKATAKATAKA*

Victoria: Machine guns? Cheating!

2:57 PM
Caleb: Hurt my girlfriend and I stab you, bro. Stabbee-stabbee, heeheeheehee … stab is a funny word, Himari.

Himari: Yup, okay, that's great. Keep trying to like, actually put your feet quasi in front of each other.

Caleb: Heeheehee, my feet are following the leader.

Billy: Hi-ya, Liam. I know you wanted to give me the day off, but I figured you could use a nice cheese pizz—uh, who are you?

Billy: Calling all backup. I repeat, calling all—augh!

2:58 PM
Caleb: Heeheeheehee. Himari stabbee-stabbee our pizza friend.

Caleb: Buuut … no pizza now?

Himari: Oh my gosh. I just … stabbed him. Is he dead? Ohmygosh ohmygosh.

Caleb: Himari? Ope, I'm on floor now. Heeheehee. Himari?

Kevin: Not to be rude, but whatever chatter is happening in my ear is distracting me from the mission at hand.

2:59 PM
Kevin: Okay, who's breathing really heavy? Himari, that sounds like you.

Kevin: Himari? Doing all right?

Himari: Did I kill him? No. He's breathing. I think? Omg, so much blood. Omg omg omg.

Kevin: Okay, Himari, you're breathing really fast. It's okay. Just get Caleb out of there. It seems like Billy gets knives thrown at him a lot anyway.

3:00 PM
Himari: Okay. Yeah. Right. V threw a knife at him too. Oh gosh, Caleb's on the ground. Sorry for dropping you, bro.

Caleb: It's okay. Floor comfy. Nap time?

Himari: Yeah, nope, not nap time. Come here, you. Oof.

3:01 PM
Caleb: Heeeheeeheee. Oh. Head hurts. Okay, feet, follow the leader again.

Kevin: Wait, what are they doing to the car? No, stop! Stop ... oh, little buddy, I wasn't yelling at you. No! Don't run away!

Victoria: *ping ping ping TAKATAKATAKA* ... You ready with that vehicle, Kevin? Things are getting really tense up in here. I'm pretty sure backup is coming.

Kevin: Haha, yeah, good thing I'm a dependable kind of guy.

3:02 PM
Kevin: Hypothetically …

Kevin: If someone happened to tow the car, since I apparently parked in a no-parking zone, and got distracted by something super threatening outside the car, what kind of trouble would we be in?

Victoria: F-*THUNK* you, Kevin.

Caleb: Oooooh, V gonna kill Kevin.

3:03 PM
Victoria: There any other cars around, Kevin?

Kevin: Huh, let me use my eagle eyes to scout the situation.

Kevin: Oooh! I do see some cars. Lots of them.

Kevin: Right across the street, actually.

Kevin: … In a parking lot.

3:04 PM
Victoria: I have no words. Himari, you got that car-hacking gadget thing on you?

Himari: Always.

Victoria: Head there. I'll meet you all. Just let me know when you're in the clea—aaagh!

Kevin: V? You doing good there?

3:05 PM
Himari: Oh my gosh, V is dead too. Oh my gosh, this is bad.

Kevin: Himari, V's probably fine. Focus on getting Caleb out of there, and we can freak out once we're out of here.

Himari: Right. Come on, Caleb. Almost out the door, buddy.

Caleb: Ack, sun so bright. Curse you, summer. I'm going blind, ack!

3:06 PM
Himari: Always such a drama queen. Oh dang. Look at your neck though. That's freaky.

Caleb: You should see Kevin's birthmark on his knee.

Kevin: It's my beauty spot, okay?

Himari: I've seen it. It's shaped like a deformed porpoise. Okay, step down here, buddy. I can see the parking lot. Liam literally built his secret lodge next to a strip mall, the freak.

3:07 PM
Kevin: Which of these bad boys should we hijack?

Kevin: There's one with a dinosaur eating a stick figure family. I vote this one.

Himari: Grab it.

3:09 PM
Himari: I see you. Here, catch this. Stick it on the door lock.

    Kevin: Wow, not a bad catch. Haha. I mean, I've never missed a thrown object ever. Okay, stuck on the door lock. Now what?

Himari: Here, hold up Caleb while I work. And call for V.

    Kevin: Wowza, he smells weird.

Caleb: Kevin always smells weird.

    Kevin: V, where are you? Himari is hijacking a car. We need you to get out to the parking lot ASAP.

    3:10 PM
    Kevin: V?

    Kevin: Whoops, looks like another car's rolling into Liam's driveway. Who paints their car plaid?

    Kevin: Wait a minute, plaid … there was a guy at TechieCon who wore plaid.

    Kevin: V, I think that might be Liam. We need you to get out of there now.

Unknown Source: What's this little thing? An earbud?

    3:11 PM
    Kevin: V, either you just trained yourself to sound like a Southern man, or I'm not talking with V anymore.

Unknown Source: Hey, Pete, check this out. I don't know what this—*BANG*

> **Victoria:** K-Kevin. I'm coming. Hold on one ... one second ...

Kevin: I'll try, but some dude in a dinosaur T-shirt's approaching the car. I think he noticed that we hijacked it.

> **Victoria:** Just ... just get in and get rolling. Open a door and I'll ... jump in.

Caleb: Car ride, wheeee!

> 3:12 PM
> **Himari:** We're in, car's all revved up.

Kevin: Vroom, vroom. Coming for you, V.

3:13 PM
Kevin: Yikes, looks like V's limping down the driveway, and something's trailing behind her. Shoot, is that blood?

> **Caleb:** No!

> **Caleb:** Oh, God. V. Get her in now.

Himari: Opening the back door ... Oh my gosh, it looks like she got hacked with an axe or something! And is that a bullet wound to the leg? Holy—

> **Caleb:** Did you pack the m-med kit? Wow it's hard to talk. What did he put me on?

3:14 PM
Victoria: Look out! Ugh! Ah!

Kevin: Hypothetically …

Kevin: If someone who was supposed to pack the med kit left it back at Caleb's house …

Kevin: What exactly would happen?

Himari: All right, give me extra clothes. We're gonna try to stop this blood. Kevin, killing you is going to have to wait. We just have to keep V alive long enough to get back home. Then the fast-heal kit can stabilize her. Unfortunately, since that's AN HOUR AND A HALF away, it's not going to be very fast-healing by the time we can use it. It has to be a fresh wound.

3:15 PM
Caleb: Just keep her alive o-okay? And Kev-Kevin, she dies, and I'll make sure you personally have a s-slow, agonizing death.

Kevin: I'd normally say something funny, but—

Caleb: You put her in jeopardy. You almost cost us the mission. Now drive.

Victoria: H-he … he was f-fighting some … thing. N-not his fault … Himari, I don't think I can stay awaaa …

Himari: Shoot, she's out. What was that thing anyway, Kevin?

Kevin: …

3:16 PM
Kevin: We've all agreed that killing a driver could be potentially really hazardous to all the passengers in the back and is likely not the best course of action at this present moment, correct?

Caleb: Kevin.

Kevin: And perhaps things perceived as threats may have turned out to be benign after investigation?

Caleb: Kevin, what were y-you fighting?

3:17 PM
Kevin: …

Kevin: So there was this really cute dog outside the car.

Caleb: …

Caleb: I'm turning this thing off. I don't want my next few words to be on it.

SIDEKICK SUPPORT GROUP FORUM

TOPIC: SO MY HERO LOST HER POWERS??

Freya: Heyyyy, so a funny thing happened on the way to this sidekick forum.

My hero—some of you may have heard of her (humble brag: it's Vale. Uh-huh, yeah, the chick who can knock people out when she kisses them)—got tangled with some of the wrong folks. I guess her villain has been eyeing some secret group for a while and ended up betraying my hero's secret identity to get an in with their headquarters or whatever.

So my hero. She's fighting. She's kissing a bunch of bodyguards and whatnot. All of a sudden, some dude in flannel walks up and jabs her in the neck with this yellow liquid.

Lucky for her, she has a powered sidekick (I mean, come on, a girl like Vale ain't gonna take on any folks without gifted abilities), so I managed to confuse them with my party powers.

For those who don't know what party powers are, you're missing out. Basically, they get lost in the celebration and forget about the fight.

They're jamming. They're bumping to the music. They're vibing, and I have to limp-walk Vale out of this warehouse.

Then things got weird. When we made an escape back home, Vale realized she'd lost her powers. She tried kissing the mailman, the goldfish, everything. Nothing.

On the bright side, she has a date with the hunky mailman on Thursday.

On the downside, this worries me about job security and all that. Sure, I can work for a B-list hero, but sort of a downer when you work for THE Vale.

Plus, she keeps getting all moody. I think she hates the fact I have powers and she doesn't. The parties I keep throwing her don't help.

Please help before I lose my job!

ANSWER THREAD

Tyr: Wow, that sounds rough. I wish I could help, but I'm honestly answering just to follow this thread. Something similar happened to my hero. Some blond dude showed up, in went the needle, and now, no powers.

Tyr: Also, the guy handed me a bag of scones his henchman made. Not really sure what to think, but doesn't help that they taste incredible. Man, can that henchman bake.

Idun: Weird! Same thing happened to my villain. (Sorry if you wanted to keep this thread to just sidekicks, but I figured since you hadn't made an exception ...) But I did manage to hear the dude in flannel mutter something about how he was losing money flying to all these places to inject heroes and villains.

Freya: Weird that it's happened to multiple people. Has anyone's heroes/villains gotten their powers back?

Tyr: Nope, but he has joined a local book club to help fill in the time he usually does savings. Reading some book called Wraith-wood. Says it's pretty darn good.

Idun: My villain doesn't have any powers back yet. It's been two weeks, but hopefully he can recover. Maybe I should give it two more before seeking employment elsewhere.

KEVIN'S LOG
JUNE 11

6:37 PM
Kevin: You ever mess up really bad?

6:38 PM
Kevin: Caleb's back and stabilized, but coming to meant he said a lot more things to me that probably can't go on these little chats. Made V look and sound like a church girl.

Kevin: Can't really blame him, though. Whatever stuff Liam injected him with seemed to drain him of his powers. We hope it's temporary, but knowing villains … Cortie ain't gonna fry any motherboards anytime soon.

6:39 PM
Kevin: Which Himari was very keen to tell me several times on the drive home wouldn't have happened if I remembered to stick to Cortie like fly paper at TechieCon.

Kevin: And she also reminded me that remembering the med-kit could've spared V from four-plus weeks of recovery. Apparently taking a machete to the side is pretty serious. V's not going to be stabbing too many Unknown Sources for a while.

6:40 PM
Kevin: Dear Manly Diary, I wish I could remember things more. I've always had problems with this sort of thing. Doctors always told my mom it was ADHD or something, but I've never had a good memory growing up.

Kevin: Had to retake my temps test, like, five times because I couldn't remember the answers to the questions. Couldn't get a college scholarship because I bombed the ACT.

Kevin: Speaking of ACT, Mom stuck me in theater pretty early on in life.

Kevin: She thought that memorizing lines would help me with the whole I-forget-stuff-easily thing.

6:41 PM
Kevin: Don't get me wrong. I love the stage.

Kevin: I mean, look at me. You can't keep this baby away from the spotlight.

Kevin: But there's a reason I get panic attacks before every show.

Kevin: Because I worry I'll forget my lines. That I won't remember a cue and then bomb the whole show for everyone.

Kevin: Doesn't help that I get easily distracted.

6:42 PM
Kevin: Or that I really like dogs.

6:43 PM
Kevin: It's not that I can't remember things. I do, really.

Kevin: Like, I can tell you Himari's dad sometimes calls her "Alberta." Because, Albert Einstein, you know. They're both geniuses. Personally, I think she's way smarter.

Kevin: Some of her favorite foods are tacos and burritos and soba, and she really likes awful pop songs that always manage to land on the Top40 list.

Kevin: I can tell you lots of things about Himari. But I can't remember the answers on a test.

6:44 PM
Kevin: Dear Manly Diary, do you ever wish you couldn't be you?

Kevin: Because at this point I'd give anything to be a little less Kevin.

Kevin: And a little more like a hero.

6:45 PM
Kevin: Then I'd actually be useful.

PRIVATE MESSAGE
JUNE 11

10:09 PM
Caleb: You still cooped up in your room?

10:10 PM
Caleb: Come on, man, I'm not that mad at you anymore.

10:11 PM
Caleb: Please let me in.

10:12 PM
Caleb: Texting with thumbs seriously takes forever.

10:13 PM
Caleb: How do you peasants deal with it?

Caleb: Oh, hey. An open door.

10:14 PM
Kevin: Did you just turn on speech to text?

Caleb: Yeah, Himari forgot to install autocorrect on my phone for this super-secret thing, so texting manually takes forever. Have to keep fixing misspelled words.

Caleb: But since we're talking face to face now, I can turn it off.

> **Kevin:** No, don't. I'll probably forget this conversation anyway, so best leave it on. I really should get this memory problem checked out. I think college stress didn't help.

Caleb: Mind if I come in?

> 10:15 PM
> **Kevin:** The deflated beanbag in the corner is calling your name.

> **Kevin:** Cortieeeee, you have a cute tuuuushie. Sit on meeeeee.

Caleb: Aaaaand, now I'm sitting on the floor as far away from that beanbag as possible.

Caleb: Glad to see your sense of humor hasn't gone away.

> **Kevin:** Yeah, seems like the only thing I can do right. Make jokes.

Caleb: …

10:16 PM
Caleb: *Ding. Bzzz. Ding. Bzzz bzzz.*

> **Kevin:** That another email in your hero inbox? Your phone's going crazy.

Caleb: Yeah, a bunch of people want interviews with "Cortex."

Bzzz. I guess someone leaked on an Instagram story that the SA kidnapped me.

Kevin: How rude of whoever did that …

Caleb: I'm just ignoring them for now. Himari and V are watching Terminator downstairs to calm their nerves, and then we figured all of us would talk in the morning about a game plan moving forward. *Ding, ðing, bzzz. Bzzz.*

10:17 PM
Caleb: You know, I think I'll just put this on silent.

Kevin: Might want to do that to me, too.

Caleb: Kevin.

Kevin: Don't bother inviting me to the meeting, I'll only s-screw things up.

Caleb: Are you … are you crying?

10:18 PM
Kevin: I have to practice for an audition, okay? The part requires me to cry on command.

Caleb: Okay? What play?

Kevin: …

Kevin: It's called "K-Kevin Made Cortex Lose His Powers and V Almost Died Because He Forgot the Med Kit and He Is the Worst Sidekick Ever Known to S-Sidekick."

Caleb: Wowza, the poor graphic designer who has to fit that title on a program.

Caleb: Look, Kev.

10:19 PM
Caleb: V and Himari talked with me downstairs.

Caleb: Although you did walk right into Liam's trap at TechieCon, it's not fully your fault that I lost my powers.

Caleb: I decided to drive the car, knowing full well that Himari had installed an autopilot function. We really could've slept the whole way there, gotten up later, and I wouldn't have been super out of it at the conference.

Caleb: Honestly, I probably could've broken past the wall of SA dudes if I had faster reflexes and had gotten more sleep the night before.

10:20 PM
Caleb: And, really, if I'd dug a little more out of my college fund, I could've just booked us a flight there.

    Kevin: S-so why didn't you?

Caleb: I don't know. I like driving. The feel of control you have with the steering wheel.

Caleb: Plus, I've gotten skittish of commercial airlines after what happened with V in Albuquerque.

    Kevin: Ah yes, that event will pass on between the four of us and no one else. No one shall ever know what went down on that fateful day.

10:21 PM
Caleb: Ummm … right.

Kevin: So why didn't you let the car drive on autopilot?

Caleb: I just wanted to control … something.

Caleb: With all these booked savings and interviews I keep feeling like everyone has a grip on my life except for me.

Caleb: Figured if I had a hold of the steering wheel that maybe I could somehow manipulate the direction of my life or something.

Caleb: Only two things make me feel like I have control over even a small portion of my life. Driving and …

Kevin: Your undying friendship with me?

10:22 PM
Caleb: Was gonna say my powers, but yeah, we can go with that.

Kevin: Oh.

Kevin: Again, please don't include me in that post-Terminator meeting.

Caleb: Honestly, Kev, I don't even think I deserve to keep them. My powers.

Caleb: I mean, I freaking read your mind just so you wouldn't catch me spying on your texts to yourself. When I don't even read the minds of villains anymore.

Caleb: What kind of friend does that?

10:23 PM

Kevin: I mean, I probably deserved it. Can't even trust myself to remember simple tasks like turning on the lights to the backyard or watering V's plants when she's out of town.

Caleb: Speaking of, when did you last water them?

Caleb: Kevin?

Kevin: How does V feel about droopy brown plants? I think they really match the villain vibe.

Caleb: ...

10:24 PM

Caleb: Please come to the meeting tomorrow, okay? Everyone can use a morale boost, and something tells me that some of your awful puns can put people right in the mood.

Kevin: Darn, can't even think of one now. I'm useless.

Caleb: Not totally. Heard that you guided V through a panic attack and helped Himari keep going after she stabbed Billy. If you ask me, that goes way beyond the sidekick call of duty. Maybe even heroic.

Kevin: Really? You mean it?

Kevin: I think this calls for a hug.

Caleb: I think not. Still haven't recovered from ... whatever happened at Liam's place.

Kevin: Cool, cool, I'll just hug myself.

10:25 PM
Caleb: Wow, you're hugging yourself for a long time.

    Kevin: I'm a good hugger.

Caleb: Gonna catch the tail end of the movie. Feel free to join.

    Kevin: Nah, don't want to be around V when she just watched a violent movie.

Caleb: Good plan.

    10:26 PM
    Kevin: Caleb, you're taking this whole power-loss thing extremely well.

Caleb: Probs because the drugs from Liam's haven't fully worn off yet. Can't guarantee I'll be in this good of a mood tomorrow.

Caleb: Also, any tips on replacing drywall?

Caleb: A hole may or may not have accidentally gotten punched in a wall in the basement.

    Kevin: Put a wet wall up and wait for it to dry.

10:27 PM
Caleb: …

Caleb: Yeah, I'm gonna leave you now before the drugs finish wearing off.

PRIVATE MESSAGE
JUNE 11

11:23 PM
Himari: Yo, you can't hide from Mom forever. She's been grilling me. Especially with V all bandaged up on the couch and loopy on pain meds.

Caleb: Did you tell her it was a bowling accident?

Himari: V has a gigantic gash in her side and a bullet hole through her leg. So ... yeah. That didn't fly.

11:25 PM
Caleb: Sorry, takes so long to type with thumbs. I'm gonna do voice to text. Cool?

Himari: Sure thing. Thank your awesome sister for that capability.

Caleb: I have a sister? :O

Caleb: And yes, I just told my voice to text to put a colon and a capital O next to each other.

Caleb: I mean, what should I even say? "Hey, Mom? How was Canada? Oh yeah, I drove thirty-six hours on like ten hours of sleep over three days and got myself so tired the SA kidnapped me and robbed me of all my powers"?

11:26 PM
Caleb: That will totally go over well.

Himari: Well the current situation is she thinks you're a jerk ignoring your wounded girlfriend, sooooo …

Himari: Speaking of your wounded girlfriend … how long has this panic-attack thing been going on?

Caleb: I mean, ever since what happened two years back, it hasn't exactly gone away. It just seems to be more and more frequent now. I wonder if something's triggering it.

Caleb: Tell me more about Australia and what happened at the beach.

11:27 PM
Himari: She was saying things about her childhood. Like, stuff about when she was forced into the SA. It was … some pretty dark stuff. But she just acts like it never happened. I feel like she's not okay.

Caleb: Oh gosh, yeah, she's had an awful go at things since the start. She won't even tell me some of the training she went through.

Caleb: What do you think we should do?

Himari: I don't know, bro. I don't really know what to do with the non-murdery V. And she's been a lot less murdery lately. Except just battling a whole bunch of people this morning to save you, of course.

11:28 PM
Caleb: Yeah, I read over the transcripts. Yikes, Caleb on drugs is embarrassing.

Caleb: You know, I've noticed that too. She doesn't have the same bloodlust. You think I'm accidentally turning her into a hero?

Caleb: Nah, I'm glad she didn't read that. She'd throw a knife at me.

Caleb: You don't think she's ... lost motivation about being a villain, do you? Because she used to get so excited about things like the rack and popping people's bones and stuff.

Himari: I don't know. All I know is at the beginning, she was excited to teach me every fighting move in the book, and now we spend all our time singing to sharks.

Himari: Anyway, you should probably come down here. She keeps asking about you, and I think Mom just finally went to bed.

11:29 PM
Caleb: Good idea. Maybe she's just in a rut. We'll have to get back into the hero and villain swing of things anyway, with how much my phone is buzzing with interviews.

Caleb: I guess we can talk more about that tomorrow. Coming downstairs.

THE FABULOUS FOUR
JUNE 12

10:03 AM
Caleb: Okay, glad to see everyone's up. Now, Kevin requested that we put this meeting on voice to text so he can remember it.

>**Kevin:** Never been in V's room before ... cute angler fish stuffed animal. Do you smooch it at night? Mwah mwah, Caleb, I wooooove you.

V: Her name is Angie. I have Caleb for smooching. Agh! Gosh, Kevin, careful please. Don't bump my leg trying to play with my plushies.

>10:04 AM
>**Kevin:** Who has dino AND unicorn stuffed animals? Weirdo.

Himari: Back to the topic at hand ... bro, what did you and V want to talk about?

>**Caleb:** Number of things. If my phone buzzes any more, I swear I'm going to throw it in the pool. We need to deal

with the press now, before they create a story they like and we don't.

> Caleb: V, really, a llama? How are you even fitting on the bed with all those? They're eating you alive.

V: Can we stop commenting on my animals EVERY TIME you're in here, Caleb? This is why I don't usually let any of you in here. If I could actually walk …

10:05 AM
> Caleb: Okay, okay, fine. But let's talk about the press thing. Now, obviously we have to respond to these emails, and they're wanting both me and V on talk shows, podcasts, you name it. What should we do?

Kevin: I could go in disguise as you.

Kevin: 'Ello, I am Cortex. I am sexy herrrrro.

> Caleb: Is that a Spanish accent? Also, why are you making your index finger into a mustache? I don't even have any facial hair.

V: Just that sexy scar.

> Caleb: Awww, babe, I'm blushing. So obviously Kevin can't go as me. I can make an appearance and just not use my powers so I don't strike fear into the super community. People usually freak out if they find out the Rookie of the Year got bested by some midwestern dude. But what about V?

10:06 AM
V: I'll be fine. I can probably walk and stuff. And wear real clothes.

Himari: No. You've got a lot of healing to do. And you lost a lot of blood. You can't even sit up without getting dizzy.

Kevin: Again, I still think Kevin going in disguise can really be helpful here.

Kevin: Hello, I'm Veeeeeee. I'm so prettyyyy. Let me stab you with this knife while I whip back my long flowing hair into the gentle wiiiiind.

V: I don't stick out my butt like that. However … I think there might be something to this disguise idea. Just, not disguised as me.

10:07 AM
Caleb: What do you mean?

V: So obviously we need to take down this Liam guy, but he's buried deep in the SA. Besides, he may not even be the mastermind here. We need to figure out where they got this power-sucking stuff and stop them. And of course, finding those nukes would be good. But you and I are way too high-profile to do anything sneaky. But Kevin … no one knows who Kevin is.

Kevin: Excuuuuse me, but the Marion Public Theater very much knows my name.

Caleb: Kevin? I don't know, V. Do we really want to put him in … that much danger?

V: We'll send Himari with him.

Himari: Whoa whoa whoa. Sneaking into the SA? Like,

THE SA? I've heard some of your stories about their initiation rituals.

10:08 AM
V: Yeah … maybe things have changed? Maybe you only have to dismember one person? And you can use weapons? It's probably more chill now, right?

   Kevin: So hypothetically … how long until I can send in my two weeks' notice?

Caleb: Kevin.

   Kevin: Caleb, I can't kill people. And Himari didn't do so great either when she offed Billy. I'm starting to think superhero movies make all this killing look way too easy.

Himari: Hey, first time jitters, that's all. V's been villain-training me for two years now.

   10:09 AM
   Caleb: Villain training. Huh. Wait, V, do henchmen also have to dismember people, or can they just sort of help out the villain? That may help us with the Kevin-getting-squea-mish-over-here thing.

V: Oooh, it's unusual, but yes, we could do that. Himari can be the villain, and Kevin can be her henchman. They really don't care that much about henchmen—really replaceable.

   Caleb: Oh, shoot, just had a thought. Liam really did his research on us. He knows our names and what we look like. We'd have to give them at least different names and hair colors and all that.

Himari: I call pink hair!

10:10 AM
Kevin: Just when I thought you couldn't get any prettier ... Caleb, I was talking to the angler fish. Stop hitting me with the dinos.

V: Only I get to use my stuffed animals for violence. You know this, Caleb. Okay. So that's what we'll do for getting into the SA. But if we want to take down an organization that big, we can't do it alone. Which is why Caleb and I are going to do some recruiting ... on both sides.

Caleb: Heroes and villains. Since the SA wants to take down both. We'll hopefully destroy them inside and out.

Kevin: Like Taco Tuesdays, got it.

V: That's disgusting, Kevin. All right, so you two need names and makeovers, and we need to figure out a way not to let on that I'm injured and Caleb doesn't have powers, or we'll be dead in seconds.

Himari: I've been working on something, actually. Very, very much a prototype, but a sort of communication device that works a bit like Caleb's brain used to, able to telepathically send messages to one another based on intercepting neural signals in the brain stem.

10:11 AM
V: Wow! I didn't know about that.

Himari: Yeah ... see the problem is, it's very hard to filter what you send to other people. So things could get really weird really quick.

Kevin: Again, let me know about the two weeks' notice.

Caleb: We'll be fine, Kev. That sounds good. Now, V, about that leg. Maybe you could say you sprained it or something? While doing some combat training in the backyard?

V: That works. And we just won't mention the torso wound … Himari, you HAVE to let me wear a bra on TV.

Kevin: Glad we don't have those telepathic things hooked up to our brains yet.

10:12 AM
Kevin: Ow, ow, Caleb, stop. I was worried my thoughts about Taco Tuesday would get released. That's what I meant. Ow.

Himari: We can talk about wardrobe allowances and strategic wound bandaging, I suppose. Hey, Kevin, what's your henchman name going to be?

Kevin: Well, I have given this some deep thought and have narrowed it to two choices.

Kevin: Sexy Cowboy or Amnesia.

Kevin: You know, because I forget things.

10:13 AM
Kevin: Obviously, we should go for the cowboy choice. It's the far superior one.

Himari: All right, cowboy, your name will be Amnesia. And I'll be Virus. Because, you know, I'm a villain, and viruses are the villains of tech.

V: I'm so proud.

10:14 AM
Caleb: Sounds like a plan. We'll alert the press and let the madness begin. Keep us in the loop as you head to Indy … after getting your disguises, of course.

Himari: Neat. We'll keep in touch.

TV LIVE NEWS BROADCAST TRANSCRIPT

JUNE 12

Anchorwoman Clara Bentley: And now to tonight's trending story. Last Friday morning, the rising star rookie superhero known as Cortex was kidnapped while attending TechieCon in Silicon Valley, California. We're going live to the scene. Ashley?

Reporter Ashley Harrison: Thanks, Clara. I'm standing outside the convention center where convention goers are tearing down from last week's tech convention. It appears the superhero Cortex was here with his sidekick on superhero business when he was unexpectedly captured by a villain known only as "Liam."

Anchorwoman Clara Bentley: But Ashley, villains and heroes fight all the time. What's special about this one?

Reporter Ashley Harrison: Cortex and Liam had no previous contact before the kidnapping. Instead of duking it out in a battle, reports say that Cortex simply disappeared.

Anchorwoman Clara Bentley: Thanks, Ashley. Hundreds of thousands took to social media with the hashtags "free Cortex" and "real villains fight fair." But when Cortex was freed, he came back with a shocking message. Join us after the break to find out more.

THE HERO EVENING TIMES
JUNE 12

Heroes Now "Powerless" Against New SA Captor

Three days ago, rookie superhero Cortex was kidnapped. But the nation took notice today when he escaped with a shocking new message.

"I know most heroes who try to search for enigmatic SA members are coming up short, but we might have a lead. Liam's been claiming to suck powers from heroes and villains. I just ... narrowly escaped him taking mine away from me," Cortex told the press. "I can't really go into detail yet, but rest assured that we're on it, and we need help from both heroes and villains for the final push."

Cortex has been making waves in the hero community long before this. He is pictured below with his girlfriend, a deadly villain known as Vortex, a former member of the underground villainous Shadow Assassins.

But this large-scale push for hero and villain collaboration is unprecedented.

"Villains and heroes need to work together," Vortex said. "This person sucking superpowers is bad news for heroes and villains. Listen, villains, fighting these heroes is cool and all, but let's take out the Shadow Assassins. That would be one heck of a feather in your villainy cap."

In an anonymous statement that dropped only hours ago, sources suggest that nuclear warheads were unintentionally sold to underground anarchists by global arms dealer TakahashiCorp—anarchists who may in fact be members of the Shadow Assassins. Owner and CEO of TakahashiCorp, Kosuke Takahashi, refused to comment, but some have questioned whether Cortex and Vortex know more.

When asked about whether his new approach is the result of a greater global threat, Cortex dodged the question.

"It may not be a huge résumé booster to be on a big team, but Liam, our most immediate threat, is a danger to us all."

EVENING TALK SHOW TRANSCRIPT
JUNE 12

Roger: I'm telling you, those two know something the rest of us don't. What sort of scheme is this?

Joe: Maybe Cortex has turned villain, and he's trying to make heroes weak.

Ted: Or Vortex turned hero! Taking out the SA sounds strangely … heroic, depending on your point of view.

Roger: Most heroes don't waste their time on the SA. No publicity fighting unregistered villains. Usually the government has to deal with their terrorism tactics.

Paul: Okay, but let's be honest, the people who are best at being villains tend to be current or former SA members. The villain creed is all for killing any and all heroes, other villains, or those associated with the business, but even the villain creed stops at civilians, unlike the SA. The SA's no-holds-barred approach really helps villains develop the proper bloodlust.

Joe: There's also the possibility Cortex and Vortex are working with the government. Washington has been trying to crack down on hero/villain activity in the wake of an eighteen percent increase in collateral damage.

Roger: Speaking of collateral damage, which of you fellas have been eating all my donuts? You bet I'll find out ... during this break.

ENTERTAINMENT NEWS
JUNE 12

Voiceover: What was Vortex wearing to the press conference? Were those ... FAKE CONTACTS?

Second Voiceover: Next, the truth behind singer Carlie Irish's rise to fame.

Voiceover: And coming up, is Vortex PREGNANT???

Third Voiceover: Entertainment News, happening ... now!

THE FABULOUS FOUR
JUNE 12

9:13 PM
Kevin: *Okay, I think I have this thing on. Think normal thoughts, Kevin. Normal thoughts. Not about how amazing Himari looks with that pink hair. Or how weird you look with black in yours. And the new haircut. Yeesh, I look like a sad soldier. Why did I have to have super-bright red hair? Dyes don't work well on that.*

Kevin: *Also, what a dumb plan. We're just planning on waltzing right up to the entrance and asking if we can join Liam's team. Like, he already replaced the guys with guns up front.*

Kevin: *At least I remembered to park in the parking lot this time.*

9:14 PM
Himari: You're thinking so loud, Kevin. I'm trying to concentrate on looking villainous as we approach.

Kevin: Sorry. I'll try to look like I'm out of it, which is what most sidekicks slash henchfolks look like anyway. I was born to play this part.

Himari: This black cloak is surprisingly cool and comfortable for summer. V had a great designer.

Kevin: Yeah, they were churning out garments like Project Runway pros … not that I ever watch that show. *Dang it, Kevin, be cool.*

9:15 PM
Himari: *Okay, walking between gunmen. Polite nod. Midwest wave.*

Gunman: You get the flier?

Kevin: The what?

Himari: Sorry, my henchman is stupid. Yeah, definitely. I must have, um, misplaced it, though.

Kevin: No, you didn't, boss. I forgot it. *Wink.* Like I always do. I'm such a dummy.

Himari: *Who thinks "wink"?* Right. So, uh, mind directing us, fellas?

9:16 PM
Gunman: Knock at the front door. He's still setting out dip for the party.

Himari: Uh, right. The party. Thanks! *Walk away normal, be cool.*

Kevin: *You also get the feeling that we're walking into a trap or something? What dude puts out dip for a party? Unless they made it out of the blood of our enemies.*

Himari: *Listen, nothing about Liam is normal. Probably why he's at the Indy SA outpost. Indy's lame.*

Kevin: *So wait, he isn't the head of SA? Caleb got kidnapped by some sidekick of the big boys? Maaaaan, is he gonna get mercilessly teased by the Kevin Maester.*

> **Himari:** *I mean, he's not a sidekick. He's the head of the Indy chapter of the SA. But ... yeah, we're nowhere near the level where V was.*

Kevin: *You gonna knock or we gonna just stand here like some sad little Girl Scouts in black capes? Or villain scouts. Do the villains have scouts?*

9:17 PM
Himari: *I'm working on it. Okay, Himari, bladder control. You're fine. Not nearly as scary as the SA HQ V used to talk about. Just this dweeb. K, you did it. Good job knocking.*

Himari: *I really need to tune this tech better.*

Billy: Hello, can I help —

Himari: Billy! Uh, I mean, hi!

Kevin: *Ain't that the dude you shanked?*

9:18 PM
Billy: Do I know you?

Himari: *Yup. I mean, he's alive, so that's good, but oh gosh, is he gonna recognize me?*

Himari: Uh, you deliver great pizzas.

9:19 PM
Kevin: *How the heck did he survive getting stabbed? Twice?*

Billy: Aww, I'm blushing. But judging by your costumes, you're either a little early for Halloween or got the flyer.

Billy: Liam, they got the flyer.

> **Liam:** That's great. Wow, Billy. So proud of you for posting those all over Indy, going into coffee shops and doing door to door. You really have a can-do attitude, don't you know?

Kevin: *Did he just come running to the door? He looks so excited.*

> **Himari:** *Deep breaths.* Hi! You must be Liam. I'm Virus. Amnesia and I saw the flyer, and, uh, we were really excited.

9:20 PM
Liam: Wowza, guys, have to say I feel "hashtag" blessed tonight. I had twenty or so other villains and henchfolks show up a few hours ago, and we want to get the initiation started soon.

Liam: But first.

> **Kevin:** *Oh no. What's he going to do? Brand us? Make us kill someone? Swallow a spoonful of cinnamon?*

Liam: Can't have you come inside without a nice Liam hug. Get in there. Yes. There you go. Big squeeze. Now we're friends. Okay, come inside. Feel free to leave your shoes at the door, and I have some nice snacks set up.

> **Himari:** Wow, uh, that was a nice hug. Er, thanks.

9:21 PM

Liam: Billy positively outdid himself. Way to go, Billy. Take the rest of the night off, man.

Billy: You got it, boss.

Liam: Meet us out back in five at the fire, okay, you two? Wow, it's so great meeting new people. I'll let them all know you're here.

Himari: *A fire? Are we burning a body?*

Himari: Cool, thanks, Liam.

Kevin: *You know, sometimes the best thing heroes can do is run away like brave little cowards.*

9:22 PM

Himari: *Not helping, Kevin. Look around. Anything stand out to you? Anything to do with nukes or power-sucking weapons?*

Kevin: *No way!*

Kevin: *He has a bunch of stuffed rabbits playing on a fake-grass meadow above his fireplace. Wait, are those taxidermy?*

Kevin: *We may be dealing with an absolute evil mastermind.*

Himari: *V would be upset enough to kill him just for that. In fact, pretty sure she did kill a guy with a bunch of antler racks once.*

9:23 PM

Liam: Hey, guys, everyone's so psyched to meet you. We got the white stuff and the brown stuff and the tan stuff out for some special little treats, if you know what I mean.

Kevin: *I don't. But maybe that's because I'm Kevin.*

Kevin: *Is he saying we're going to eat people of different skin colors alive?*

Himari: *V didn't mention cannibalism.*

Liam: Oh, I see you've found my little bunnies. Yeah, found those at a garage sale last year. Figured they were all sad sitting in the dust and all. So I decided to give them a nice happy warm place right above the fire, ya know?

Himari: *I take it back. V would probably marry this guy. My brother better watch out.*

9:24 PM
Himari: Cute. Uh, lead the way to the many-colored things.

Liam: Oh, you sure? Everyone's pretty antsy to get started, but I didn't want to rush you. You got plenty to eat? I can see if we have more drinks in the fridge. Anything at all?

Himari: That's really kind, but I think we're good. *I don't want to barf anything up at this initiation.*

Kevin: *Plus, maybe he's on to us and poisoned everything. I bet this nice thing's all an act.*

Kevin: *Although speaking as a thespian and theater major, if he's pretending, he's really good at it. I wonder if he does any method acting?*

9:25 PM
Liam: All righty, well if you insist, I can't turn you down. We have some seats outside, so take one, and we'll get started.

Kevin: *Are those beanbag chairs? So hard to tell in the dark.*

Himari: *Guess I'll try it out … yup, beanbag. Ooooh, super comfy beanbag. Even better than yours, Kevin.*

Kevin: *Well, for all we know, maybe he's making you super comfy so he can drug you, man. Kevin likes his beanbags sharp and hurting his tushy.*

Himari: *That … defeats the whole purpose of beanbags. Whoa. Look at this sketchy crowd. They all look ready to kill.*

Kevin: *White, tan, yup … you think we're going to have to eat each other?*

Himari: *Can I just say I'm allergic to human meat?*

9:26 PM
Liam: Okay, folks, hope you're settled in. Did everyone pass around the little baggie? Carl? Carl, stop hogging those and let the new folks get some, you little rascal.

Kevin: *What's in the baggie, Himari? Human body parts?*

Liam: All right, well I guess Carl ate the remainder of what was in the baggy. I'll have to go get some more when this is over. As you all may well know, SA is known for their mighty-intense initiations.

Himari: *Omg, here it comes. We got this. It's all good.*

Liam: So tonight I want us to sit around this fire … and talk about our feelings.

9:27 PM
Kevin: *What?*

    Carl: What?

Himari: *Oh thank God, we're not eating each other.*

    Carl: That's so stupid.

Liam: Now, Carl, everyone in this circle here is entitled to their opinions. We do want to value the thoughts of all members who came to the first beta initiation. Next week, I think I'll have Billy hand out some flyers around Muncie. But rules are rules, man, and we really like a team player atmosphere around here, you know?

    Carl: Well, I ain't doing it.

9:28 PM
Liam: Now, Carl, you're starting to push my buttons just the teensiest bit. I really do hope we can still be friends and that you participate in our initiation—

    Carl: Forget it, I'm not doing any stupid—ack!

Kevin: *Shoot, did he just stab him with a marshmallow skewer? Oooh, now I get the white and tan thing. Marshmallows.*

    Himari: *Wow, right in the jugular.*

Kevin: *Dang, the dude just keeled over. I think I'm gonna be sick.*

    Liam: Sorry there, Carl, I feel mighty sad to have to put you out like that, but we really value teamwork here, and I can't have anyone participate who wants to isolate others.

Sorry, y'all, that you had to witness the blood and all that. I know it's not always everyone's favorite liquid to see.

Himari: *BLARGH*

9:29 PM
Liam: Ope, y'all, sorry. I hear one of you throwing up. Should've given a warning beforehand. Let me know if you want a blindfold in case any of the others aren't too keen about team exercises and all.

Kevin: *Oh, Himari, I'm sorry. I'll turn this thing off. You look really dizzy and probably don't need to hear my voice in your ear.*

Liam: Anyone know any good campfire songs?

THE FABULOUS FOUR
JUNE 13

5:34 AM
Kevin: *Kevin's Log, since apparently I wasn't allowed to bring my phone with me to Liam's Lair—I mean, Lodge—which means I have to put this on the group chat. So he can't see these messages, I guess. It's something dark outside AM, and Himari's asleep. Heavy sleeper, and snorer, from the sounds of it, so she probably can't hear me. Just wanted to get all the weird off my chest.*

Kevin: *Last night, after Liam led us in some campfire tunes, he wanted to have another "sharing time." He said, "All right, y'all, this has been a mighty good campfire. Who wants to talk about their super cool powers? We'd love to see your amazing gifts." Almost no one had any, but this one chick named Willow said she could turn herself into a tree, kind of like some Greek myth. I don't know. She was going on and on about it.*

5:35 AM
Kevin: *Anyway, after she demonstrated her power for everyone, Liam stood, grinned, clapped her on the back and said, "Thanks for sharing and doing that amazing demonstration, Willow. The firelight really made it look epic. Now, Willow, here we see everyone as equal."*

Kevin: *She sort of rolled her eyes in a snooty way and said, "Uh-huh. Just some villains are more equal than others." Some villains, heroes, and even henchfolks and kickies, can get that way sometimes. They do that on the Meta-Match forums. Act all like those with powers have a one-up on those who don't.*

Kevin: *Wowza, I could miss scrolling through those forums. How do people ever survive without their phones? I get Caleb didn't want us to have our phones so Liam couldn't steal them and hack them, but still ...*

5:36 AM
Kevin: *So Willow has her nose upturned. We're all awkwardly trying not to address the fact she has a branch still stuck out of her nostril. Forgot to change it back, I guess. Or who knows? Maybe it's a fashion state-ment where she's from. She did have an accent.*

Kevin: *While she ain't lookin', Liam reaches into his belt, pulls out a syringe, and jabs it into her neck.*

Kevin: *So she's screaming, wailing, the nostril branch shriveling, and at last she slumps to the ground and goes night-night.*

5:37 AM
Kevin: *Liam has a real weird look in his eyes. He says, "Thought Billy included it in the flier, but we don't want any folks with powers here. Makes everyone feel excluded, less than whole, you know?"*

Kevin: *Then he claps a hand on her shoulder, not that she can really tell, and says, "Here we make sure everyone is equal."*

Kevin: *So glad Himari doesn't have any powers. If he did anything to hurt her ...*

Kevin: *I wonder what Liam would look like as a taxidermy bunny.*

5:38 AM

Kevin: *After all the weirdness of last night's bonfire, Liam sent us to a number of cabins. Each room has a bunkbed. He wanted everyone to pair up with someone because, "We share to care, here. Mama always said, 'Roommates and bunkbeds make today some life friends.'"*

Kevin: *I think Mama needs to stop trying to be Dr. Seuss. She didn't even come close to rhyming with that one.*

Kevin: *So now, Himari's on top, and I'm on bottom.*

Kevin: *Of the bunkbeds. It's weird that we're in the same cabin, but I think we were too scared of Liam to ask to be put in separate ones.*

Kevin: *Oh shoot, someone's opening the door.*

> 5:39 AM
> **Liam:** Mornin', Amnesia. How's one of my best of friend-os?

Kevin: *Huh, Himari's still sleeping. Guess I'll whisper just in case.* Good, Liam. Trying not to wake the roommate.

> **Liam:** Look at you, all polite. What a great pal you are. I wanted to show you something.

Kevin: *Uh-oh.*

> **Liam:** Found this at a garage sale yesterday. Thought you'd like it since you were staring at the mantle and all.

5:40 AM
Kevin: *A taxidermy fox?* Wow, Liam, you shouldn't have.

> **Liam:** I'll just put it by your things. Wow, a pair of Spider-

Man boxers on the floor. Man, do I have the coolest friends or what?

Kevin: *Okay, no one can act that well this early. Something seriously isn't working right up in this dude's head.*

Liam: Now, Amni—mind if I call you that? Want to help me collect firewood? I thought we could make some tin-foil eggs at the fire this morning with all our new friend-os. Billy taught me the recipe. Learned it in Scouts, that resourceful little moose.

5:41 AM
Kevin: *Not really, but maybe I can learn more about you. You didn't share much at the campfire last night, after the skewer to the jugular incident, bro.* Yeah. I love me some firewood.

Liam: Great, let's set off for an adventure, Amni.

Kevin: *Sleep well, Himari.*

5:42 AM
Liam: Thanks for closing that door slowly, man. It squeaks and would've given your poor friend a nasty little headache. Once Billy comes back, I might see if he wants to oil the hinges, if it doesn't put too much of a strain on him, you know? Don't want to abuse the employees.

Liam: But at this point, why even call him an employee? He's like family. You're like a brother to me, Amni. After you shared your heart at last night's fire.

Kevin: *Oh, right, forgot I had to make up a story on the spot about my "origin." Good thing I took those improv classes. And also, thank God he let Himari sit that one out, after her throwing up and all.*

Haha, yeah, too bad I "forgot" most of my memories—Virus really took me under her wing and helped me get on the path to villainy.

> 5:43 AM
> **Liam:** That's all well and good, friend. Sounds like she's a lot nicer than what I saw at the front door last night. Her calling you "dumb" lit just the teensiest bit of frustration in my chest, man.
>
> **Liam:** But that story there really set me on the right path too.

Kevin: *Shoot, should've warned Himari to be more polite.* Yeah, she just meant the dumb thing jokingly. Sometimes villains have to put on a front, you know? *"You know?" Now I sound like him!* At first, when she acted nice to me in public, people told her she needed to man up and act like a real villain by treating her henchman like ... *Oh shoot, did I step in dog poop?*

> 5:44 AM
> **Liam:** Sorry to hear that, good friend.
>
> **Liam:** Villainy doesn't work like it used to. People used to hatch evil schemes and—
>
> **Liam:** Oh, grab that stick. Yes. Amni, my man! You've done it. Look at that beauty.
>
> **Liam:** —and heroes would try to stop them. Wow, look at that sunrise. Beautiful above the lake, don't you think?

5:45 AM
Kevin: *How did this guy manage to fit all of this in Indy? Then again, we are in the greater-Indy area. And Indy is pretty big. But still, I think*

157

the strip mall in the distance sort of ruins the campground feel. Yeah, wow, so orange.

Liam: But the definitions got all blurred. Take those heroes V and Cortex, for instance.

Kevin: *Shoot, I hope he didn't see me tense. Relax, Kev. Shoulders down. Breathe.*

Liam: V turned from villain to hero in an instant, killing a bunch of SA members, and I heard rumors that Cortex killed a dragon henchman. Not all that hospitable, if you ask me. Heroes don't do that kind of thing, my good man.

Kevin: *Oh right, Bernard. I almost forgot Caleb accidentally electrocuted V's old henchman.*

5:46 AM
Liam: And those are just two teeny-tiny examples. More and more, we see villains and heroes turning in their capes for publicity stunts, and—yes, that's a beautiful stick. Man, can you find some good specimens of wood, Amni!

Kevin: *Wonder if these things can even burn. Dew's drenched them.*

Liam: Even take my own parents.

Kevin: *Oh boy, parents. Here comes the backstory.*

Liam: Dumped me into Mama's lap when I turned two because kids can't enjoy the show-biz life. And I didn't have an inclination for powers, so they didn't really want to bring me along. They had great powers and all, but used them mostly to star in movies and pose for action figures. Really, the weird power craze started with them.

Kevin: *Wow. Himari did mention once or twice that she feels a little lonely being the only one in her family without powers. Maybe she'd understand Liam a little.*

Liam: You may have heard of my dad. He was more famous than Mom. Went by the name Dimension.

5:47 AM
Kevin: *Dimension, Dimension? Oh, wait! Bingo. Caleb used to idolize that hero, until he showed up to a party at Caleb's house all washed up. I guess hero work did a number on him.*

Liam: Years later, some villains and heroes with better powers replaced them. When the media turned their eye, parents didn't react all that well. Mom disappeared and, well, Dad pursued side gigs.

Liam: By the time they'd retired, I was in college. They didn't know me, nor I them. Saw them more in movies than in real life.

Liam: Wow, really sorry there, Amni. Didn't mean to dump all that on you. Hadn't even practiced that bit in the shower. Boy, do I feel embarrassed.

Kevin: No, man, it's all good. *Okay, Kev, slide into those DMs nice and easy.* Bet that provided some good reasons to join the SA, huh?

Liam: Sort of. Leveling with you, good friend, I don't all that much like the way they run some of their shindigs. I mean, look at their initiations. No heart to hearts whatsoever.

5:48 AM
Kevin: Yeah, weird. *Eww, this stick has mushrooms on it.*

Liam: But when they saw a chemistry major in college had some ideas about a formula to drain heroes and villains of their powers, they gave me a business card. A really nice one too. You know those cards that have the nice textured embossed letters? Man, did they put their all into those little babies.

Kevin: *Did he just jump up and down talking about a business card?* Yeah, wow, entrepreneurship.

Liam: Said when I graduated to take up the mantle on the Indy chapter. How could I say no to running a business in the best place in these United States?

Kevin: *Ask him, Kev. Ask what SA wants to do with that formula. Breathe. He just clapped your back real hard. Prob means he trusts you.*

5:49 AM
Kevin: What does —

Liam: Oh, partner, looks like I see another Liam friend poking his head out of his cabin. Better go greet him and give him my favorite stick I picked up. Whoopee! See you at breakfast, good friend.

Kevin: *Aaaand, there he goes bounding down a hill. Our deranged camp counselor who sounds like he's pretending to be Southern.*

Liam: Morning, best friend-o. Man, did you just make my day by showing your wonderful face.

Kevin: *Better turn this thing off and hope we didn't wake Himari.*

VORTIE AND CORTIE

JUNE 13

5:13 PM
Vortie: *I'm glad we figured out we can do the mind-text thing in PMs too. Although Kevin's personal diary this morning was entertaining.*

    Caleb: *Yeah, too bad he can't really read it back with no cell phone and all. Let's hope poor Himari slept through that.*

    Caleb: *Speaking of things I wish I could've slept through. How about that lecture I just got downstairs from Mom a couple hours ago, eh? Riveting stuff.*

5:14 PM
Vortie: *Yeah … Oh gosh, how do I even respond to him? I mean, you! Oof, this mind thing.*

    Caleb: *Glad we didn't turn it on when I first saw you in that dress. That plunging neckline got me. Oooh, don't think that out loud, Caleb. Now, walk me through why we had to go to this function anyway?*

Vortie: *Eyes are up here, love. Anyway, we need to mingle, you know?*

Be all, winsome or something. We gotta get these heroes on our side.
Thank goodness your parents were already planning on hosting a hero
party tonight. Even though it's kind of turned into an everyone-grill-
Caleb-and-V party.

> **Caleb:** *Yeah, just glad Dimension isn't here. That guy knows*
> *how to ruin a shindig.*

5:15 PM
Caleb: *Sorry people keep trying to hug you with the wound and*
all. You'd think Liam sprinkled some hug dust on them or
something.

Vortie: *You know, I'm just glad they don't all watch me like I'm about to*
kill them anymore. Remember that first party? Oof.

> **Caleb:** *True, I guess that's what you get for "betraying your own*
> *kind." People get weird about hero and villain labels. Now, if*
> *people would stop asking me to do party tricks with my powers.*
> *I keep having my mom flicker the lights on and off just to make*
> *people think I'm doing it.*

> **Caleb:** *Wouldn't it be just easier to say, "Hey, Liam can drain us*
> *of our powers?" I feel like this whole putting on a façade thing*
> *could backfire. Oooh, might grab some of that veggie dip.*

Vortie: *Of course we want them to know he drains powers. Just not*
YOUR powers. I'm not in the right shape right now to protect you when
a bunch of villains find out you're vulnerable.

5:16 PM
Caleb: *Yeah, well, glad my parents invited a bunch of heroes*
and not villains.

Vortie: *What's wrong with villains? We need them too, remember?*

Caleb: *Sorry, still stuck in the old definitions. We're all fighting the SA. Not villains. Okay, you can stop gripping my hand that tight. I get the point.*

Caleb: *Although, don't you think it's weird that Liam only invited villains and henchies to his weird bonfire bonanza? Like, why couldn't I get some white and tan munchies? Oh, yuck. Why does this dip taste like blue cheese?*

Vortie: *Ewww. You think any heroes are going to be down for stabbing people with anti-power serum? Besides, he's technically aligned with the SA. A villain organization.*

5:17 PM

Caleb: *True. So the villains will be harder to convince to fight against them.* It's great to see you too, Coral. How are the little guppies doing? *Glad I have you to try to sway them.* Yeah, I know. Potty training is the worst. I mean, I'm not a parent, but. *Oh, okay, and now she's gone.*

Caleb: Hiya, Rex. Oh, you want to see my powers? *Wave at Mom. Ignore her eye roll. Oh good, she's by the light switch again.* Ready to see these babies flicker? Yeah, that's right. SA better look out. Or they'll get weird vision problems from watching these things strobe. Good to see you too, Rex.

Vortie: *We do not kill people at parties. We do not kill people at parties. We do not—WHY IS A GROWN MAN PICKING HIS NOSE?*

Caleb: *Whaaat? I definitely don't ever do that. Okay, Mom's back now. She looks frustrated. Let's hope no one else asks to see me do anything other than flicker the lights. Heroes can be Kevin-dumb sometimes.*

5:18 PM

Vortie: *You're getting a hardcore death-glare from your mom, my dude. It's a good thing he doesn't know what she said to me. Whoops. Oh look, grapes!*

> **Caleb:** *V. You hate grapes.*

> **Caleb:** *What did she say?*

Vortie: *Not a big deal, just something along the lines kind of that if she didn't like me so much, she'd tell me to dump your sorry a*—Oh, hi! Yes, nice to see you too—*because you're an idiot, and you're going to get us both killed. She was probably just overreacting. Or joking. Probably joking.*

> **Caleb:** *Yeah, my mom can't tell jokes to save her life. And my "ah" does feel a little sorry.*

> **Caleb:** *Yeesh, I can't please her. One moment she wants me to save the world, and the next she wants me to save for college. I can't do both, woman.*

5:19 PM

Vortie: *Your dad could probably buy half the country if he wanted to. With those gold powers and whatnot. Why on earth do you need to save for college? Oh, yeah, the responsibility thing. Guess that could be helpful … for some people! But you're very responsible. I'm proud of you. Stupid devices, hate these.*

> **Caleb:** *When you read minds for a while, you learn how to filter properly. Oh, please tell me that isn't a slit in Ms. Edmondson's dress. She's sixty-two.*

> **Caleb:** *I guess my parents are a little like Liam. They had their powers before the weird publicity craze, so they actually had to*

do real hero work without any social media following or movie deals. They want me to save and all for college because they don't want me getting lazy like other heroes.

Vortie: *Yeah ... kinda hard to be heroic when it's all for publicity and no one is really helping real people. Like, fighting heroes is fun, as a villain, but my parents got to actually rob banks and stuff. Now that's considered impolite. You're only supposed to fight heroes.*

5:20 PM
Caleb: *Weird as it sounds, maybe Liam does have some good points. I think forcing people to hug and drugging them ain't polite either, but maybe when all this mess is over, we can figure out what we really want to do in terms of hero work and—*

Caleb: *V, who's the weird dude in the gray cape? I've never seen him here before.*

Vortie: *Oh my ... How did he ... I thought I lost him a long time ago.*

Caleb: *SA? But he looks just like a hero. There could be more of them in disguise here. I think I see an unknown by the punch bowl.*

Vortie: *Not good. It's been too long since I was in the SA—I don't recognize enough faces. But the guy in the gray cape? I ... know him ... a little too well ... This is not good.*

Caleb: *No kidding. Most people in here are out of their prime or rookies. Don't even think we have any C-list heroes.* Hi, Blast, yeah, we'll have to catch up sometime. *Do you know if anyone here has any formidable powers? Enough to take down SA? Shoot, I think my mom and dad left. Maybe to clean up one of the other rooms. And they never have their cell phones on them ... I wish they'd get over the hating-tech thing.*

5:21 PM
Caleb: *V? Oh, crap, you're shaking.*

Caleb: *Is it one of those panic attack thingies? Himari said … shoot, what did Kevin say to do? Breathe, maybe?*

Vortie: *Chains. Dark. Cackling. Dark. So dark. Very dark. Pain. No no no no no …*

Caleb: *V, I need you to stay with me. I don't get these attack things, so I don't know what all is helping, but you need to stay calm, okay? Inhale? Exhale? Shoot, the guy in the gray cape is coming toward us. Shoot, stop thinking, Caleb, you're freaking her out even more.*

Vortie: *Can't see. No-no-no-no-no.*

Caleb: *Oh, aww, V, you sure you want to hug right now? I mean, don't get me wrong, I just don't want to hurt your wound. OH, okay, you're clinging tighter. I guess that answers my question. There, there, just breathe. We should be out of this mess soon—Oof!*

Unknown Source: Die, villain!

Vortie: Aaagh!

5:22 PM
Caleb: V! Get off her, you freak.

Unknown Source: You killed my sidekick, villain. Prepare to meet your demise.

Caleb: Get off her. I'm warning you. *Shizz, his eyes have a certain glint. Like he knows something he shouldn't.*

Vortie: Aaagh! No! Ah, ow-ow-ow!

Unknown Source: Tell you what, hero. Since you betrayed your kind, why don't you use your powers against me to stop me from killing your girlfriend, eh?

Vortie: Grim, please, no ...

Party Guest: Come on, Cortex! Use your powers to stop him. Flicker the lights. Something!

> **Caleb:** *He knows my bluff. But I gotta do something. Come on, there's gotta be a weapon somewhere. The table. The knife to cut the cake. Maybe I can cut his hand or something and he'll let go of V's neck.*

> 5:23 PM
> **Caleb:** Let her go now, or else.

Unknown Source: Hmm, where to dig my blade in first? You don't mind if I slice those pretty little eyes, do you? After all, the contacts are fake.

> **Vortie:** *This is it. He's gonna kill me this time ...*

Caleb: *I'll show you not to threaten her. Take that. And another one to the arm. To the leg. Get off her. You're gripping her like a spider. And another, and ... what just happened?*

> **Vortie:** Caleb, stop ... stop stabbing ... he's ... dead ... *Whoop, can't ... see straight ... is that my blood too? Dang it, bleeding on my favorite ... dress ...*

Party Guest: Cortex lost his powers.

Other Party Guest: And he just killed a hero.

5:24 PM
Caleb: Shoot, V, we have to go. Now. Can you stand?

Vortie: Tr-trying … think the—agh—stitches ripped … help please.

Caleb: I got you. We'll mend these on the helicopter. I think Himari managed to install the autopilot function. But we have to go.

Vortie: W-where are we going?

Caleb: I—I don't know. Anywhere but here. I think I just … *Save thinking for later. Turn your mind off, bro. Let's get to the helicopter. Is anyone chasing? No, I think they're just standing around in shock. Hate hearing my voice in my head. Echoing … echoing … echo—*

EVENING TALK SHOW TRANSCRIPT

Roger: I guess Cortex did turn villain after all, eh, fellas? I mean, this hero swoops in, says his girlfriend killed his sidekick, and Cortex just slices his throat in front of this huge party.

Joe: Yikes, sounds worse than my parties when my relatives get together.

Ted: What do you think drove him to it?

Roger: I'll bet Vortex's been having quite the influence over him for some time now. We've shown time and time again that you can't trust villain and hero romantic relationships. One always manages to convince the other to join their side.

Paul: Well, thoughts and prayers go out to the unknown hero's name. His family requested that his hero identity not be unveiled to the general public until they've been able to have a private funeral.

Joe: We don't even have a last name? A secret identity?

Paul: I think they mentioned two initials: an A.S. Maybe it's Adam Sanderblock, who coincidentally died of "choking on a taco" around the same time, as mentioned in a post by one of his family members.

Ted: So Cortex killed Adam Sanderblock in cold blood is what you're saying.

Roger: I'm saying there's no way Cortex is a hero now. No hero kills other heroes. We've seen vigilantes kill villains, and sometimes henchmen, but that's rather out of the norm or accidental.

Joe: Didn't he kill a henchman two years back? A Bernard something?

Ted: You know, I think you're right, Joe. Maybe he's been a villain this whole time. I heard his parents are supers too. You think the pressure of having two super parents got to him?

Paul: I'll tell you what's getting to me: this pizza the studio ordered for us right before we went live. We best be heading for a commercial break before things get … messy.

THE FABULOUS FOUR
JUNE 13

9:12 PM
Himari: *Mm, sticky marshmallow. All right, Kevin, we on?*

Kevin: *Were you and I ever off?*

Kevin: *Okay, you didn't need to pelt me with a marshmallow. Yes, we should be on.*

Himari: *I'm going to be honest—this day of personal reflection was actually pretty relaxing.*

Kevin: *Speak for yourself, man. When Liam decided we needed to have bonding time by dumping everyone into the lake, I had to chuck this communication device thingy under a log. Glad it didn't rain today.*

9:13 PM
Himari: *See, he told us this morning we would be doing that, but you didn't listen. I left mine safe and sound under my pillow. You really should treat my tech better.*

Kevin: *At least your tech didn't get fried by the sun. Looking at you, sun! I even put on 50 SPF. But noooo, Liam was all like, "Take the 100, bro. We all look rather dashing when we look like we just slapped paint on ourselves, you know?"*

> **Himari:** *Well, you look like you didn't put any on at all. I've never seen a human that color red. Except for that one villain, Mr. Mad, or something? Who turns red when he gets super-powered?*

Kevin: *Maybe I do have powers and you just don't know it.*

9:14 PM
Liam: Wow, Billy, putting Peeps marshmallows in the fire. You've done it again, my pal. Why they don't put you on some fancy cooking show, I'll never know, man.

Kevin: *So I don't know what you got out of today, Himari, but I learned the bottoms of manmade lakes are super gross when your feet touch them. So, so slimy. Shudder. Also, my feet touched something hard with a handle. Like Liam threw a door at the bottom of the lake or something. What a weirdo. And that Liam either needs a new hobby or someone to date, because clearly he has way too much energy.*

> **Liam:** Now, Billy, how did you heal from that sunburn so fast? I guess I can't really tell in this lighting. Was going to say, thought you had powers for a minute. Yeah, you silly moose, Liam's going crazy over here, isn't he?

Himari: *I learned that Liam is nuts, but I don't think he's our biggest worry. He just wants his nice little club. I'm worried about that shipping box I saw in his garage.*

Kevin: *What do you mean he's not our biggest worry? I definitely saw him stab some dude last night. Maybe you forgot. Throwing up and all. And he probably just shipped in more taxidermy. Also, I saw you put a hat on the fox earlier. Isn't it weird that he packed our cabins full of clothing?*

Himari: *Moving on from the fox, and the incident of which we shall never speak again, it wasn't taxidermy. It was full of serum, and it looked like he was ready to ship it out to the SA HQ. Which is literally what the address said. "To SA HQ."*

9:15 PM
Kevin: *Hard to argue with that, but yeah, that does sound sketch. Too bad we're stuck here, huh? Since we don't really seem to be getting many leads from the Liam loony.*

Liam: Good idea, Rover. You guys start on the round of Kumbaya. I want to talk to two of my best friend-os.

Himari: *Speaking of, here he comes.*

Liam: Hiya, Vir and Amni, wow. You guys both look so … ah, Amni, you silly moose, you. Not putting on enough sunscreen. Mama always said, "If you don't want to burn in the sun, put on 100 SPF." It doesn't rhyme, but I think it's grand advice. No worries, man. I think you still look great. Makes your black hair really glow in the firelight.

Kevin: *I have no words. Can he just stab me and get it over with?*

9:16 PM
Himari: Yeah, our good friend-o Amnesia gets fried pretty easily. Poor guy. What's up, Liam?

Liam: Well besides the fact that I am so blessed to talk with some of the coolest people sitting around this fire—that's you, by the way …

Kevin: *Did he just wink?*

Liam: I really wanted to talk with both of you. Mind if we go somewhere a bit more secluded, so we don't disrupt this beautiful rendition of Kumbaya?

Kevin: *Sounds like dying cats, I'm game.*

Kevin: *Wait. Shoot. Himari, what if he just found us out and wants to kill us somewhere away from these people?*

9:17 PM
Himari: *Yup, that was my first thought, but you have a point. Might be better than listening to Kumbaya.*

Liam: You both keep staring into each other's eyes. I think we know what that means. But I'd better get in on the action too. Let's all hold hands as we walk around the campsite.

Kevin: *Himari, you're standing in the middle.*

Himari: *Ugh, fine. Or we could put Liam in the middle. ;)*

Kevin: *Oh wait, he just grabbed both of our hands. I guess that answers that question. Wow, he has really soft hands. I think I saw him put on some hand sanitizer earlier WITH ESSENTIAL OILS. How extra.*

Liam: Vir, which direction should we go, left or right? Each is equally important, equally correct, and equally amazing. That Robert Frost has simply no idea what he's talking about.

9:18 PM
Himari: Right. Um. Let's go right, then.

Liam: Wow, such decisive action. You sure blow me away, Vir. Billy doesn't have many faults, except that he gets down on himself a lot. Reminds me of a burrito. Lots of great stuff on the inside, but bruises kind of easily on the outside. Now, let's skip-dee-doo to the right. Okay, aaaand, now we're far enough away from the singing. I'd love to talk with you both about something. Something secret that I don't want the others to know.

Kevin: *Shoot, he definitely knows. Himari, we're going to die.*

Himari: *I'll stab him. And you stab him from the other side. And then we run.*

Kevin: *Good plan except we have nothing to stab him with. Except our intellect. And by "our," I mean "your." Mine would be like an anti-stab. A hug.*

Liam: You two sure are awfully quiet tonight. Shows me you have great listening ears. Wow, just when I thought you couldn't get any cooler.

Liam: Now, Vir, I saw you doing your reflection journals in the garage earlier and noticed your legs were propped up on a certain box of mine.

9:19 PM
Kevin: *Busted.*

Liam: And that got me thinking, you know what the three of us haven't done that could bring us into a super level of bonding time?

Himari: Ritual sacrifice?

Liam: Oh, you just crack me up. Such a kidder. No, a road trip!

Kevin: *YAY. Oh, wait. No.*

Liam: I have a fun mission I'd love to take y'all on if you're up to it, but it's fine if you say no. I won't cry too much.

9:20 PM
Himari: *Dear God. But it could be a lead.* That sounds super fun, Liam!

Liam: Oh dear, the tears are coming anyway. I could just hug you if we weren't already holding hands. Now, I'm mighty pleased to hear that. First thing in the morning, let's hit the road. Shall we get back to the campfire for the final verse of Kumbaya?

Himari: Yeah, wouldn't want to miss it. By the way, where are we heading for our road trip that I'm so excited about?

Liam: Silly Virus. You forgot to put your listening ears on earlier during our trust exercises in the woods. Mama always said, "The key to friendship is not telling them anything and letting everything be a surprise."

Kevin: *I'm starting to think Mama is just a figment of this dude's imagination.*

9:21 PM
Kevin: Yeah, silly Virus. We can't wait to be surprised with whatever destination you have in store for us.

176

Liam: Great, now that we're back at the campfire, I'm going to put on my inside voice when I tell you this, but pack lots of clothes and get ready for some fun. Amni, don't forget the Spider-Man boxers.

Kevin: *Did he just wink again?* No problem, Liam. But I do forget a lot.

Liam: Haha, what a kidder. Okay, Kumbaya, my Lord. Kumbaya.

Himari: *Oh Lord. I'm turning this off.*

VORTIE AND CORTIE

JUNE 13

11:37 PM

Vortie: *Okay, we have to do mind texting so we don't scare my little friends. No loud noises.*

Caleb: *Yeah, so, so many questions, but first. Where are we? Once you got your stitches, you sort of went all command-mode and stole the controls and everything. It was hot, scary, and weird, all at the same time.*

Vortie: *Stitching myself up was invigorating. Never try needlepoint—you suck at stitching. We're almost there. Are you sure you want to be carrying me down this rocky path? I can probably walk.*

11:38 PM

Caleb: *I'm trying to protect you from the bats.*

Vortie: *Silly, those are my friends.* Chitter-chitter-chitter-chrik!

Unknown Source: Chitter Chitteree peep.

Caleb: *So remind me how you know about this villain's cave? Can we barge in here without them noticing us? I'd rather not get stabbed in my sleep.*

Vortie: *Oh, it's my cave. I built it after I lost my house two years ago, just in case your house exploded or something. Always good to have a backup lair.*

Caleb: *Oooookay, it's too late for me to compute or ask questions, so I'll simply go with it. All right, now entering another room, and ... V.*

Caleb: V? I thought you took all your plushies to my mom's house. What happened to the creepy lair vibe?

11:39 PM
Vortie: Well, the first few chambers with the chains and spikes and stuff are because the bats really like that aesthetic, makes them feel all cool, but in here I wanted all my little friends. That one is Carly, that one's Shelby, that one's Steven ... Yeah, I probably won't give you all twenty-five names. You'd forget them.

Caleb: Well, Kevin has been rubbing off on me. And is that a pink plush comforter? Who are you?

Vortie: Okay but listen, it was half off and it's SO SOFT. You must try it. But not wearing that. You're all bloody. Here, put me down.

Caleb: Oh, but it's dried up at this point, and ... No. Absolutely not. I'm not wearing that.

Vortie: We can match! They were eighty percent off after Valentine's Day, matching fuzzy hearts and flowers jammies.

11:40 PM

Caleb: Why do you even have one in my size? That's weird.

Vortie: I told you I was prepared for your house blowing up or something. I have a pair for you, Himari, your mom, your dad, even Kevin. It was a great deal.

Caleb: Again, too late to comment or question. Fine, turn around. I don't want you to see me putting these monstrosities on.

Vortie: Heeheehee, okay, I'll wait for the big reveal.

Caleb: Wow, footie pajamas too, huh? Now what's the plan since everyone thinks I killed a hero? *Okay, Caleb. Left foot. Okay, now right foot. Don't fall.*

Vortie: Well, you kind of burned the hero bridge, so I figured we could reach out to some of my villain friends. Oooh, I forgot I had this little sleeping cap. You want it?

11:41 PM

Caleb: Man, needlepoint did give you a rush. And no, I think this is plenty. Ta-da.

Vortie: Oooooooh, SO CUTE! Heeheeheehee, you're like a giant plushie.

Caleb: I'm both ashamed and feeling complimented. But back to the villain thing. Do you think that's the right way to go? I mean, won't they hate me, even if I've killed only one hero?

Vortie: Oh, they hate everyone. It's okay. You just have to convince them it's in their best interest to work together. And most of my villain friends are ex-SA anyway. Got bones to pick. Ugh, why can't I find my pair? Too many cute jammies in this drawer.

Caleb: You could always just wear the mask.

11:42 PM
Caleb: Wow, okay, why do these plushies hurt more when you hit me with them?

Vortie: OW. I should not exert myself or throw things right now.

Caleb: Maybe we should return to planning tomorrow when we've had time to think. *And have hopefully turned off this mind chat thing so we don't think too deeply about the fact that I purposely killed someone. Not accidentally. And oh gosh, this is showing up on mind chat, but now I can't stop thinking about the theater, and Bernard, and the lights, and please stop me …*

Vortie: Hey, hey, listen. You saved my life. Either Grim was going to die, or I was.

Caleb: True, and Grim would've looked terrible in these jammies. The glass eye would've thrown the whole thing off.

Vortie: And Bernard and I both know it was an accident. Stuffed Bernie told me. It's all okay. Thank you for saving my life. I kind of … froze.

11:43 PM
Caleb: Honestly, would do it again in a heartbeat. And you couldn't help it. After everything SA did to you … no one blames you.

Vortie: Yeah … I guess it just … keeps coming into my mind lately. And then I imagine …what if … Never mind. We should probably sleep.

    Caleb: Oh—okay. But we should probably come back to this when we both have the energy.

    Caleb: And when a creepy hyena stuffed animal isn't staring into my soul.

Vortie: You can put Henrietta in the closet if it makes you feel better.

    11:44 PM
    Caleb: Nah, I think she might be growing on me.

    Caleb: Goodnight, I guess.

    Caleb: Sleep tight.

    Caleb: Don't let Henrietta bite.

THE FABULOUS FOUR
JUNE 14

4:56 AM
Kevin: Who da heck is knocking at the door this early … oh no.

Liam: Good morning. Hope you guys don't mind Billy coming along. Would feel like a third wheel and all with the way you two looked at each other on our special little walk. Now wakey wakey and meet us in the driveway in precisely three point five minutes. Toodles!

4:57 AM
Himari: I'm going to kill him.

Kevin: Great, now my pants are on backwards. I'm so disoriented. Himari, any idea how long of a drive we have to look forward to?

Himari: Nope. *Oof, it's too early for pants.*

Kevin: *Best go without them then.*

Himari: I wish I had something to throw at you.

Kevin: Oh, whoops, forgot I had the mind thing turned on. It's been a habit just turning it on the moment I hear knocking. So Caleb and V can know how we hit our endly demise.

4:58 AM
Himari: "Endly?" It's too early in the morning for me to even be sure if I should make fun of you for that one. Hey, you should put sunscreen on, just in case, Mr. Tomato.

Kevin: Haha. We're going to be inside, you doofus.

Himari: You should have at least let Liam rub some aloe on it last night, hahaha.

Kevin: Stop, I'm having flashbacks. That's so weird he offered to do that.

Himari: Rub, rub, rub-a-dub.

4:59 AM
Kevin: We should probably rush to the car. I have no idea how much time we have left. I'm guessing point seven minutes.

Himari: Wow, specific. Okay, got your Liam's Lodge logo-embellished duffel all packed?

Kevin: If by "all packed" you mean I shoved in whatever clothes I had in my dresser in the last ten seconds, then yeah. I thought by "early" he meant, like, nine.

Himari: All right, let's hit the road then, friend-o. Hey, I'm going to turn our tech off.

Kevin: What, you don't want Liam's Mad Libs and Twenty Questions to take up screen space? He was all giddy about his new Mad Libs book he got at a garage sale. "Only half filled out, what a steal!"

Himari: Over and out, Caleb and V. Hope things are a little more normal on your end.

VORTIE AND CORTIE

JUNE 14

7:49 AM
Unknown Source: Would you like to purchase a jar of premium eyeballs?

> **Caleb:** Umm, V, why's there a salesman at the mouth of the cave? Do I want to know? He just woke up all your bats, by the way, so we could probably just speak now.

Vortie: Noooo, is that why the doorbell rang? It's not even eight yet! I should put up a sign. "Do not knock before 10 AM if you don't want to be stabbed."

> **Caleb:** Okay, but please explain the eyeballs. Does it come with a monthly subscription to Evil Vogue or something?

7:50 AM
Vortie: The Villain Scouts came around last year selling body parts, and I bought some to be nice, but now they won't stop sending people. And they aren't cute little kids anymore.

> **Unknown Source:** I'll come back later!

Vortie: Bet you a million bucks that was Harold. He should've graduated Villain Scouts thirty-five years ago, but he's still at it.

   Caleb: Well, I guess we all have our hobbies. Now that we're awake, what's the plan with the whole Cortex-turned-villain-gasp! thing?

Vortie: Noooooooo, we're not awake yet! Noooooo! Come back and snuuuuuggle, pleeeaase.

7:51 AM
Caleb: Tempting as that is, my phone is blowing up with notifications. Hate mail and fan mail. Disturbing. We should probably get a jump on this early.

Vortie: Fine. But I might kill people. I don't have my no-murder filter on until after ten.

   Caleb: As long as you don't kill me and end up with Kevin.

Vortie: Nah, he and Himari have a nice road trip now to get to know each other. What? Stop glaring. I think it's kinda cute.

   Caleb: Listen, if I wasn't a gentleman, I'd be flinging these stuffed animals at you.

7:52 AM
Vortie: Poor babies. Ugghh, I'm still a little loopy from those pain meds. Anyway, what were we planning? Oh, yeah, helping you make villain friends! Gasp! I have costumes!

   Caleb: Did you just say "gasp" out loud?

   Caleb: And no. I think I had my fill of outfits from you, missy. You're going to put me in an Easter Bunny outfit or something.

Vortie: No, silly, these are of my own design. Ouch, still hurts to move much. Hey, open that closet, will you? Take a look. And will you hand me my phone? Gonna text some villain friends.

Caleb: Sure thing. Here.

7:53 AM
Caleb: Whoa! Okay, you've been holding out on me. Seriously, where did you get the money to afford this fabric? This is the stuff the pros use.

Caleb: Then again, your parents did rob banks ...

Caleb: Remind me why you worked retail again?

Vortie: Bernard recommended it for increasing murderous rage. Anyway, I didn't afford this fabric. Juan stole all my assets, remember? I kind of ... permanently borrowed it from someone who didn't need it anymore.

Caleb: Oh, gotcha. And yeah, sorry. We haven't heard Juan's name in a while. After he crossed us and it turned out he was working for SA, I've sort of tried to block any memory of him.

7:54 AM
Vortie: Come on, I've seen you sneak in and throw darts at his face on my dartboard when you think I'm not paying attention.

Caleb: Well, he does have a very impaleable face. Okay, does the red cape work for me? Or green? I just need to avoid purple, since … you know, that was the color I wore as a hero.

Vortie: Sigh, but you look so sexy in purple. Hmmm. Green? But now I'm picturing you as Barney. Probably go with red.

Caleb: Barney and sexy. Whoosh, I've hit bottom. Red it is.

7:55 AM
Caleb: Does it look all right?

Vortie: Turn around, let me see. Heeheehee, I think it looks great.

Caleb: Well, I guess it doesn't really matter anyway. Heard back from any of your friends yet?

Vortie: Yeah, Slicer just responded. He said they're having a bash today at his lair. He really wants me to come see his new interior decorating. Oh, wait … that's flirting. OH. That … was really flirting. Anyway!

Caleb: How does Slicer feel about getting sliced? I've killed once and will kill again.

Vortie: That's adorable. Anyway, I texted him back that we would love to come to his bash. Oh, who's we? My boyfriend and I. Oh, he stopped texting. Dang it.

7:56 AM
Caleb: Eh, he's probably a sucky villain anyway.

Vortie: That's just rude of him. We've been friends for years. Oh, look, Pulse texted back. Heehee, she's going to Slicer's bash and invited me to come with. Looks like we're in. Just asking the time.

Caleb: So I've never really been to a villain event before. Any tips? Do I just brood and avoid eating in case everything's poisoned?

Vortie: Wow, is that really what you think we do? Villain parties are LIT. We play Russian roulette, throw knives, show off our new torture gadgets, and play poison pong.

Caleb: Right, so it's EXACTLY what I thought villain parties were like. Let me know when you have a time for the event. I'm busy trying to get these shoes on. Stupid spandex.

7:57 AM
Vortie: Got it! Party starts at three. Oooooh, that's different! A daytime party! Edgy! Slicer has always been edgy.

Caleb: Great, so I put on this spandex for nothing. What do you say we watch some movies on that huge TV you have in the main area and get back in these costumes before the party?

Vortie: Sounds good. I have some spare black cloaks in there for myself and plenty of disposable contacts.

Caleb: Are they prescription? I'd kind of like to see at this thing.

Vortie: Gasp! My time has come! Open that drawer.

7:58 AM
Caleb: Niiiiice, sweet glasses. And they're actually my prescription. These look cool. I hope. There are no mirrors anywhere.

Vortie: They look fabulous. I told you I was prepared. So … what sounds good for movies? I've got Axe, Logan, Terminator, and Frozen.

Caleb: Well, obviously, since I need to get in the mindset of a villain.

Caleb: Frozen it is.

THE FABULOUS FOUR
JUNE 14

1:25 PM
Kevin: *So Mad-Libs was interesting. I was curious why Liam could only alternate between two verbs, "hug" and "stab."*

Himari: *Also, I told you to put sunscreen on. Who knew it would be a convertible?*

Kevin: *Well, now that we're here I gotta say Liam's Lodge looks just the teensiest bit more cozy. You know, with the huge looming building, electric fence, and men with machine guns, I think I want to go back to the lake.*

Himari: *So this is what's hiding in the middle of Pennsylvania. Not where I imagined a global villain slash terror group would have their headquarters, but okay.*

1:26 PM
Kevin: *On the bright side, we got to stop at a tourist cheese place on the way. So if we die, we at least ate happy.*

Liam: All righty folks, here are your name badges. And these big fellas here want to give us a nice good pat down. Pat, pat, pat, good, good. Now, sorry, but they don't want to hug you, so don't try. Okay, everyone got a good pat down? Were they thorough? We want to make sure to give them the best opportunity to do their jobs.

> **Himari:** Well, pretty sure I've never been so thoroughly … patted down before, so I think they did a great job.

1:27 PM
Liam: Great job. I'm going to fill out the company survey later and give y'all five stars. Okay, now that everyone has their name badges, we can head on inside.

> **Himari:** *Through the gigantic metal doors flanked by what look like automated spikes. Awesome. This is chill. All is well. Totally fine.*

Liam: Wow, they sure did a great job with this place. I think I even see a rooftop garden. No wait, that's just graffiti. Onward we go.

1:28 PM
Liam: Oooh! Got to stop by the front desk first and say hi to the secretary. Hi, Hulga, did you do something with your hair? I love how you made it look like snakes. So environmentally conscious. A woman with a mission. How are you doing this beautiful afternoon?

> **Hulga:** Mr. Gladkins will see you in two minutes. Sit.

Liam: What a nice reception area. These hard seats really make me appreciative of the comfortable ones we have in the convertible. Is everyone full? Had enough to drink? We can always make another stop at that cheese place. Billy, you silly, eating all the samples.

Himari: I think we're fine. *Mr. Gladkins? Is he anything like Liam? Maybe this steel and black marble waiting area is just a façade. Maybe the entire SA is different now? Maybe they won't brand an SA on our butts? That would be nice.*

1:29 PM

Kevin: *Speak for yourself, sister. I got some nice cheeks. But yeah, the name Gladkins doesn't exactly strike fear into you. I don't even know if V would name one of her sharks that.*

Himari: *My brother said the worst part of the branding is the kerning. And it's in Papyrus. What do you think Mr. Gladkins wants from us?*

Kevin: *Well, if he suspected us, Liam would've let on by now, unless he really wanted us to endure that car ride with him just to have us meet our endly end. Makes sense. All those Mad Libs were torture of some sort. Especially with the pages flying all over in the wind.*

1:30 PM
Hulga: Mr. Gladkins will see you now.

Liam: Wow, right on the dot. What a polite little fellow. Come on, folks. Up the rickety staircase. Let's see if we can make some music with our feet.

Kevin: *This stuff looks like it's rotting. Any chance we could plummet to our death?*

Himari: *I'm just annoyed Liam walked right past the elevator.*

Kevin: *Probably feels like we have to earn the trip to the office. He's the kind of a "pull yourself up by your bootstraps," "rode a dinosaur to school" kind of guy, it seems.*

1:31 PM
Himari: *Oh gosh, look at those gigantic double doors covered in rivets. This is like the movies.*

   Kevin: *I don't know what movies you're watching. Mine are mostly the ones with musical numbers.*

Himari: *V likes movies with a lot of screaming. Look how burly those guards are.*

   Kevin: *Yeah, those biceps could squish my head like a grape. Okay, they're opening. Breathe. His name is Gladkins. He's probably a super small smiley kind of guy.*

Liam: Okay, folks, the moment we've all been waiting for. We're here!

   Himari: *I can hardly see, it's so dark. Oh man, that's a big chair behind that desk. Slowly spinning around …*

1:32 PM
Himari: *Slooooooowlyyyyy. Wow, it looks way better in the movies with ominous music playing in the background. It feels really weird with just silence.*

Liam: Oh, sorry, Mr. Gladkins. I forgot in my excitement to play your tunes. Feel free to start over. Guys, we have to re-enter to not spoil the entrance. Everyone out of the room? Great. Playing the tunes … now!

   1:33 PM
   Unknown Source: *Dub-DUN! DUN DUN DUUUN. Dub-DUN!*

Himari: *Oh … wow. That's a big man.*

Mr. Gladkins: You can turn the music off, Liam.

Liam: Yes sir. Thanks for recommending that soundtrack, Billy.

> **Kevin:** *He doesn't look all that glad. Maybe because of that scar running from his eye all the way to his lip. Any chances that's a birthmark?*

Mr. Gladkins: So these are your best hitmen?

1:34 PM
Liam: If by hitmen you mean the most dependable, superb listening, and most attentive best friends an SA branch head could ask for, then yes sir. Sorry, Billy, but you're too young and vulnerable for this kind of mission. Not after I found out you got some blood on you when some people invaded Liam's Lodge.

Kevin: *Umm, Himari. Didn't you stab him? That's a little more than some blood.*

> **Himari:** *Well, you know Liam. Everything's a bit more sunshine and rainbows in his rendition of life.*

Mr. Gladkins: Hmm. Well, if these are your best, they'll do. I assume you two know the Indy area fairly well?

1:35 PM
Himari: Yes, sir.

Billy: They had to know it, Mr. Gladkins. I only posted fliers in the city.

> **Liam:** Post them you did, you little sucker. Now, Mr. Gladkins, these are some of my best friend-os, so can we have an

idea of what sort of trials and tribulations they may encounter on this fine mission you're putting them on?

Mr. Gladkins: You may exit, Liam and Billy. I want to speak to these two ... alone.

Liam: Well, you do know best. Say hi to Kara for me, and let me know if you want me to send another fruit basket arrangement to your house. Oh, oh, yes, these guards are very strong. You certainly know who to hire, oh —

Unknown Source: *THOOM*

1:36 PM
Kevin: *Call me crazy, but I felt a little more protected with Liam in the room.*

Himari: *Yup. It's really dark now. And this guy ... yeah, he looks like an SA director.*

Mr. Gladkins: Ugh, that kid ... He really does know his way around serums, though. But you two. I'm putting together a team for a special mission, and I need members from your area. Surprisingly, we don't have many branches around there; Indiana is pretty boring. So you two will be my Indy Assassins.

Kevin: *Think we're going to take down race cars, Himari?*

Himari: *Shut up, Kevin! I'm trying not to pee my pants. Dang it, mind text!*

1:37 PM
Himari: So what do you want us to do, Mr. Gladkins?

Mr. Gladkins: Have you ever heard of TakahashiCorp?

Himari: *Oh, crap.*

Kevin: *Don't your parents own that?*

Himari: *Wow, Kevin, great job noticing.* Yes, sir. The biggest independent arms dealer in this hemisphere. What about it?

Himari: *Wow, now that's an evil smirk.*

Mr. Gladkins: I need Kosuke Takahashi. Here. But I have reason to believe he is guarded by the superheroes Lux and Aurumque. Every time I send forces to kidnap him, those two get in the way. I need them out of the picture.

1:38 PM
Kevin: *Himari, those are your parents' superhero names, right?*

Himari: *Yup. So this is no bueno.* What do you need from us?

Mr. Gladkins: I'm glad you asked. I have a PowerPoint.

Unknown Source: *Click. Click. Click.*

Mr. Gladkins: Oh, come on. Where's that intercom? Hey, I need someone up here to fix my projector! Sorry about that, you two.

1:39 PM
Kevin: *I think I just went deaf. Never give that man a megaphone.*

Himari: *Hahaha, runs an evil corporation but can't use Power-Point. Okay, Boomer.*

1:40 PM
Juan: Yes, Mr. Gladkins?

Himari: *WHAT. Are you seeing what I'm seeing?*

Kevin: *I said deaf, not blind. Shoot, do you think Juan will recognize us? He knows our faces, even with the new hair and suits.*

Juan: Ah. The projector again. I see, sir. You just need to hit this power button first. Yes, excellent.

Mr. Gladkins: A pleasure as always, Juan.

1:41 PM
Himari: *Is it just me or did Juan give us a look on his way out?*

Kevin: *And a wink, yeah. Maybe he has a lazy eye. Let's hope. It is really dark in here.*

Mr. Gladkins: All right, sit down. The presentation is about to begin.

Unknown Source: *BADADUUUUUM*

Unknown Source: *BA-DING. BA-DING.*

Himari: *Okay, for all of our sanity, I'm going to turn this off so we don't have the slide noises recorded on here every time he clicks on something. Who does that?*

Kevin: *Yay! Clipart!*

VORTIE AND CORTIE
JUNE 14

2:59 PM

Vortie changed name to V

V: Sorry, can't take myself seriously with that name.

Caleb: No worries.

Caleb changed name to Cortex

Cortex: Since we're in costume and all, might as well act the part. So that's a creepy mansion. Did he paint the outside black?

3:00 PM
V: It's supposed to help keep it warm in the winter. Environmentally friendly!

Cortex: Also all the rose bushes are painted black. How is that even possible?

V: No, it's a special breed! He gave me clippings. Haven't you seen them growing in my fox-in-socks pot?

> **Cortex:** Not going to comment on that. Also, your voice is in my ear. Did I accidentally click on the voice-to-text function on this thing? I'm so helpless when I can't control tech. Hope we can figure out a way to get my powers back soon.

V: Must have been when you looked at the notification that I changed my name. But it's fine. Then we can mind-text, you know? In case you think someone might kill you and I have to challenge them to single combat.

3:01 PM
> **Cortex:** See, hero parties aren't like this. At hero parties you just roll your eyes while everyone tries to one-up each other with stories of saving people, and you take selfies with some heroes you've been following. That's literally it. No combat.

> **Cortex:** Unless a member of the SA happens to crash, and then … things get bloody. Let's hope these new disguises will help keep them at bay?

V: I think it's going to be great. I always wanted to bring you, but I didn't think you would really be down.

> **Cortex:** Babe, you know I'd go into SA HQ with you. I think I was just less keen on getting killed. No one has seen me as villainous until now.

3:02 PM
V: Nice. Well, maybe we'll go to these parties more often. Hey, there's Briar. Hey, girl! Nice thorns you've got going there. Looking real good.

Briar: Thanks, Vortex. Omg, is that your boyfriend? Yeah, he does kind of look like a villain. Look at that facial scar. Nice to meet you, Cortex! Welcome to villainy.

Cortex: *Literally, how does someone respond to that?* Umm, thanks. *Nailed it.* Nice skull decorations. Looks like Halloween came early. Haha.

V: Oh, those are probably some recent hero kills.

Cortex: Wow, so morbid. I love it. *V, can we please leave now? These lovely folks probably won't join the SA or anything. We go up the stairs now?*

V: *You're fine.* So Briar, have you seen Pulse? She's the one who invited me.

3:03 PM
Briar: Oh, bad news, girl. She just challenged Venoma to poison pong.

V: Ohhhh. Not good. She dead now then?

Cortex: *Internal screaming.*

Briar: Of course. Happens literally every time. Don't know why people try challenging her anymore.

V: Hmm. Maybe I should try sometime. She's had the record for ten years.

Cortex: *Yeah, this is just small talk, right? You won't try that challenge, right? V?*

V: *What? Oh, probably not today. Gotta stay focused. I'm pretty good at poison pong, though.*

> **Cortex:** *Gonna put that under the list of things Caleb didn't really know and probably would've had a happy life not knowing.*

3:04 PM
Cortex: *Okay, so shall we start recruiting people to team up to defeat the SA? Because I'm getting worried that your friend also hung a bunch of skeleton arms and legs from the ceiling like streamers.*

Slicer: O to the M to the G! Is that mah girl Vortex? Hey, there, beautiful!

> **Cortex:** *Any chance I can kill him without doing poison pong?*

V: Oof, careful on the hugs there, Slicer. *Detangle. Detangle. Oh, there, put his arm around Briar's shoulders, perfect.* Hey, good to see you. Uh, Slicer, this is my boyfriend, Cortex. Cortex, Slicer.

> **Cortex:** Nice to meet you, man. *Yikes, he's trying to break the bones in my fingers. Get him off. Get him off!*

Slicer: Yeah, so great to finally meet you. Thought you'd been a little, well, too chicken to come. You know, couldn't keep up with your girlfriend. But, guess I might have been wrong. Welcome to the party.

3:05 PM
Cortex: *What does he mean "keep up"?* Yeah, haha, whoo.

V: Thanks, Slice. Hey, I was wondering, are there any new people here? Not the regular partygoers?

Slicer: Nah, this guy's the only odd one out. Usually don't let outsiders in, but anything for you, Vort.

Cortex: *Eww. Vort? Also, outsider? Aren't I a "villain" now?*

V: *This crew has known each other for a long time. A lot of ex-SA. Not exactly dealing with it in a healthy way. Hence the poison pong.*

Cortex: Yeah, you know me. The weird kid. Well, we're glad there aren't any weird characters bopping around. *Did that dude just eat a tarantula?* Because we heard an SA member crashed a hero's party. Zapped some peeps of their powers. Weird stuff.

3:06 PM
Slicer: Oh, man, yeah, I heard about that. Only a hero would be that dumb, ha!

V: Well, there have been some villains too.

Slicer: Eh. Not very good ones. Come on, you two! I've got a place at the arachnid buffet for you. Oh, and a vegan option, just for you, Vort. Spider plant soup. It's a little spicy, but I feel like that's up your alley.

V: *Here comes the wink. Yup, there it is.*

Cortex: *Please let me kill him.*

V: *I appreciate the thought, but I'm not sure how well that would work without your powers. Although, let's be honest ... it's probably best for everyone you can't read his mind right now.*

3:07 PM
Cortex: *You don't think I can take him? Of all people. You, V?*

V: *You know that's ... that's not what I meant ...*

    Cortex: *Fine. Whatever. It's fine. Just recruit them and let's get this over with.*

Slicer: Hey! Courtney! My man! Did I say that right? Have some spider guts on the rocks. A delicacy.

    Cortex: Wow, thanks. You're a real slice, man. I can't wait to chug this in a dark corner over there. *Be right back, V. Gonna dump this when someone isn't looking.*

V: *Good. It's horribly cruel to poor spiders.* So, Slicer. *Oh wow okay he got a LOT closer.* I know we've all been out of the SA for a long time, but do you ever still worry they'll come back for you? *Oh, that's not a polite place to look, you fool.*

3:08 PM
Cortex: *I'm dumping! I'M DUMPING AS FAST AS I CAN!*

Slicer: Sure, baby, I mean, they can always come after us. That's why you gotta live it fast, you know? Live in the moment.

    V: *Dodge the arm. Dodge.* Right, ah —

Cortex: *Heyyyy, V. Question. Some dude walked down the stairs with a gun. Aren't villains more about medieval torture weapons or powers? That seems out of place.*

    V: *Yeah that's a little —*

Slicer: Why you staring into the distance, Vort?

    V: Sorry. Um. Like I was saying. You ever think maybe we should just take down the SA so we don't have to deal with them anymore?

3:09 PM
Slicer: Ha. Ha. HAHAHAHAHA. You're so funny, Vort.

Cortex: Hey, folks. I'm back. Wow, what great spider guts. Stuffed to the brim. Gonna just put my arm around my beautiful GIRLFRIEND. Babe, I love you forever. Let's get married someday.

V: *Wow, overboard much?* Love you too, babe.

Cortex: *Well, I'm sorry, but I guess that's the only thing I'm good for without my powers. I'll just be a stay-at-home dad while you go out and play poison pong or something.*

V: *What? Where is this coming fro—*

Slicer: Ha, get a room, you two. Heh. So what were you actually trying to say about the SA? I know you must've been joking about actually taking them down.

3:10 PM
V: Well, no, actually—

Unknown Source: *BANG BANG BANG!*

Cortex: Get down! *V? You hiding under the pool table? Is this normal for a villain party?*

V: Slicer! Who is that wacko? Don't they know there's a no-guns rule at parties?

Slicer: I don't know him, Vort. Whoa. What's he stabbing people with?

V: Look out! Another one from the other direction. Cortex, watch out!

3:11 PM
Briar: Ugh, I'm not dealing with this cr —

Unknown Source: *BANG!*

Cortex: *Are they shooting with bullets or ... shoot, I know that smell.*

V: *They have it weaponized now?*

Cortex: *Liam did say I was a beta tester. Maybe I was the last one? I guess they've moved on to bigger and better things.*

V: *Fantastic. Come here, get under the arachnid bar. I think I left a few knives here last time.*

Cortex: *So that's the plan. Just make me cower? Don't you think I'm immune because I lost my powers? Shouldn't you be the one to hide?*

3:12 PM
V: *It's fine, there are ... um ... okay, five of them and I have ... yup, two knives under here. I'll make it work. Wow, everyone is dropping like flies. They have real weapons too. Ugh, what is this sticky stuff? Oh look, I'm bleeding again, whoopsies. These stitches suck.*

Cortex: *Yeah, well, you did them. Stay down, I'm going after this guy.*

V: *Yeah right, I'm not staying here. Be back in a minute.*

Cortex: *No wait—ugh, great, now she's tackling one of the guys. Okay, well, one down, four to go. I like those odds.*

3:13 PM
Cortex: *Shoot, one of them is aiming a gun at her from behind. Sorry, V, I'm going in.*

V: Die, you shadow scum!

Cortex: *This guy's stronger than he looks. Oh, snap, that's a really jagged blade.* Augh! *Dang it, he got me on the arm.*

Cortex: *Yeah, tech powers would've been great right now to dim the lights. Or to read his mind and anticipate his actions.*

Cortex: *Wish there was a serum to reverse this …* Augh. *Shoot, that's the leg. Oh, crap, I think that's a bigger vein. Yep, this outfit's toast.*

V: *Two down. Caleb, what are you doing? Don't let him sit on you!*

3:14 PM
Cortex: Oof! *Ah, crap. Why does this guy weigh so much? What's he doing with that knife?*

Slicer: Whoa, man, you can't just go offing my best girl's boyfriend. That's my job.

Unknown Source: *SLICE SLICE SLICE SLICE*

Slicer: There we go. You look like some nice sandwich meat now.

Cortex: *Yeah, and now the rest of the outfit is covered in blood.*

3:15 PM
Cortex: *Crap, V. Look out behind you!*

    V: Wha—augh! Let go! Agh! Right to the side … that's the wounded side … *cough cough*

Cortex: *Ugh, can't get this corpse off me. He's heavier dead than alive.*

    Slicer: Vort! I got you, bay-bee!

Unknown Source: *SLICE SLICE*

    Slicer: Ah! Dude, you're pretty much dead. What did you just inject me wi—ooooh no.

3:16 PM
Cortex: Ugh. Finally got him off. V, are you okay?

    V: Oof! Got an unconscious Slicer on top of me … can't breathe …

Cortex: Pulling him off. Ugh, ugh, okay, off. Yeah, and stay off her, you creep.

    V: Hey, he saved me. He can't be too bad. *Cough cough.* Ugh, I'm never going to heal at this rate.

Cortex: Yeah, let's not really talk about that creep saving you, all right? It's embarrassing enough he had to kill the dude on top of me.

    V: Aww, he did? See, he's not that bad. Anyway, can't really see straight at the moment. What's the damage? Anyone still up?

3:17 PM
Cortex: Looks like they got everyone but you.

Cortex: The SA's sending a clear message.

Cortex: Villain or hero, the SA can take you down. So much for trying to recruit villains. Once they find out the best of the best were taken out … oh, boy.

V: Hey, they didn't take me out, at least.

Cortex: Yeah, but your power is stealing other people's powers. If SA gets to heroes and villains before we do …

3:18 PM
V: Oh. I'll be just as helpless as you.

Cortex: … Yeah, that.

THE FABULOUS FOUR
JUNE 14

3:47 PM

Kevin: *Okay, whew. Himari, I just ended my sprint trials. They basically had me run around for the past ten minutes and go retrieve weapons. One of the dudes almost hit me over the head with a mace since I didn't know what a flail was. Apparently it is NOT a dance move. He said yours might be a little longer because "Henchmen usually just die, so their trial is simply picking up whatever object we tell them to." Glad Liam packed some extra shirts. And sandwiches for lunchtime while Gladkins had all those meetings. I guess our trials took a bit of time to set up.*

Kevin: *How are you holding up with your trial? Did they make you get a flail?*

3:48 PM

Gladkins: It's simple. If you want to be a full-fledged member of the SA, you must be well-versed in our tactics. Torture is one of them.

Himari: Right. Um, what about bribery?

Kevin: *Shoot, torture?*

Gladkins: Ha! I should have known a friend of Liam's would be a joker. Now, show me your technique. Your physical trials and weapon-wielding tests were impressive. I'm excited to see what sadistic things you can do here.

3:49 PM
Himari: Right. Definitely. Um, hello, you tied-up, chained-up person. You're going to tell me everything, you know, or else!

Unknown Source: As if. *Ptew!*

Himari: Ew. I mean, how dare you spit at me!

Gladkins: Sighhh, I have another meeting soon ...

Himari: Okay. Yes. So, um, you're part of the secret service, right, mister? So tell us the secret things of the secret service.

Kevin: *Yeah, I'm not quite sure that's how a villain would talk, Himari. That sounds like something I would say.*

3:50 PM
Gladkins: If he's not talking, show him you mean business. Like this.

Unknown Source: *SMACK!*

Gladkins: See? Now, hurry up.

Himari: Uh, tell me where the president eats breakfast, or else I'll, um, cut off your toes!

Kevin: *That seems extreme.*

Himari: *I know, ack! I was trying to sound scary to Gladkins.*

Unknown Source: We don't negotiate with terrorists.

3:51 PM
Gladkins: Well? Do it.

Himari: Oh … really? Maybe we should give him a chance to consider?

Gladkins: Listen here, "Virus." If you don't have what it takes, we can always use another test subject in the labs. Your choice.

Kevin: *I really hate to say it, Himari, but you might have to do something you hate right here. Remember Juan? Everything he said to us outside the room? Believe me, I wish I could go in there for you, but guards are blocking the doors. I'm in some waiting area with no windows.*

Himari: *Okay, Himari. You can do this. You're a villain. V killed people all the time. It's fine. It's just toes.*

Unknown Source: AGH! AAGGGHHH!

3:52 PM
Himari: *Ohmygosh-ohmygosh-ohmygosh.* Just tell us what you know!

Kevin: *Do you need me to turn this thing off to focus better? I don't know how much I'm really helping, and I clearly caught you at a bad time.*

Gladkins: Hahahaha! Yes! Now, the ultimatum. If he doesn't talk … kill him.

Unknown Source: I'm not t-talking.

Himari: Please don't make me do this. Please.

Gladkins: Do it.

Himari: *Kevin. I have to. I have to do it. I ... Turn it off, Kevin.*

3:53 PM
Kevin: *I'll see you out here soon. No one blames you ... remember that. I don't blame you.*

THE FABULOUS FOUR
JUNE 14

11:23 PM
Kevin: Himari, everyone went to bed. We can talk now.

Kevin: Himari?

Kevin: Listen, I know you're not asleep, because you're not snoring. You have a cute snore, by the way.

Kevin: Himari?

11:24 PM
Kevin: *Yo.*

Kevin: *You can't ignore my voice in your heeeeead.*

> **Himari:** *Leave me alone. Please. I … I don't know if I can speak to another human ever again.*

Kevin: *Well it's a good thing I'm an elephant. Speak to me, Mari. We don't have to talk about it. We can talk about how we were awkwardly* *playing board games in the lobby with Liam. He really likes Monopoly for some reason. The PB&J sandwiches he packed were cute.*

11:25 PM
Himari: *Maybe if you keep rambling in my ear it will drown out my thoughts. Or ... the sounds of ... screaming ...*

Kevin: *Now don't get me wrong, I love the sound of my voice in your head, but maybe we should go about this a different way. I don't want you to hurt. And trust me, if I talk and talk and talk, it's going to hurt. I've been told my voice is "annoying."*

Himari: *Honestly, Kev, I've never found your voice annoying. In all this crazy stuff, sometimes the only thing keeping me sane is your stupid jokes.*

Himari: *Um, Kevin?*

11:26 PM
Kevin: *Um, George?*

Himari: *I always thought I wanted to be a villain. But ... I barely didn't puke all over the place. And ... I just ... I couldn't look into that man's eyes without thinking he could be someone else's Kevin. Or Caleb. Or whatever. And ... and then I k-killed him.*

Kevin: *Oh, Mari, I want to give you a hug, but also don't want to ...* Oh, okay, you're down for a hug. All right. Come here. Look at me. What Gladkins wanted you to do ... people have got the definitions of heroes and villains all mixed up. That was something else, but that's not V or any other villain. Movies and Instagram make out this hero and villain stuff to be glamorous. It's not. I know for a fact Caleb gets flashbacks from everything he's seen.

11:27 PM
Kevin: What Gladkins did is something that shouldn't have happened. And I'm so sorry I couldn't rescue you. You won't believe how helpless I felt in that waiting area.

Kevin: I should've been the villain and you the henchman.

> **Himari:** There was nothing you could've done. At least …
> at least I trained for this sort of thing. Or … I thought I did.
> Stupid me. I don't have a villainous bone in my body. I
> just … I wanted to do SOMETHING. Caleb's always been
> so cool with his powers and everything. Like, everyone
> knows Caleb. But me? I'm just the nerdy kid sister, or that
> girl you cheat off of in Engineering 101. I thought …
> maybe I could be something special too. A scary villain. So
> much for that.

11:28 PM
Kevin: Hey, hey, hey, let me tell you, you're a lot cuter than Caleb.

Kevin: And oh my gosh, if people don't know your name, don't know what you're capable of, their loss.

Kevin: Personally, I think powers are overrated. Caleb's getting a sharp kick-in-the-tushie lesson about that.

> **Himari:** I guess. It's always been weird to be the only one
> without superpowers in the family. Like, my dad hasn't
> even THOUGHT that maybe I might want to be part of
> TakahashiCorp. I have so many ideas. But I feel like
> everyone just goes, "Oh, that's little Himari. She just stays
> upstairs making fun little toys." But I guess that's all I can
> really do. I'm done being a henchman, Kev. I'm going to
> turn in my resignation to V as soon as we get home.

11:29 PM
Kevin: Whoa, whoa, speaking as someone who has had their two weeks' termination repeatedly rejected by his hero, let's not jump down that road too fast.

Kevin: You really seemed like you liked henchwork. What about it really made you excited?

> **Himari:** Honestly? I just liked hanging out with V. I liked being part of the crew, not just the kid sister.

Kevin: You know, I feel the same way about being a sidekick with Caleb. As much fun as putting coffee beans in hot water is, I think I enjoyed it because I at last had friends.

11:30 PM
Kevin: Believe it or not, but a theater kid at a frat house doesn't turn out to be the greatest mix. Sure, I had to get internship credits for class, but I wanted some friends who didn't talk nonstop about theater things and the only exciting thing they did was go to Steak 'n Shake after performances.

> **Himari:** To be honest, you're probably the best sidekick my brother could have had. Someone to keep him honest. The last thing he needed was a … well, I mean this in the best way possible … a competent sidekick.

Kevin: Eh, no offense taken. It's literally me.

Kevin: V couldn't have asked for a better henchie. But maybe when all this craziness finishes, we can go bowling without having to whack some SA dude with a pin. Something tells me Caleb and V might not keep up with hero and villain work forever.

> 11:31 PM

Himari: I think I understand where V is coming from now, at least a little bit. It seems glamorous, but then ... the real stuff, the stuff you don't see in the media, it's not glamorous at all. It's ... a-awful. I d-don't know if I'll ever s-stop hearing that poor man's screams ...

Kevin: Maybe, Himari, but each time you do, find me and I'll hug you until you stop shaking. Like this. I can't fix it for you, but I can sit with you.

Himari: You are a really good hugger. And ... hey, Kevin?

Kevin: Yes, George?

Himari: I just wanted to say ... don't let anyone tell you you're stupid. I think you supporting your friends is way more important than remembering everything.

11:32 PM
Kevin: Well, you know, I don't ALWAYS forget. Sure, I can't remember the events exactly, but there's no way I can forget how you guys make me feel.

Himari: Awww, Kevin!

Kevin: Man, did you just give Liam a run for his money with that hug. I suppose we should get some sleep now.

Kevin: Hate to bring this up, but they did debrief us afterward about the kidnapping. Still can't believe they want it to happen tomorrow. Everything happens lightning fast at SA, I guess.

Himari: Can we ... just not talk about it, for now? And go to ... sleep ... snorrrrrre.

11:33 PM

Kevin: Sure thing. Tell you what, you can keep my bed. I guess I'll go up top. Night, Mari. I really do hope you have good dreams.

THE FABULOUS FOUR
JUNE 15

4:05 AM

Kevin: *Kevin's log: We got back a few hours ago from ... yeah, I'm sure you read all about it. Himari conked right out when we returned to Liam's Lodge, before the kidnapping later today, but she keeps whimpering in her sleep. Every part of me wants to go to the bottom bunk and hold her, but that would be weird, since she's asleep.*

4:06 AM

Kevin: *She even stopped snoring just now. Hopefully this mind-text thing won't wake her. It's apparently impossible to whisper on this thing when you think thoughts. But somehow you can still yell? Brains are weird.*

Kevin: *Maybe that's why Caleb calls himself Cortex, a part of the brain.*

Kevin: *Oh wait, she started snoring again. Okay, I guess I can have my thoughts in peace. And, well, hopefully V and Caleb will see these before the kidnapping. They want us to leave Indy in, like, two hours, so hopefully Caleb is his normal morning-person self and gets up in time. Or maybe he's listening now.*

4:07 AM
Kevin: *Nope, chatty Cortie ain't listening.*

Kevin: *With all the fun trauma that happened in the last few hours, I thought I'd fill you two in on something that went down at HQ. As you may have heard on the transcript before the PowerPoint, we ran into Juan. We'd hoped he didn't recognize us in our disguises. After all, Liam, who did extensive research on us, didn't manage to.*

Kevin: *But when we ran into him outside the office, we found out otherwise.*

Kevin: *Liam was chatting his ear off about his two new best friend-os "Amni" and "Vir," and Juan glanced at us with a certain glint in his eye and smirked.*

4:08 AM
Kevin: *Liam excused himself to go use the little evil mastermind's room and asked Billy to come with because he wanted company. What a weirdo.*

Kevin: *Anyway, Juan waited until they'd disappeared before saying, "Kevin and Himari. So you turned to the SA, eh?" He didn't sound all that convinced.*

Kevin: *Himari cleared her throat and said, "Yeah, but we want to keep our secret identities hidden. That's why Liam only knows our villain and henchman names."*

4:09 AM
Kevin: *Juan rolled his eyes. "Liam also mentioned you got assigned the Takahashi kidnapping. But something tells me you may accidentally screw things up and let Takahashi go." He leaned in real close, breath all minty. "Tell you what. You don't try to screw up the kidnapping, and I don't tell Liam your little secret, eh?"*

Kevin: *Basically, he called our bluff. He knows we don't really work for SA, and he wants us to stay out of the mess.*

Kevin: *Of course, Himari and I were thinking about trying to find a way to help her dad escape, but that definitely throws a wrench into the mix.*

Kevin: *I mean, yeah, Liam wouldn't do what SA just forced Himari to do, but he still stabbed a dude in the neck for not sharing his feelings at a campfire. Something tells me Liam will not take the news well that Himari and I are here to simply learn about the SA and bring back any intel we can.*

4:10 AM
Kevin: *Much as I'd like to help your dad escape, Caleb, I'm worried what will happen to Himari.*

4:11 AM
Kevin: *You know what? If Juan gets wind about us trying to help your dad, I'll take the blame for it. Say Himari had nothing to do with it. I don't care if that ends up getting me killed.*

Kevin: *Because she's worth saving, and I'd rather her walk away from this, even if that means I can't.*

Kevin: *I guess it's time for the Kevin Maester to finally be a hero. The first and last time.*

VORTIE AND CORTIE
JUNE 15

8:43 AM
V: Caleb? Are you in the living room?

Cortex: Huh, what? I'm awake! I totally did not sleep in.

V: Um, okay. So … are we talking now?

Cortex: Sure, yeah, the bats are awake and alive. Talk, talk, talk. What do you want to talk about? We can talk about this fun pink carpet you have. So fluffy. Wow.

V: You know what I mean. You hardly talked to me at all last night. Granted, I bled a lot and was having a hard time staying conscious. What's going on?

8:44 AM
Cortex: Besides the fact we had to hear Himari torture some dude?

V: That was rough. I would never wish SA trials on anyone. At least hers was shortened. I'd hate to think of her doing the full assassinations circuit … anyway. This is about you right now. What's going on?

Cortex: I'm fine. Let's just check and see if we have any texts from Kevin or Hima—hey! It's rude to karate chop people's phones out of their hand.

V: Nuh-uh. I did not hobble all the way out here for you to ignore me.

8:45 AM
Cortex: Wow, the phone landed on the hardwood. Probably cracked. Fine, you want to talk? Let's talk about the fact that you were all like, "Oh, Slicer. You're my hero. You cut that dude into nice human bits." *Eyelashes fluttering on my soft, pale cheeks.*

V: What? You're jealous of Slicer? We're just really old friends.

Cortex: I'm not jealous of him. Who wants their hands replaced eighty percent by blades? Have you ever seen Edward Scissorhands? No, I'm mad because you told me to cower during a fight and then … Slicer happened. It made me feel … like nothing.

V: I … oh. Caleb. That's not why. I just … I'm scared. I'm terrified.

8:46 AM
V: I lost my parents. I can't lose you. I just can't.

Cortex: Look, I … understand on some level. Before I knew Tamora was an evil villain trying to actually kill me, I got all soppy on you, asking you to leave her out of our fights. Because I thought being a hero would put her in danger.

Cortex: But without my powers. I don't know, V. I want to feel useful. For once, I think I understand how Kevin feels.

Cortex: I did not EVER want to be a Kevin.

> 8:47 AM
> **V:** I get it. I really do. But Caleb ... I don't care if you're a Kevin or a Dimension. I just want you. Here with me. Alive.

Cortex: And same with you, V. That's why I didn't want you fighting those SA guys either.

Cortex: Not having powers has made me really think about why I got into the hero business in the first place. Because my parents did it? Because I had the abilities so how dare I not use them to help save people?

Cortex: Being a hero meant I was something ... but also, it made me feel like a nothing. Like a shell, you know? People dictating my scheduled savings to me, my interviews. I didn't get to do a whole lot of actual helping people. Actual heroism.

> 8:48 AM
> **V:** Right. You have a good heart. I know that. But ... sometimes being a hero makes it hard to be ... a hero. There's ... something I've been wanting to talk to you about.

Cortex: About how red really isn't my color?

> **V:** Um ... no. I think you look good in every color. I wanted to tell you that ... I applied for the Peace Corps. And ... they accepted my application.

Cortex: Well, that's. I mean, that's great, V. I didn't even know you'd been considering it.

> **V:** I just ... I love school—now that I transferred, anyway. I love marine biology. And I love writing children's books, of course. But I feel like, after everything I did when I was part of the SA, after everyone who got hurt, I want to do something GOOD in the world for a change.

8:49 AM
Cortex: Well, you've already done so much good. Tolerating me, for a start. But that's wonderful. I'm glad you have a next step. Most villains and heroes don't. That's how we end up with Dimensions and people playing poison pong.

Cortex: I haven't even thought about my next step. Didn't know I'd retire this early.

> **V:** Heehee, I'm dating an old man, I guess.

Cortex: Maybe do something cool with graphic design. I mean, after all, I am paying for my education.

8:50 AM
Cortex: Good talk, I guess? Sorry, my family doesn't have many of these. Dad doesn't ever talk, Mom just gives lectures, and Himari usually shuts herself in her room.

> **V:** It looked like Kevin and Himari had a good talk last night, teehee.

Cortex: Ugh, let me see.

8:51 AM
Cortex: Wait, scroll up.

Cortex: What's that about kidnapping my dad?

V: Oh, shoot. I got distracted by my ship sailing.

V: Dang. I think it might be hero time for both of us.

Cortex: Right when I'd booked the retirement cruise. Okay, but this time I'm wearing purple.

V: Good. It's your best color.

THE FABULOUS FOUR
JUNE 15

10:12 AM
Kevin: *We're rolling up to Caleb's neighborhood. Remind me one more time about our plan to try to save your dad whilst looking like we tried, and alas, failed to kidnap him?*

> **Himari:** *Right, so if I only had a phone or SOMETHING I could contact him with, but since I don't ... old-fashioned way, I guess. Can you get your best friend-o Liam to honk the car horn or something?*

Kevin: Hey-a, Liam. I love this car of yours. Man, do you have so many cars! This one even has a sweet roof. Raise it, raise it. Anyway, I bet you also have an awesome car horn. Does it sound amazing?

> **Liam:** Hey, Amni, I sure do, good friend, but remember? We have to be sneaky. Blaring that sick car horn would alert them we're coming.

10:13 AM
Himari: *Ooooh, Juan's giving you the death glare.*

Kevin: *Got it, strike one. We need another plan. Probably should've talked about it on the ride here, but nooooo. Liam was all like, "Let's do more Mad Libs."*

Himari: *Is that a phone in Juan's pocket?*

Kevin: *Why are you looking at Juan's pocket when he's busy staring at me with those beautiful but soulless eyes?*

Himari: *Figured he'd have some tech on him. Hmm. Maybe I can reach it if someone distracts him.*

10:14 AM
Kevin: *Good luck getting Liam to distract him.*

Kevin: *Ohhhhh.*

Kevin: Hey, guys, look outside. Cows! So many cows! I win all the cows.

Liam: No fair, I didn't even know we were playing the cow game. Well, all righty, Kevin, you bested me this round, but when we drive back, best believe I'll see more cows than you.

Juan: What the … there aren't even any cows out there.

10:15 AM
Himari: *Perfect distraction! He's squinting out the window … almost got it … ugh, why are men's pockets so deep?*

Kevin: *Because our thoughts are not.*

Kevin: *Crap, he's looking away from the window.* Wow! Windmills. So industrial.

Juan: That's ... a telephone pole. Liam, where did you pick these guys up again?

Liam: Wouldn't you know it, these friend-os showed up fashionably late to my bonding night of fun and friendship. And everyone knows the ones who show up the latest are, in fact, the most important guests of the night. The Queen doesn't show up on time.

10:16 AM
Kevin: I'm a queen.

Himari: *That hurt me inside. Almost ... there ...*

Kevin: *Yeesh, how long does it take to pick a pocket? I was in a production of Oliver Twist, and we stole from pockets like ten times in one musical number in the time you haven't even picked one.*

Himari: *Have you ever picked a real pocket before? It's a slow process if you can't distract them with some other sort of physical force like bumping into them. You have to do it incrementally, otherwise they feel it. Got it!*

Kevin: *I don't even want to know how you found that out.*

10:17 AM
Kevin: *Explains why Caleb always loses things he puts in his pockets ...*

Himari: *V actually taught me. I don't usually pick his pockets, but she does all the time. She has a stash of random crap she's stolen and is just waiting for him to finally notice.*

Kevin: *Y'all need therapy or something.*

Himari: *Okay. Trying to figure out his passcode. Keep him distracted. You're doing great.*

Kevin: Oh, dearie me, I think I have to pee.

10:18 AM
Liam: You sure there, friend? We stopped at the gas station on the way over here.

Kevin: Pre-kidnapping nerves, you know? Oh, Lordy, I don't know if I can hold it. I would sure hate to mess up this beautiful car with these nice leather seats.

> **Liam:** Understandable, friend-o. My first kidnapping, I was so nervous, I forgot to give the sidekick a scone after I injected his hero. I felt so embarrassed. Getting injected and not even having a scone baggie to take home. What kind of monster am I?

Kevin: Mind if we pull over to the side here? Back in a jiffy.

10:19 AM
Juan: I ... think I'll step out as well.

Liam: Man, even Juan has the jitters. Reasonable, though, folks. I mean this is a BIG kidnapping. I say we get some nice food to eat on the way back to celebrate. I sure hope the kidnappee doesn't have any food allergies.

> **Himari:** *Yo, Kev, you better pee, my man. You're gonna make Juan even more suspicious.*

Kevin: *Probably suspects I want to make a break for it or something.* Great, Juan and I will have an excellent pee. Come on, Juan. *And* *no worries, Mari. I always have to pee. You have no idea how much college wrecked my bladder.*

10:20 AM
Himari: *Thanks for sharing. All right, got through his first two passcodes. This dude is so paranoid.*

Kevin: What a beautiful morning, Juan. I'm singing in the raaaaain. Look at those nice flowers right there. We're all having a good time.

Juan: You're that guy who makes small talk at the urinal, aren't you.

Kevin: I'm also that guy who sidles on up to the urinal next to you, instead of giving people space. Instead of 1, 5, 3, I'm 1, 2. If you're a guy, you know what I mean. I'M YOUR WORST NIGHT-MARE, JUAN. La la la la la.

Himari: *This is a whole new type of pissing war. Okay, pass-code number four aaaaand ... I'm in. Sending a text now ... "Dad, we're coming to kidnap you as bad guys. You should probably hide or get suited up or something." That's a weird text to send.*

10:21 AM
Kevin: *Whoops, just ran out. Going to zip up these pants nice and slooooow.*

Himari: *Kev, I don't need this detailed of updates. Why is this text not sending?*

Kevin: So clumsy! I can't even get this zipper up. Man, what have I been eating? Juan, buddy, I might need some assistance here.

Juan: No hablo ingles.

Kevin: Gesundheit. *Any luck, Himari? I can only zip up these pants so many times. And Juan quirked an eyebrow at the "eating" comment. I think he's on to the fact that I'm skinny.*

Himari: *Wow, he must be so perceptive. Ah! Finally sent. Terrible service.*

10:22 AM
Kevin: Welp, zipper went right up. Guess the ninth time's the charm. Into the car we go!

Liam: You look mighty refreshed. Glad to see you had a good time out there. Okay, we should be pulling up to the driveway momentarily. Temperature okay back there? Need me to crank up the AC?

Himari: Think we're good, thanks. *Although you look a little flushed, Kev. Or is that still the sunburn?*

Kevin: …

Liam: And here we gooooo. Wheee! Oh wait, sorry, folks. Probably should whisper that … wheeeeee.

10:23 AM
Juan: … Right. Okay, couldn't get into the security feed here because of that blasted Himari chick, but at this time of day, Kosuke is always in his office on the first floor toward the southwest side of the house.

Liam: Juan, good sir, I like you already. So on top of everything. Okay, speaking of, we should probably run through our checklist. Stuff to tie him up with? Check. Stuff to tase him with to disorient him? Check. Some snacks in case he gets hungry? Check. Yay, Red Vines. Okay, some serum for any heroes who try to protect him? Check. Missing anything?

Himari: Ice-cold beverages, maybe?

Kevin: You're right. How could we have forgotten those? Liam, this kidnapping is a straight-up impolite bust if we can't hydrate our captee.

10:24 AM
Juan: Dios mio. He'll be FINE. We have bottled water. Let's go. Virus, Amnesia, lead the way.

Kevin: *That look looked like strike two. I don't think we can get away with much more before he tells Liam, Himari.*

Himari: *Great. Hey, can you play stupid one more time? Go ring the front doorbell?*

Kevin: *Okay. Anything for you, sweet thang. Wheeeee, up the driveway, up the stoop, and—*

Unknown Source: *DING-DONG*

10:25 AM
Juan: What the actual f—

Himari: What? It's the polite thing to do. Liam taught us.

Liam: You know, I feel mighty conflicted about this whole situation. See, to be polite or not to be polite? I'm afraid we have to hide in these bushes over here before someone sees. Boy, do I hate ding-dong ditch.

Himari: Right. Off we go. Ah, whoops! Just tripped on the step. Having a hard time getting up. Hey, Amnesia, lend a hand? Wh—Juan, ow! That bush is poky!

10:26 AM
Unknown Source: *click creak*

Dad: Hello?

Juan: What? He's answering the door himself? Where are those heroes who usually protect him?

Liam: Well, folks, I know we planned to break in and tackle him. But it seems an awful shame to ruin that nice front door. What say we tackle him now?

Himari: Yeah, definitely. Go for it, Liam. Wouldn't want to, ah, rob you of the honors.

10:27 AM
Dad: Hello?

Liam: Wow, so kind of you, friend-o. All right here, I—ugh! Now just where did that tree root come from?

Kevin: *Tripped him, Himari? Niiiiice. And now Liam's sprawled out on the path to the door, and your dad saw him.*

Dad: Oh. Um. Are you okay?

Liam: Wow, thanks for asking. I'm doing great. And yourself, sir?

Dad: Fine. Oh, hold on, sorry. I think I have a text from someone …

10:28 AM
Kevin: *Lucky he actually has his phone on him. Don't your parents hate tech?*

Himari: *Yeah, but he didn't READ IT YET. What has he been doing?*

Juan: What are you waiting for, you fools? Get him. Now.

Liam: So sorry about this, sir, but I'm afraid the next few moments might be the teensiest bit unpleasant.

Kevin: *And ... Liam pulled out the taser.*

Dad: Agh!

10:29 AM
Kevin: *What should we do? Your dad's down for the count, and Juan's wrapping him up in those ropes like nobody's business.*

Himari: *I don't know! Poor Dad. That's going to leave rope burns.*

Liam: Come on, y'all. It's not a kidnapping if there isn't teamwork.

Dad: Whoa. Oh, hate to do this, but —

Unknown Source: *Shing!*

Himari: *Yes! Gold powers!*

Juan: Kosuke IS Aurumque? Give me that serum! My poor golden ropes.

Himari: *Come on, Dad, break through them.*

10:30 AM
Liam: Here you go, friend. Don't forget to use a sterile wipe on his neck. Don't want him to get any infections. That would just ruin his day—kidnapping and an infection.

Juan: Yeah, okay.

Kevin: *No sterile wipe. Bold choice. I think Juan enjoyed stabbing him a little too much.*

Unknown Source: *thump*

Juan: He's out. I trust you three can manage to get him back to the transport at the lodge? The two of you over there must have a lot of energy left after doing NOTHING.

10:31 AM
Liam: Oh, Juan, don't go too hard on them. It WAS their first kidnapping, after all. Maybe we can't go to a really fancy restaurant on the way back, so they can learn a lesson in teamwork, but I'm not completely inhumane. Tacos, anybody?

Himari: Um, yeah, tacos. Uh, where are you going, Juan?

Juan: I have some … other business to attend to.

Himari: *I didn't like the sound of that.*

Kevin: *Curse his smooth, beautiful, suave voice.*

10:32 AM
Himari: *Kevin, stop being attracted to the bad guy.*

Kevin: *Any way we can avoid taking your dad's body back to the car?*

Himari: *If we want to stay undercover? Don't think so.*

Liam: Okay, I'll grab his feet, and you guys get the fun part, the shoulders. Ready? On the count of three, lift. One, two, three. Ugh. Wow, great job. Take that back, we're getting really fancy tacos on the way home.

Himari: *You know, Kev, I might turn this off for a little bit. I don't feel like my panicked brain is going to pick PG words.*

VORTIE AND CORTIE
JUNE 15

2:44 PM
V: Well, just checked the chat. They got your dad.

Cortex: You decided to do that AFTER we flew six hours to get here?

V: My phone battery died.

Cortex: And I guess Himari fixed one of the bugs. It says "Dad" now instead of "Caleb's Dad." Not that it matters.

V: Caleb, are you okay? You're shaking.

Cortex: I don't want to think about this right now.

V: That doesn't seem healthy.

2:45 PM
Cortex: Neither is you sleeping with knives. This hero and villain business is messed up.

V: Fair point.

Cortex: Okay, well, I guess we can hide out here for a while. Don't know how long until the police show up or something to take me away for killing a hero and whatnot.

V: Nah, the police know Caleb Takahashi lives here, not the superhero Cortex. You think your mom is here, though?

2:46 PM
Cortex: She's usually out at this time. Has a local hiking group, and I think they're at Turkey Run today. She's pretty far away. Good thing. If they took her too …

V: Oh, yeah … I was texting with her last night. She was debating leaving the house, hoping you'd come back. But I told her we were okay and she should do things anyway. Glad that happened.

Cortex: So what now? They've already taken Dad, and Kevin and Himari haven't had a chance to get out of Liam's Lodge yet.

V: Well, first of all, I need to find Himari's special first aid kit with stitches that will maybe actually stay. Been a little lightheaded.

2:47 PM
Cortex: Right. Sorry. Should've thought of that first. Let's go check Kevin's room. I think Himari said he'd left it there last. How are you doing? You don't really talk about your pain.

V: Eh, it doesn't hurt too bad, just keeps bleeding all over. Had to use some old pink bed sheets for bandages. It was sad. Liked those.

Cortex: The burn-your-eyes-out ones? Uh-huh. A tragic loss. Okay, Kevin's room. Don't know why Himari put the med kit back here after she used it last time. Maybe because her room is stuffed full of things she's working on. Might not have had space.

> **V:** Yeah, her room is insane. She has more gadgets than I have plushies. Agh, think Kevin would mind if I take a break to sit on his beanbag?

2:48 PM
Cortex: Better that than his bed. Seriously, how many wrappers does he have on that thing?

> **V:** Oof. Yeah, that's disgusting. I'm just not gonna wonder what that sticky spot is.

Cortex: Let's see. Under the sheets that fell off the bed? Nope. Under all these comic books? Nuh-uh.

> **V:** Hey, once you find it, would you mind doing the stitching? It's awkward for me to get to my own side.

Cortex: No problem. Makes sense why it keeps splitting open since you had to stitch the wound at a weird angle. Oh, bingo, underneath the stack of play programs. Dang, this dude's been in a lot of shows. Let's stitch you up.

> 2:49 PM
> **V:** Okay, I appreciate how calm you're being, but if you need to throw up like last time, that's okay. Just … not on me, please. Not sterile, you know.

Cortex: Yeah, well, the stench of Kevin's room ain't helping. All right, walk me through this.

V: Okay, don't freak out when you see it, okay? It's probably not THAT infected. Just … a little bit. K, gonna take the shirt off now.

Cortex: *Oh gosh, it looks like those videos we saw in history class. Eww. Eww.* Looks great, babe. No worries at all.

V: Great. Okay, so this healing kit is a little weird. It will do most things automatically, but you've got to get these old stitches out of the way or it will jam. So … scissor time.

Cortex: *Don't puke. Don't puke.* Cool. Snip, snip. *Oh, I can't look away, but I so want to.*

V: Whoa, make sure you hold the flesh together while you do it.

2:50 PM
Cortex: Anything for you, babe. *Ugh, I'm apologizing to Kevin for ever having to patch any of my wounds after fights. Then again, he did make them much worse … never mind about the apology.*

Cortex: *Ugh, shudder.* K, babe, the stitches are out. Yay.

V: Okay, cool, now before everything starts falling apart, go ahead and get out the —

Juan: Oh, excuse me. Looks like I found you at a bad time. Should I come back when you have all your clothes on and not as much blood everywhere?

2:51 PM
Cortex: Stay down, V.

V: Don't have much of a choice. I move, things aren't gonna be pretty.

> **Juan:** Oooh, nasty wound there. Was that from Liam's place? Nice. Nice to see you again too, "Cortex." It's been a while.

Cortex: *Right, no powers. I can do this, right? Just gotta not remember the villain party. When Slicer ... yeah, won't think about that.*

> **Juan:** You know, I really don't have a problem with you, hero boy. You're no more threatening than a housefly without your powers. How about you back away and just let me do what I need to do?

Cortex: Wow, Juan, never took you for stupid before, but let's just say you're making my sidekick look like my sister at the moment, in terms of smarts.

> 2:52 PM
> **Juan:** V, you can't hide behind your pathetic boyfriend for long. This time, you're mine.

V: The heck, Juan. I don't get this. Why the bloodlust? You already took basically everything I owned.

> **Juan:** Maybe. And maybe I got a really cool house with dungeons and lots of money. But I still have NOTHING. No leadership in the SA. You know how long I've wanted to be a district boss? Too long. It was supposed to be my chance. Turn you in. And then everything in Vegas went down the toilet. But. Heh heh heh. If I kill the unkillable Vortex, one of the top members on the SA hit list ... they'll have to put me in charge.

2:53 PM

V: Ah, got it now. Thanks for the monologue. It helped.

> **Cortex:** Kevin would've done it better. Now, get out, or we'll make you regret stepping foot in here. *Sorry, babe, a bit rusty on the threatening. At most of my "savings" they give me a script beforehand.*

V: *Hey, improv is hard. You're doing great.*

> **Juan:** Ha! Step aside, boy. I've got a special blade just for you, V!

Cortex: *Gotta find a weapon. There's a trophy from when Kevin did speech. Oh gosh, he's swinging the knife. Let's smack his head with the trophy.*

> 2:54 PM
> **Juan:** Agh! Fine, I'll kill you too!

Cortex: Aww, I'm honored. *Watch the knife. Keep hitting him over the head with the trophy. Scoot back. Hit. Duck. Hit. Dang it, the top broke off. Stupid trophy.*

> **V:** *You're doing great, babe ... hey, is the room spinning? That's weird.*

Cortex: *No, don't pass out on me now.*

> **Unknown Source:** *ploof*

Cortex: *Well, SOMEONE is bad at following directions. All right, let's find a new weapon and keep Juan from swinging his knife at the conked-out V. Weapon, weapon ... is that a police stick?*

Juan: Backed into a corner, boy. What now? Heh heh.

Cortex: *Let's thwack Juan on the head with it.*

2:55 PM
Unknown Source: *THUNK!*

Cortex: Huh, sounds wooden. Must be a stage prop. Well, works for me.

Juan: Uggghhh, ohhh, ouch ...

Unknown Source: *THUMP*

Cortex: Slumped to the floor, eh? *Well, might as well get a few more hits in case. Safety first.*

Unknown Source: *Thunk. Thunk. Thunk!*

V: Babe? Whoa ... you look sexy fighting. Heeheehee, my hero ... oh gosh, things are super blurry. Hey, how much blood can a person lose and be okay?

2:56 PM
Cortex: I think he's out. We need to get you stitched up. Any chance you can walk me through it, or are you losing consciousness again? You don't look like you can hold your head up.

V: Hey ... I hate to say this, but ... I think for once I actually need ... medical attention ...

Cortex: Good thing we're in civilian clothes, so the hospital doesn't ask any questions. Keep these clothes I found on his floor pressed against your wound.

Cortex: First calling the ambulance, and then …

Cortex: *Give Juan a significant look. Hold it. Perfect.*

Cortex: … the police.

EVENING TALK SHOW TRANSCRIPT

Joe: You mean to tell me Cortex DIDN'T kill a hero? It was a member of the Shadow Assassins, a deadly group to both heroes and villains?

Ted: That's what it looks like. Party guests who were closest to the scuffle said it seemed like the guy tried to take out the villain Vortex. You know, Cortex's girlfriend.

Roger: Roger that. Well, I guess that means Cortex is vindicated.

Paul: Sure, but it still doesn't look good for anyone. The Shadow Assassins are everywhere. Heroes and villains are losing their powers all over the place.

Ted: And it must have affected those heroes Lux and Aurumque who always hang around TakahashiCorp. That was some breaking news right there. Kosuke Takahashi, kidnapped. Weird stuff. Wouldn't have happened if they were around.

Joe: Well, what do you think this means for heroes and villains? From what we've been able to tell, most of the A- and B-listers have lost their powers. Anyone left can maybe transform into an iguana or sneeze pepper. Not exactly formidable against the likes of SA.

Paul: I think what it means is if we actually face a national or global threat, we're toast. These heroes haven't had much to do lately, but it's always comforting to have them around, just in case something happens like what used to happen thirty years ago.

Roger: Not to mention, apparently the SA is also going after the most promising henchmen and sidekicks too. They're leaving no one out, making no distinction between hero and their lesser counterpart. The only ones left have pretty much useless powers.

Ted: Well, it looks like we may be fresh out of the heroes we need ... just like we're fresh out of coffee. Coffee break, gentlemen?

THE FABULOUS FOUR
JUNE 15

10:57 PM
Himari: *We're going to die.*

Himari: *We have to. Right? Juan is going to tell.*

Himari: *Even though we did get Dad handed off to the transport—sorry, Dad—Juan knows we tried to sabotage the mission.*

Himari: *So he'll tell Liam. Wonder where he's been this whole time ...*

Himari: *Speaking of wondering ... why exactly do they want Dad? I mean, he is a major arms-dealer dude. Maybe they want him for that?*

10:58 PM
Himari: *In any case, we're going to die.*

Himari: *But we can't exactly run. We have to stick it out. Figure out how to take these guys down.*

Himari: *I think I'll be okay. I can take it. But ... what if they do something to Kevin?*

Himari: *I don't know if I could take that.*

Himari: *When I'm around Kevin, I feel like things might not be too bad. Like I don't have to take everything so seriously. He's like a big golden retriever. Just the thought of bad things happening to him ...*

Himari: *Unlike Caleb, Kevin actually knows how to have heart to hearts. That's a new one. My family doesn't really do that.*

10:59 PM
Himari: *Also he's a really good-looking dude. Not loving the black hair, though. Does not complement the skin tone.*

Himari: *Still, you can't hide that Kevin charm.*

Himari: *Ack! What am I even thinking right now?*

Himari: *I'm just a nerd. No one thinks of me like that. Kevin flirts with literally everyone. It's just how he is.*

Himari: *He fangirled over Juan's voice, the weirdo.*

Himari: *Although, if someone was actually going to like me ... I'd like it to be Kevin.*

11:00 PM
Himari: *Wait. Why is my voice echoing in my head?*

Himari: *Oh, crap.*

Himari: *What do I do? Crap crap crap. I've gotta spam this chat.*

Himari: *PONIES.*

Himari: *PONIES.*

Himari: *CRACKERS.*

Himari: *Oh gosh, what would none of them ever want to read if they scroll back?*

11:01 PM
Himari: *Aha! The quadratic formula. Over and over.*

Himari: *X equals negative b plus or minus square root of b squared minus four ... wait, did Kevin just groan?*

Himari: Kevin?

Himari: *That was a really loud snore. Okay.*

Himari: *WAIT. Kevin doesn't snore. And I did that to him last time to make him think I wasn't listening.* Kevin? You awake?

    Kevin: *Sleeping noises. Snore.*

11:02 PM
Himari: Wow. Okay. Um, hi, sorry, turned on the mind-text thing accidentally. You can go back to sleep ... Um, how long have you been awake?

    Kevin: *Kevin is not here right now. Please leave a message after the beep.*

Himari: Kevin! Come on. Don't make me come down there.

    Kevin: I don't know, Mari. I think I only caught something about a formula. What a rotten way to spoil some good dreams.

11:03 PM
Kevin: Hypothetically …

Kevin: If I were to stop accidentally flirting with people, would this weirdo have a chance at taking you out for fancy tacos? I mean, fancier than where we went tonight?

Himari: *Is he asking like as a date, or like as friends? I'm bad at this.*

Kevin: OMG, Himari. You think I'd take Juan out for tacos? No, he may have a sexy voice, but you … you … wow. I wish I had the words. Maybe some writer can come up with better ones.

Himari: So … you definitely heard … pretty much everything? *Oh, crap, that's embarrassing.*

11:04 PM
Kevin: I don't know what you're talking about. I was just dreaming about flying when suddenly a quadratic formula to the tune of Pop Goes the Weasel popped into my head.

Kevin: Anything said afterward was completely coincidental.

Kevin: Also, I hate the black hair too.

Himari: Hahaha! Kevin. I … I'd love to get fancy tacos.

Kevin: Granted, if Liam doesn't kill us tomorrow.

Himari: Well, yes. They can be celebratory tacos. For living.

11:05 PM
Himari: Kevin?

HOPE BOLINGER & ALYSSA ROAT

Himari: What are those weird noises?

Himari: Are you squealing?

Kevin: Is there a word for a manly squeal? Like a manly diary?

Himari: A what now?

Kevin: Well, anyways, sweet dreams. I know I ain't getting any sleep now.

Himari: Haha. *And he thinks I am? Oh my gosh, way to rock my world right before bed, Kevin. Oh, shoot. This stupid mind-text thing. Why did I invent this?*

11:06 PM
Kevin: *Yeeeah, I'm gonna turn it off now. Hoping none of my thoughts slip through—*

THE FABULOUS FOUR

JUNE 16

8:30 AM
Unknown Source: *KNOCK KNOCK KNOCK*

Liam: Morning, you two. Thought I'd let you sleep in a little. Feeling well rested? Enjoyed those s'mores and tacos last night?

Kevin: *Sleep in?*

Himari: Yeah, it was great. Thanks, Liam! *It is after eight, dude.*

Liam: Can I get you two anything while I'm asking? Don't want to be rude and all that.

Himari: Appreciate it, but I'm good. Amni?

Kevin: Peachy.

8:31 AM
Liam: Great. Now, Kevin and Himari, do you have any

preference on what type of blade I stab you with? I have a whole belt full of them but thought you'd want to have your first choice. Kevin, I found a nice curvy one. Could look kind of neat going into your chest.

Himari: *Oh. Oh, no. Who's Kevin?*

Kevin: *... We're going to die.*

Liam: Now, you don't have to pull the wool over this silly fella's eyes anymore, Himari. Juan texted me when we stopped for tacos on the way home.

Liam: Thought it would be rude of me to stab you in the restaurant. Some poor worker, who doesn't earn enough, would have to clean up all that blood.

8:32 AM
Liam: And then I figured with the campfire last night, you two looked mighty traumatized from whatever happened at SA the day before. Figured you should at least get a s'more or two before you meet some angels.

Himari: *Knew I should've gone to see the priest before we left. I'm sorry, God.*

Kevin: *Himari, stay in bed. And bolt out of here when you get a clear shot at the door.*

Kevin: *Liam, I think I know which knife I want you to use. But mind if we do it outside, bro? Would hate for Billy to have to scrub this cabin or something.*

Liam: You know, that's very thoughtful of you. He's coming up the hill soon with some bacon he made. I'd offer you some, but you look kind of pale. Don't want to upset your tummy before I stab it.

8:33 AM

Kevin: Sure, man, now let me get a clear look at those knives in the beautiful daylight.

Kevin: *Himari, his back's to the cabin. Book it!*

Kevin: Wow, so many to choose from. Where'd you find all of these, man?

Himari: *Just gotta slip behind him ... grab a knife from his belt ...*

Kevin: *I'll distract him.* Oooh, wow. Is that a heron on the lake? Gorgeous.

Liam: Huh, is it? You know, me and the bird watching club have been—oof!

Kevin: *Decked him in the stomach. Get the knife, Himari!*

Himari: *Got one!*

8:34 AM

Liam: Not going to lie, Kevin, that punch right there made me the teensiest bit upset. I'm sorry, pal, but I think I'm going to have to choose your knife for you. How about this one?

Kevin: *Wow, that's jagged.* Augh! *Okay, and now my face feels jagged. Did he get my cheek?*

Himari: Kevin! *Oh no. Gave myself away.*

Liam: Himari, sorry, but you might have to share the same blade.

Unknown Source: *Shtwlunk*

Liam: B-Billy? I d-didn't see …

Kevin: *Yikes, right in the chest. And the plate of bacon in the grass. A lot of losses.*

8:35 AM
Billy: Boss, it's fine. I've been stabbed like three times in the past two weeks.

Liam: Y-you what?

Billy: Yeah, I have, like, dragon skin. It's sort of a lame power, considering healing takes several hours, but I'm good. A little owy, but good. Want me to make some more bacon?

Liam: You—you have powers?

Himari: *Awkward.*

Liam: Sorry, folks, but I'm at a loss for words. I need to retreat into Liam's Lodge for some … introspection.

8:36 AM
Kevin: I guess that makes sense how you and V couldn't kill him.

Kevin: It's probably time we head home. Before we have to do any more kidnappings, or before Liam finds another blade to stick in my face.

Himari: Or tells SA HQ what he knows. We'd better get out of here, reconvene with Caleb and V, and go rescue my dad.

8:37 AM
Kevin: Himari, if you go get the car started, I think I can convince Liam to come with us.

Himari: Wait ... what? You're still bleeding from him stabbing you IN THE FACE.

Kevin: Just trust me, okay? He might have more SA intel. Worst case, maybe we can bring him along to find a way to reverse that power-sucking serum.

Himari: Oh ... okay. I'll trust you. But be careful.

Kevin: *Now, where did that weird little lumberjack go?*

8:38 AM
Kevin: *Found him, by the fireplace. Is he playing with those taxidermy bunnies?*

Liam: No, Mr. Hopper. You mean to tell me that you haven't been a rabbit this whole time, but rather, a hare? Boy, do I feel betrayed.

Kevin: *I don't know whether to find this adorable or disturbing.* Uh, hi, Liam. Oh. No, you didn't have to throw those bunnies behind you.

Liam: I was just practicing for a, uh, play I'm in. Haha, no worries. Didn't want you to feel all uncomfortable, good sir.

Kevin: What is the play called? I love theater.

Liam: It's called ... I've Been Betrayed by Three of My Best

Friend-os, but I Probably Deserve It Since Everyone Abandons
Me Anyway. Wow, sorry there, Kevin. Didn't mean to unload all
that on you. Please feel free to dump on me.

8:39 AM
Kevin: No, really, that's fine.

Liam: Go ahead, bro, let it all out. Dump on Lonely Liam.

Kevin: Ummm, Liam. No, I'm okay. We don't need to hug.
Liam, I'm really sorry about having to lie about my name
and the backstory I told at the campfire. We just thought
you'd try to … you know, kill us otherwise.

Liam: Yeah, I guess it wasn't polite of me to wake you up this
morning and try to send you away from God's green earth.

Liam: Did you know Billy had powers?

8:40 AM
Kevin: The power to cheat off of Calc tests? No, my dude,
hadn't a clue. But I guess now it all makes sense with V and
Himari both impaling him.

Liam: V and Himari doing what?

Kevin: Either way, he healed, slowly. Like what he's doing
outside right now.

Liam: Right. It's just … do you mind if I have a rock-my-world
kind of moment? If you want to make your escape in the car with
your friend, I would understand.

8:41 AM
Kevin: We can wait a few more minutes. Go ahead, man.
Let it all out.

Liam: When the SA stopped by my college, they'd talked about
the dangers of heroes and villains who had powers. Gave a very
convincing lecture series, and I got some bonus points for my
philosophy gen ed, so that was a plus, you know?

Liam: Rambled on and on about how lazy they'd made society and
how they didn't actually do a whole lot of saving and villainy. And
those who actually wanted to got lost in the shadows of these influ-
encer heroes.

Liam: You sure you don't want a glass of water or something?
How about some stitches for that wound on your face?

   Kevin: I might let it scar. V thinks Caleb's scar is really hot.
   Maybe I'd have a chance with a certain lady. Really craving
   tacos right now.

8:42 AM
Liam: Well, holler if you need anything. Anyway, this lecture
series clicked with me. I'd worked my whole life for everything,
you know? 4.0, varsity athlete in four sports—I do hope I'm not
coming off like I'm bragging.

   Kevin: No, man, you earned it. Besides making the leads in
   some shows, I've accomplished squat.

Liam: And here I watched supers like my parents and others skirt
by with half-baked savings. They couldn't even parent right
because they chose the spotlight over their non-gifted kid. That did
hurt me the teensiest bit, you know?

Kevin: Sure.

Liam: Gosh darn, you're a good listener, whether you're Kevin or Amnesia. So when the SA recruited me for Indy, everything made sense. They loved the formula I'd spent years making, and I'd actually earned this spot.

8:43 AM
Liam: But then, along came Billy …

Liam: Maybe he does cheat on Calc tests, like you said, but he put one hundred and ten percent effort into everything. And I should know that's impossible. You do a lot of math as a Chem major.

Liam: So I thought, "Here's this kid without powers trying his hardest. Why can't we have more people like him in the world?"

Liam: Only to find out he did have powers. He had an advantage. But he still worked hard. Can you see the fuses misfiring in my brain? I feel like I can smell smoke or something, you know?

Liam: Now I don't know what to think, man. SA had convinced me heroes and villains had gotten lazy because of powers. But then, Billy. He has powers and isn't lazy at all.

8:44 AM
Kevin: Cortex too.

Liam: What?

Kevin: Yeah, the hero I sidekick for. You know, the one you researched and injected with serum somewhere in this house?

Liam: Ah, yeah, he got some of Billy's cinnamon pancakes too, the little rascal. What about him?

Kevin: Well, he worked retail, is pushing a 3.8 GPA in his graphic design major, and had to pay his own way through college. Mind you, his dad can literally create blocks of gold out of thin air. Talk about tough parenting.

8:45 AM
Liam: Huh, I hadn't really done that part of the research. Mostly searched about his power and publicity stunts all over social media.

Kevin: Don't get me wrong, he may have lost his way a bit in herodom, but he does try hard. I mean, he works diligently at school, actually saved people who needed saving these past two years, instead of just staging photoshoots with celebs who need "saving." And he endured me for the past two years. That takes perseverance.

Liam: Now, partner, I don't want you getting down on yourself—

Kevin: V also's worked hard. Studying like crazy for marine biology and has really trained Himari well. And don't even get me started on Himari. No wonder her dad calls her "Alberta." Alberta Einstein.

8:46 AM
Liam: Huh, let me see if I can get this all to compute. Feel free to eat one of Billy's breakfast scones on the table over there while I process all of this.

Liam: Powers can make people lazy or impolite. Like my parents and so many superheroes on social media.

Liam: ... But there are exceptions like Billy, V, and Cortex.

Kevin: Yowza, these chocolate chips are still warm. So good!

Liam: So maybe the problem isn't the powers.

Liam: Maybe it's the people who have them.

8:47 AM
Kevin: I think you just had a breakthrough, buddy.

Liam: So I shouldn't have taken the powers of some of those folks. And now the SA ... they're going to do some mighty impolite things, my friend. Not just the serum, but the nukes too.

Kevin: Nukes?

Liam: You don't know about the nukes, friend?

Kevin: Do you?

Liam: Oh, I know loads of good things. I guess it happens when you talk to what some people think are "little folks," like Hulga the secretary. Even though Hulga doesn't divulge much, the others do. I know more about the SA than I think the SA knows themselves. I do like to do my research, you know.

8:48 AM
Kevin: Mind taking some of that research on the road? We could implement that intel. Cortex and others could use it for some actual heroism. Real save-the-world kind of stuff.

Liam: ...

Liam: Can I bring Mad Libs?

Kevin: Sure, buddy.

Liam: And the bunnies?

Kevin: As long as you bring Mr. Hopper. *Awww, he's hugging a rabbit corpse. I think that's cute? Maybe?*

8:49 AM
Liam: I could never leave him behind.

GROUP CHAT
JUNE 16

Caleb added Himari

Caleb added Kevin

Caleb added Liam

Caleb added V

10:57 AM

Caleb: V, can you hear us from the hospital room? Himari, good thing you made an extra communication device so Liam can hop on. Why'd you just happen to have that on hand, again?

Himari: Always prepared, bro.

V: I'm here. Luckily the nurse finally left. They think I'm dying or something, lol.

Liam: Can you feel my hug all the way from the cafeteria, V?

V: Umm, sure, Liam. Thanks. Very nice.

10:58 AM
Caleb: So Kevin, you mentioned you guys have more SA intel?

Kevin: Liam does. He managed to get some info by talking to a lot of the "sidekicks" they have working at that building.

> **Liam:** Yeppers, all except for that secretary. She's a bit of a tough nut to crack. But I know enough to understand things are about to explode soon if your dad starts talking all nice for Mr. Gladkins.

V: Fantastic. So the SA has those nukes. Really, your parents should have known the Canadians weren't in the nuclear warfare market.

> **Caleb:** Yeah, right.

10:59 AM
Liam: Well, although they do have the nukes, they don't have the correct codes to activate them. Hence our little adventure the other day to Caleb's house. By the way, love what your mom did with the decor. Beautiful columns at the front entrance, my friend.

> **Himari:** That was Dad, actually. He loves interior design. But back to the topic at hand. Where are the nukes right now?

Liam: Oh, haha, where aren't they? The SA really likes to spread the love, you know? I want to say they have one scattered anywhere they have an SA branch. The one for Indy has a little race car painted on it. I think they had fun decorating the nukes.

V: There are thirty-two SA branch headquarters. No way we can be that fast.

Himari: Thirty-two?

V: They didn't see any point in having one in some areas. Like Wyoming, that sort of thing.

11:00 AM
Kevin: Also, maybe I should've paid attention in history more, or honestly most of my classes, but don't nukes usually have a pretty wide range? Even if one of those goes off, we're talking millions of people.

V: And with that many? The radiation is going to affect the whole world, and who knows what else. The SA are really on an apocalyptic bent this time.

Caleb: Here's what I don't get. Won't that affect SA people too? Like, you can't just stare at a wave of radiation and say, "Not in my house, sister."

V: They're psycho. The idea is to remake the world with a new order, run by them. They're villain extremists. And I don't think they care how many of them die in the process. The bigshots like Gladkins probably have super special bunkers or something.

11:01 AM
Liam: For sure, every branch head has one. Mine's at the bottom of the lake you guys had a nice dip in. I guess the other folks don't have a stash of Twinkies in theirs. I think if you want end-of-the-world food, you might as well have something to enjoy as you think about the entire earth being destroyed.

Kevin: I'm really glad we turned off the mind-reading thing. I don't want to know where your brain goes, man.

Liam: And I'm anticipating your next question—no. We can't fit too many bodies down in those bunkers. Maybe a couple dozen, but I was going to save those for my best friend-os.

Himari: Okay, so all the SA HQ are in the US, right? So worst comes to worst, we go all British?

V: Well, I guess, but then the SA have control of the US, and we know what tends to happen when good ole America joins world wars.

11:02 AM
Kevin: Again, looking at a dude who skipped all his history 8 AMs, but I'm guessing it's a "stop all the nukes or hang out in Liam's Twinkie Land" kind of deal? Man are these cafeteria peaches weird. So slimy. Good thing everything else was covered in mayo, so I can't eat them. The sandwiches here look NAS-TY.

Caleb: Yeah, but we can't exactly be in thirty-two places at the same time. If we deactivate one, they'll probably get word and set off all the others.

Himari: Right. So from when I may or may not have been poking around with the nukes before, I found that you can actually set each one off individually, but you need a master code to do it all at once. And, fun fact, even if someone gives override codes on one nuke, the master code can override it. I think that's what they want Dad for. Set them all off at once, no one has time to stop you.

Liam: Yeah, heard that from the janitor Ms. Henshaw. All this info checks out. You'd need people at the sites of the nukes and inside HQ to actually make those fun little nukes fizzle out.

Caleb: Wait, Himari, when'd you have time to research this?

11:03 AM
Kevin: Oh, Liam filled us in on the ride over. We'd already finished his Mad Libs book and needed something to talk about. He mentioned the nukes as one of the "nouns," and that's what got the whole discussion started.

Himari: Also, bro, I've been poking around the missiles and stuff since I was like five. I'm sneaky. And Dad is very unobservant.

Kevin: Liam also mentioned a serum could take months to get right to reverse the effects. We can't exactly storm in with a bunch of heroes, guns blazing.

Liam: Really sorry about that. I can pay for the cafeteria lunches for a start, but I know this will take a lot of tacos to make it up to you.

11:04 AM
V: All right. So. Master code and Mr. Takahashi have to be saved, or all the nukes go off. Each nuke has to be taken down, or it will individually go off. We've got thirty-three places to be and five of us. It's time to drum up some moping heroes and villains and get this party started.

Kevin: Or … it's about time Himari reveals she can clone herself thirty-three times. Come on, Himari. I know you're holding back on us.

Himari: Yeah, haven't experimented much with cloning technology. Feels a little unethical. But where are we going to get these recruits?

V: Well, there's plenty of media wanting to talk to us right now. Oh, hi, Susan. Yes, I'm feeling great, thank you. That's really okay, I don't need you to do that. Who am I talking to? Oh, just some friends, haha.

Caleb: We can pick up this convo later. I'll start emailing some of those talk shows back. Kevin, you wanna try to recruit some folks on Meta-Match since you use that app religiously?

11:05 AM
Kevin: Whaaat? I'm never on ... fine. I'll get my phone back at home and get started.

Caleb: Y'all ready to be heroes? Probably for the last time?

Liam: Sounds like a great bonding experience with my best friend-os. Anyone up for a hug?

Liam: ...

Liam: Anyone?

SIDEKICK SUPPORT GROUP FORUM

TOPIC: WHO WANTS TO TAKE DOWN THE SA WITH ME?

Kevin: So usually I lurk in the shadows of these forums, but SPEAKING OF SHADOWS, I really need your help.

I know I've been filtering through your pouty posts of "Woe is me! I have no powers! Now I have to work at a local coffee shop!" But listen up, folks, I'm only going to say this once.

We have a chance to actually defeat something evil. Not defeating some evil lighting for a selfie or people with red contacts in their eyes. But an awful organization who makes their recruits torture and slice off limbs of innocent men, just as an initiation ritual.

I mean, something that can genuinely blow up the whole United States, and then who knows? Probably talking about a World War III situation, and I know we all ain't fans of zombies.

So if you want to get off your sorry little tushies and do something about saving that little coffee shop that pays you minimum wage plus tips, then we need you now.

Calling all Heroes, Villains, Henchies, and Kickies. If you live somewhere in the United States, I need you to email Cortex at the address below. Based on your location, he may have an important job for you.

No, you're not going to throw punches, knock out some dude's teeth, or get wedgies from your spandex.

But you will have a chance to actually, for once in your lives, make a difference.

Please?

Okay, thanks, here's the email: CortexLuvsLife567@heromail.com

ANSWER THREAD

Syracuse: This site may have blocked me — pathetic trolls — but not long enough to stop me from saying no thanks, pal. Moving to Canada and going to try to figure out life. You wish you had powers like mine before they got sucked away. Don't know why anyone would jump on this last hurrah little bandwagon. If they do, I'm telling them to "get your head checked, pal." We don't need any pity parties here, and whatever you have planned is likely beneath even sidekick work.

> **Vega:** Ugh, Syracuse isn't even worth engaging anymore. Kevin, I live in Gatlinburg, Tennessee, and I could use something to add to my résumé. I also kind of like this country and don't want it blown up and stuff. Besides, the hero kicked me out after I started dating a henchman, anyway, so anything for another thrill. Emailing Cortex now.

Lumos: I agree with Vega. My hero got returned to me from their kidnapping without their powers, and man, I've never seen someone so bummed out. I'll see if I can get them on board, but you can count me in, as long as it doesn't involve any amazing powers. From what I can tell in the forums, most sidekicks and henchmen have lost theirs, at least any powers that could actually threaten an evil organization. SA really does work in the shadows. Talk soon, from Portland!

> **Idun:** Villain's in and so am I. If you need someone from the Wisconsin area, I got your back, friend. Sharing this across as many forums I can. Want to get as many eyes on it as possible.

This answer thread has 54 replies. See more.

GROUP CHAT
JUNE 16

11:29 AM

Caleb: Have to dash for a talk show. Guess they could squeeze me in really fast. Something about, "Anything for a superhero who we thought had turned into a villain. Sorry for showing all those pics with you in bad lighting, man. How about a talk show to make up for it?"

Caleb: Anyway, from what I can tell, V, they ain't too keen on you leaving the hospital. Liam's grabbing the nuke in the Indy area, and I figured you and I could get the one in Arizona, since you know that area best.

Caleb: But I would need you.

Caleb: So I'm sending some help!

Caleb: Please don't kill me. Or him.

Caleb: Love you, bye.

11:30 AM

V: Sorry, babe, I was talking to the nurse. Well, arguing with. Kind of shouting. Not letting me leave. But, um, I'm looking forward to the help … whatever it is.

Liam: 'Ello. I am doctor. I come to help you get better, patient.

V: Oh my gosh. You've got to be kidding me. What is that on your head? Doctors don't wear those reflective mirror thingies anymore.

Liam: Oh, patient funny. We did not stop by the theater costume shop nearby hospital in the past ten minutes, no. Now, we go get you X-ray, yes?

11:31 AM

V: Okay, sounds great, Dr. What-the-heck-is-that-accent. Um, you wanna grab me some cotton balls and gauze? Gotta pull these IVs out.

Liam: Oh no, that be very messy. Let me see what I can find. Hmm, some purple gloves. And oooh, some stickers. Have you been good patient for doctor?

V: Aaaand now I'm uncomfy. Just hand me those. Oh, and can you reach the button on the heart thingy? Gotta turn it off so it doesn't start screaming that I'm dead once I take these sticky things off.

Liam: 'Ere you go. Now for some tunes to keep your mind at ease. Doo doo doo doo, oh no. Is not good to hit doctor.

11:32 AM

V: That was a tap, not a hit, Dr. Doo Doo. Okay, IV out, cover in cotton ball, wrap the tape, good. And all these stupid sticky things EVERYWHERE, ugh. Okay, I think I'm all disconnected.

Liam: All good. Patient can stand now, yes? Oh, patient can no stand now. No good.

V: Hey, maybe you can get "patient" a wheelchair, huh? There's a bunch of them at the nurses station.

Liam: O-ho-ho, patient knows too much about hospitals. Be back soon.

11:33 AM
Liam: 'Ello, colleague. I need chair with wheels. Give me one now, yes?

Unknown Source: What's your—sir, do you even work at this hospital?

Liam: Oh no, your coffee mug spilled all over the papers here. I hope they no important, yes?

Unknown Source: You have got to be kidd—hey! What are you doing? Where are you going with that? Come back here!

Liam: We run now. We very scared now. We can drop accent now because they know. THEY KNOW.

11:34 AM
Liam: Hiya, V. We might need you to sit in this chair right here pretty fast. Otherwise, I have a feeling I might get arrested a little earlier than I thought today.

V: Omg, how hard is it to act normal long enough to get a wheelchair? Oof. Okay, let's go. Oh! Wow, a little fast, bud. Ah!

Liam: I'm sorry! So sorry! No amount of tacos can make up for this, friend-o. Maybe stroganoff. How do you feel about stroga— oh, sorry, sir!

11:35 AM
V: Are you offering stroganoff to random nurses?

Liam: They work 15-hour shifts—they deserve only the best pasta creation money can buy. Oh, whoop. That was a sharper corner than I thought.

Liam: Oh no, front desk lady is chasing us now. She has some other people with her. They don't sound all that happy.

V: Hey, sorry to break it to you, but stealing people from hospitals is a pretty big no-no. Here comes the police officer too, and it looks like he's calling for backup.

11:36 AM
Liam: I don't suppose those officers want any stroganoff too? Talk about a lot of work without a whole lot of gratitude.

V: The elevator's opening. Quick!

Liam: Wheeee. Oh, sorry, didn't mean to run into that wall. Okay, click, click, click, click, click, click. Goodbye, Mr. Officer. Let me know your favorite kind of cheese. And oh no, he can't hear us.

V: Good thing you pressed the "close door" button about twenty times. Everyone knows those are super effective.

Liam: So now when we get downstairs, we're gonna take a leisurely roll, right?

11:37 AM
V: Yeah, doubt it. They've called down, for sure. We're going to have to make a dash for the exit. You have a getaway car?

Liam: Oh yeah, Caleb told Himari and Kevin to be stationed at the door. Said for me to do the doctor thing because he was worried Kevin couldn't pull off the whole part of a professional doctor. And Himari looked too young. Good call, if you ask me.

V: Uh-huh. Makes sense ... Gonna be having a few questions for Caleb ...

Unknown Source: Ding!

Liam: And we're off to the races. Dodging around that lady. Swerving around that officer. Hi, officer. Okay, focus. No stroganoff. Only the doors.

11:38 AM
V: Himari, get the door open, quick! Everyone in! Oof!

Himari: In? Okay, Kevin, go, go, go! Woohoo! Is this what robbing a bank feels like?

V: No, usually the getaway driver is fast. Kevin! You can break the speed limit right now!

Kevin: Well, sor-ry. Probably should've put Liam at the wheel since he drives mighty fast. But nooooo. Kevin can't act like a doctor. He's been a pirate, a fairy godmother, and a wolf, but no. Doctor is where we draw the line.

11:39 AM

V: I had questions with that decision as well. I'm thinking maybe Liam just looks older? Sorry, Kev, you don't look old enough to have gone through med school.

> **Kevin:** Okay, well if we were trying to lose anyone, we probably lost them. Doesn't look like we have anyone to worry about, except some Volkswagen that's tailing me. HEY, LADY, GET OVER INTO THE OTHER LANE. SOME OF US HAVE PRECIOUS CARGO.

Liam: Y-you think I'm precious cargo? This has been the best day of my life.

> **Kevin:** Right. Yes. I had only Liam in mind when I said that.

Liam: It's all right, buddy. The other two are precious cargo too. Don't you forget that.

> 11:40 AM
> **Himari:** Weeell, okay, now that we've had that heart to heart. Where are we going, V?

V: To the airport. I've got to get to Zona ASAP. We didn't get any volunteers from that area. Not surprising. One of the biggest outposts, pretty scary stuff.

> **Kevin:** Caleb'll meet you there after he does the talk show. They're filming right by the airport and should be airing any time now.

V: The fact that we have anyone at all is all thanks to you, Kevin. Thanks for being a Meta-Matcher. Guess it comes in handy.

Himari: Kevin got the sidekicks, and hopefully Caleb will get the heroes. In the meantime, V, they probably won't let you fly in a hospital gown.

11:41 AM
Liam: Costume change!

Kevin: Ever consider theater, dude? That accent? You're a natural.

Liam: We'll talk later, my friend. Time to get your friend-o some new clothes.

V: Oh dear. I'm going to turn this off before anything weird happens.

.

EVENING TALK SHOW
TRANSCRIPT

Ted: Folks, you'll have to excuse Roger's absence. Turned out some of the snacks in the green room gave him food poisoning. Glad we have a hero to fill his seat tonight at the last minute. Welcome back, Cortex.

Cortex: Good as always to be back, Ted.

Joe: You'll also have to excuse the fact that we bumped the evening news to the afternoon—ignore that heading, folks. Anything for a hero. Please don't sue us for using those pictures of you.

Paul: Now, Cortex, let me see if I can get all this straight, because you talked rather fast on the phone. The SA has a plan far worse than taking away powers from heroes and villains everywhere?

Cortex: Right, we believe that was only the first part of the plan. A certain friend-o of mine has some intel. They used a serum developed by a college student to take away powers, yes, but robbing us of our powers was the starting point.

Joe: Now, when you say "us," does that include you?

Cortex: ... Yeah, actually. On June 11th, the same college graduate who developed the serum injected me with it. I ... I couldn't figure out his identity. He was wearing a mask.

Ted: Didn't you appear on TV afterward saying you escaped with your powers intact?

Cortex: Some friends did rescue me. A henchman, villain, and sidekick —

Paul: Look at that, inclusivity. Heroism knows no distinction or boundaries.

Cortex: But they didn't get to me in time before he took my powers.

Joe: So why did you insist on live television that they hadn't taken away your abilities? At the party where you killed a member of the SA, someone who wished to remain anonymous said you managed to make the lights flicker that night.

Cortex: Vortex and I were worried that if I showed they'd taken away my powers, the SA would try to attack me because I'm more vulnerable. And as for the lights ... I got someone to turn them on and off. You'd think people would've gotten skeptical, because I only had the one party trick. I guess some had at the end. I think someone even shouted something about me missing my powers.

Ted: You know, that explains why you went for the knife on the table. If you had your powers, you would've been able to read his mind. Probably could've taken him down in a less-bloody manner.

Paul: Didn't some partygoers say they were confused why you didn't use your powers in the fight?

Joe: That they did. So the SA made you vulnerable, and you didn't want the world to know it.

Cortex: But after a little run-in with another SA member, I discovered I don't need powers to take down this organization, and neither do other heroes or villains. We don't need powers to be powerful. Or super abilities to be superheroes. We can take them down. We just might have to actually put in effort this time. No scheduled savings or photoshoots. Actual effort.

Joe: ...

Paul: ...

Ted: Gotta say, Cortex, I don't know if that's computing. Sure, we've had some dark horse villains and heroes enter the world's stage without any superpowers, but they really had to have some standout abilities to compete with the rest. Like a really good eye for target practice or be incredibly tech savvy. Although you've not uncovered your secret identity, I imagine if you had some special talent outside of your powers, you would've used it by now.

Cortex: I respectfully disagree.

Cortex: My sister loves the Einstein quote, "Everybody is a genius. But if you judge a fish by its ability to climb a tree, it will live its whole life believing that it is stupid."

Cortex: One summer she made me paint that quote on the wall of her bedroom, so that's why I remember every word, but if we judge everyone by their ability to suck powers or flicker lights with their brains, we're missing the point. We've lost heroes because we've overlooked them.

Cortex: The SA has thirty-two nukes stationed around the United States, which we probably should've mentioned right off the bat. Way to bury the lead, guys, talking about your buddy's food poisoning.

Joe: It was really bad food poisoning ...

Cortex: And, they would be setting off those nukes right now, if they happened to have a certain code from a man they kidnapped. They don't.

Paul: Getting a little misty-eyed there, Cortex?

Cortex: Point is, we need heroes and villains to step up, stop moping, and station themselves near the nearest nuke on the map. If they want a copy of that map, it's floating around the Meta-Match forums. If you search my name and click on my sidekick's link, you'll find the forum. Most heroes and villains still have accounts on that app.

Cortex: And thanks to a helpful little henchman I know, SA hasn't been successfully able to hack the app and delete the map. For now. Overheard their director can't even work a PowerPoint. Talk about a bad dude. Must have a wicked backstory.

Ted: This all sounds noble, but if we're being realistic, powerless heroes and villains marching into war zones? Yikes. We don't know how many SA folks are stationed at these nukes, if they even do exist and aren't some scare tactic. You might be walking into an army, or at least a handful of gunmen.

Cortex: Hence the need for as many villains and heroes as possible.

Joe: And with you publicizing this on television, the SA will know you're coming.

Cortex: Joe, this is the SA. If you so much as think about tweeting something about them, they'll know. How do you think they managed to track down all those with A-list and B-list powers? They've kept tabs on all of us for a while. I'm sure they're anticipating someone will try to stop them.

Cortex: The question is: how many?

Paul: You're asking them to lay down their lives against a formidable foe who by most odds will likely wipe them out? You're asking them to enter a suicide mission?

Cortex: No, Paul. I'm asking them to be heroes.

VORTIE AND CORTIE

JUNE 16

8:56 PM
Cortex: *Plane just let out. Where are you?*

Cortex: *Sucked being on a different flight than you. Had some dude sit next to me and talk about his sci-fi book he's writing. It was awful.*

> **V:** *I'm over here, sitting on the end. I see you. Nope, keep looking. Keep turning. See the horrendous orange seats? Yup, right here.*

Cortex: *Heading your way.*

8:57 PM
Cortex: Wow, it's still bright outside. And what a sad little airport. Oh, right, forgot about the time change. How far behind is Zona?

> **V:** Three hours behind. And yeah, it's summer, so it's still bright out. Come on, let's get walking.

Cortex: Yeah, maybe Himari can fix the clock on this thing once we've finished everything. Oh, that couple over there really misses each other. They're going for it.

Unknown Source: I can't believe I'm not going to see you for another six months.

Cortex: Huh ... six months. V, I'm bad at math. How many months in two years?

8:58 PM
V: Really? Haha. There's ... twenty-four. Dang, that's kind of a lot of months.

Cortex: Yeah ... Um, wow. There's like no place to eat here. Indiana airports are better, and we're smaller.

V: Eh, Tucson. What you gonna do.

Cortex: Two ... yeah. So Peace Corps, huh? You get to wear any fun uniforms? Probably no black capes.

V: Yeah ... I'll probably have to turn that in for a couple years. Ah, baggage claim. Did you pack anything? I didn't, haha.

8:59 PM
Cortex: Well, considering I rode an ambulance to the hospital and Ubered to the talk show and then here, didn't have much time to head home and pack a bag. Good thing there was a Cortex costume at that costume shop near the hospital. Looked a little cheap, but those reporters seemed flustered, so they didn't notice.

Cortex: So ... Peace Corps.

Cortex: Any chance you can postpone that for a little bit and stay home?

V: Sigh. I know. I don't really want to leave either. But ... after everything I've done, I feel like I owe it to the world, you know? I don't really deserve to just stay here and have my happy life and all.

Cortex: I'll bet there's a lot of good you could do back here.

9:00 PM
Cortex: Oh, wonder why that kid's crying over there.

Cortex: Even though I'm not the biggest fan of kids ... he looks really sad. Like a little lost Kevin or something.

V: Hey, buddy. Where are your parents?

Unknown Source: *SNUFFLE*. I don't know. *SNUFFLE*.

V: Oh, it's okay, bud. We'll help you find them. What's your name?

Unknown Source: *SNUFFLE*. Carson.

9:01 PM
V: All right, Carson—oh, yes, thank you for the boogery face on my leg—where did you last see your parents?

Carson: I went to go potty, and then I came out, and they were g-gone.

V: Okay. Um. Were they going potty too?

Carson: *SNUFFLE. SNIIIIIIIFF*. Daddy had to go poopoo, but he said I could wait for him, but then I looked under all the doors and I couldn't find him.

    Cortex: *Internal screaming.*

9:02 PM
V: SNORT—I mean, I'm sorry, buddy. Why don't you and nice Mr. Caleb go check again?

    Cortex: Sure, come on, little Carson. Oh, you and Liam like holding hands.

    Cortex: Okay, we're at the bathroom. Let's head in … No, we should probably just call out his name. No, we shouldn't look under the stalls. It's not—*dang it, Liam*—polite.

V: *Hahahahaha.*

    Cortex: What's your dad's name?

9:03 PM
Carson: Um, Tim.

    Cortex: Is there a Tim in here?

    Cortex: Tim?

    Cortex: Perhaps goes by Timothy? Timon of Athens? Timothopolis?

Unknown Source: What's wrong with you, dude? Can't a guy take a piss in peace? And no, I ain't Tim!

    Cortex: Clearly you haven't met my friend Kevin. Be glad you have that urinal all to yourself. And watch the language around the kid. Okay, Carson, he's not in here, but we still can check around. I'm sure he hasn't gotten far.

9:04 PM
Cortex: *Coming back to you V. You see us?*

V: *Yup. And guess what? Turned off the audio for a minute because I was enjoying your bathroom exchange, but I found a nice, frantic man named Tim out here looking for a kid.*

Cortex: *Balding guy? Wearing a baseball cap?*

V: *Looks like every white guy in Tucson? Yup.*

Carson: DADDY!!!!

Tim: Oh, thank goodness. Hey, buddy!

9:05 PM
Carson: Daddy! I got saved-ded by heroes! Nice lady and bathroom guy!

Tim: That's great, buddy. Hey, thanks, both of you. Look at us civilians, doing some real hero work. Don't suppose you've seen the news ... but I won't talk about that in front of Carson. Thanks, folks!

Cortex: Zona is wild.

Cortex: Are you—are you tearing up?

V: No! I'm just ... incredibly disgusted by this booger on my pant leg. From the cute little curly headed boy. Look at him smile ... I mean, ew, gross!

9:06 PM
Cortex: Uh-huh. Well, Uber should be picking us up pretty soon. Cool with an Airbnb? I hear the house is Harry Potter themed.

V: No way! You had time to book that?

Cortex: Listen, there's a lot of time between sets on talk shows. And I had to do something other than hear Paul talk about his gastrointestinal problems.

V: Oof. You were on THAT talk show? I bet you're even more excited to chill with good ole Harry and friends.

9:07 PM
Cortex: Eh, I figure if we die tomorrow at least we stayed somewhere fun. Which of the Harry Potter movies should we watch tonight before our impending doom?

V: Which one is longest? I want to snuggle as long as possible.

Cortex: Hypothetically …

Cortex: If I were accidentally playing one after the other, that would still count as only one, right?

V: Heehee. I would pretend to notice nothing. Oh, look, there's the Uber.

THE FABULOUS FOUR
JUNE 16

Kevin changed group name to "Taco Tuesday for This Day Only"

9:37 PM
Kevin: So since we've checked into the hotel and all, and since our whole world may crash and burn as of tomorrow …

Kevin: And since it's Taco Tuesday …

Kevin: You're leaving me hanging here.

Himari: You put "…" That usually means more is coming. By the way, did you get into your room okay?

9:38 PM
Kevin: Haha. The dude you heard across the hall dropping his key and putting the wrong end into the scanner thing … totally not me.

Himari: Cool, not too far apart then. But I don't want to get up from this comfy bed until I have to. So by all means, please continue your ellipsis.

Kevin: Since it's Taco Tuesday, we should eat the PB&J sandwiches Liam packed for us … yay.

Himari: Okay, okay. Well, I just so happen to see a taco shop on the map here, a bit down the road.

9:39 PM
Kevin: Is it super sketch? Will the Kevin Maester have to pull out the big guns and protect you?

Himari: Ummm … what answer would make you happy?

Kevin: Well obviously the Kevin Maester is a master crime fighter, but I would rather not get blood on my fists before tomorrow. I like to keep them clean for the fight.

Himari: Fair. Well, it's called Los Burritos Felices, so I think we're good.

9:40 PM
Kevin: That door slam was definitely not me getting too excited about tacos and then locking myself into the hallway.

Himari: Omg, Kevin. All right, just putting my shoes back on, and out the door … Ah, hello. Oh. You changed shirts. Nice.

Kevin: Good thing we left our duffels in Liam's car the other day. Hope he Ubered all right back into Indy. We sort of need him to take out that nuke. Then again, a few other peeps on Meta-Match are in that area. He can use all the teamwork bonding he can get.

9:41 PM
Himari: Ha! I'm sure he'll love that. So, uh, tacos? *Shoot, did I brush my hair after lying on the bed? Dang it. Don't think I did.*

    Kevin: Oh, your voice is in my ear. Think we should turn this thing off?

Himari: Oh. Uh, actually, can we leave it on? Maybe, if one of us dies tomorrow … we'll still have one last conversation to look back on.

    Kevin: *My first taco run with a girl in over five years?* I mean, ummm, yeah. Definitely. Sure. Whatevs. Seems like a great plan.

9:42 PM
Himari: Thanks. Okay, it's this way. I have my card at least to get back in. We'll have to contact the front desk when we get back, haha, or you'll be locked out of your room all night.

    Kevin: Yeah, don't want a repeat of when our theater troupe went to the Fringe festival. Glad we're on the first floor. Man, this lobby is nice. Apples in baskets, pillars, wow. Did Liam book this place for us?

    Kevin: Anything for his best friend-os.

Unknown Source: *wʃʃʃʃʃʃʃhh*

    Himari: He did, actually. Said he'd stayed here before. Did you just pretend to use the force to open the automatic doors?

9:43 PM
Kevin: What are you talking about? These babies aren't automatic.

Haha. Okay, wow. It's literally like a block away. How did I miss that driving up here?

Himari: "Defying Gravity" came on. You were too busy singing.

Kevin: Is that a walk-up place? Like ice cream?

Himari: Oh … I guess so. Not any places to sit, either. Guess we'll have to bring it back with us.

Kevin: I'm sure the people in the lobby will be THRILLED.

Himari: Ohhh yeah … the front desk lady looked annoyed at our existence. Hey, it's fine, we can bring it back to my room. There are those little tray table thingies. So fancy.

9:44 PM
Kevin: *Okay, be cool. Think about taco things. Lettuce. Cheese. Wow, no line. Nice.* Hi, sir. I'd like a taco.

Himari: Okay, we're temporarily turning these off so we don't have a record of our obscene taco orders. *Or me kicking myself for saying it like that … stupid, stupi—*

9:50 PM
Kevin: Wow, all out of tacos, who knew? But I guess a burrito works just fine. It's like a taco, just more insecure.

Himari: Ha! No wonder he's insecure, the way you're looking at him ravenously. Poor little burrito.

Kevin: Last I checked you were going to eat yours too. Unless you're just planning on putting him on a table and dressing him in a hat.

Himari: Okay, but Kevin, I think you're drooling, haha. My burrito is less terrified than your burrito. *I wish I were only as terrified as Kevin's burrito. I am one scared taco.*

Kevin: What?

Himari: Nothing! Mexican food, yay! *Keep it together, Himari. Don't think about dying like a crunchy taco blown to pieces.*

9:51 PM
Kevin: I mean, if you would be any kind of Mexican food, it would be a taco. Because tacos are the best.

Kevin: Oh, sorry, took me a second to register that thought. Takes it a while to load sometimes. No, I don't want little Himari pieces everywhere.

Himari: Don't think anyone has ever called me a taco before. I'm honored.

Kevin: Well, sure. The reason why I think burritos are lame is they're too soft. You get to the good stuff inside too fast, and then it burns up your mouth. Tacos, you have to work at it a little. That hard shell on the outside protects all the nice stuff inside, but I really like it all. A little hurt and a little good stuff.

9:52 PM
Himari: Problem with tacos is they look tough, until you press them too hard. Then they fall all to pieces. Burritos … roll with the punches a little easier.

Kevin: Himari, have you ever HEARD of a walking taco? Where you take all the broken pieces of the shell and make it something even more delicious? Hands down, tacos rule.

Himari: Yeah, I guess walking tacos are pretty good. Burritos are still my favorite, though. Nice, warm, comforting burritos.

Kevin: Are we actually talking about Mexican food? I'm a guy, so I feel like you're saying something but not saying something.

Himari: I don't know. Are you actually talking about tacos? Because ... I don't know if I've ever spoken so glowingly about burritos before.

9:53 PM
Kevin: ...

Kevin: Well, it's not exactly the most romantic thing to say. Shakespeare doesn't go all, "Oh my love, how thou art a taco."

Himari: Poor Shakespeare. He was missing out.

Kevin: Clearly.

Kevin: So I'm a burrito, huh?

Himari: Yeah, um, hold my burrito for me for a minute? I'm going to unlock the door.

9:54 PM
Himari: There. I'll take the burrito back now.

Kevin: Wow. Nice place. Mine has a painting of a sailboat instead of flowers. Your loss.

Himari: OMG. Oh, dang. They only have one little tray.

Kevin: Wouldn't Liam be so proud? We're sharing and therefore enhancing our bonding teamwork experience.

9:55 PM
Himari: Let's just try not to get hot sauce on the quilt. Wow, this is a big burrito.

Kevin: Yeah, haha. Wowser.

Kevin: Himari …

Kevin: In all seriousness, do you think SA smashed you in the center?

Himari: We were just … talking about tacos. That's all. Mmf. Grrd burrritr. Yummrs.

9:56 PM
Kevin: Right, yeah. Sorry. Guys in my frat house would tell me I was weird because I'd make strange connections like that. I guess it's not "the guy thing to do." Sorry. You meant it literally. Tacos just fall apart.

Himari: Sorry, Kevin. It's just … this taco isn't very good at coming out of her shell. Let's try this again. Hello. My name is Himari, and I'm a taco. Is this better? I'm bad at feelings.

Kevin: Well, apparently, I'm too good at them. Hello, I'm Kevin. And I'm a burrito. Let me burn your tongue, but yet, the outside will be icy cold because microwaves don't work in the frat house. Yeah … the metaphor kind of breaks down.

Himari: Pretty sure you're an authentic burrito. No microwave burrito problems. The real deal. So. What would a taco say to a burrito if the world might end tomorrow?

9:57 PM
Kevin: This sounds like the start of a knock knock joke.

Kevin: Oh, oh, hey, no fair. Stop hitting me with those pillows.

Himari: Nooo! Hot sauce on the bed! I blame you, sir.

Kevin: *Okay, be serious, Kev.* Speaking, obviously, in completely metaphorical terms, as we are talking about literal tacos and burritos, I would tell the taco it's okay that she—it—feels like IT fell apart. Because personally, I think she gets more beautiful by the day.

9:58 PM
Himari: Well, Mr. Burrito. I think no one appreciates you enough. Everyone is out there trying to be a chimichanga or an enchilada, but at the end of the day, what's better than a burrito? A burrito doesn't expect anything from you. And burritos give the best hugs when you're scared and stressed out.

Kevin: Do you need a burrito hug right now? Oof! That's a very strong burrito hug.

9:59 PM
Kevin: Umm, Himari ...

Kevin: *Oh gosh, I haven't done this before. Except for on stage, but that doesn't really count.*

Kevin: Hypothetically ...

Kevin: Is it okay if this burrito kisses this taco?

Himari: I think the taco would like that.

10:00 PM
Himari: Mm, um, hey, Kev? Taco's gonna turn off the chat.

10:01 PM
V: Awww, not yet! Things with the Mexican food were just getting spicy.

Cortex: V, way to spoil it. They weren't supposed to know that we heard EVERYTHING. WE HEARD EVERYTHING.

V: HAHAHAHAHAHA. PAYBACK, BABY!

Himari: Noooooo, Kevin, how could you put it in the wrong chat!

V: Oh, is she hitting him with a pillow? This is familiar. I love this. Sweet, sweet revenge.

10:02 PM
Cortex: Whack him good, Himari. If you don't kill him, when he gets back home, I will.

V: Aw, come on, babe, I ship it. Let's leave them alone now. My lust for revenge is satisfied.

Cortex: All right, love birds. But, Kev. If I'm not the best man, I'm hitting you over the head with the cake.

Himari: I hate you both right now. Goodbye!

TACO TUESDAY FOR THIS DAY ONLY

JUNE 17

Kevin changed group name to "Taco + Burrito (and ... the others)"

5:47 AM

Himari: *All right, folks, I'm halfway up the back wall. No guards have seen me yet. Everyone else in position?*

> **V:** *I hate everyone. It's completely dark out here, and Caleb and I have zero backup. This whole "we attack at dawn" thing was a mistake for everyone on the west coast.*

Himari: *Okay, but who expects an attack at six in the morning? Or ... three? Kevin, all your friends on Meta-Match in position?*

> **Kevin:** *My phone's probably going to crash with all these tabs open, but yeah, looks like it. Good thing I'm easily distracted. If I were a focused person, this would be insanely overwhelming.*

5:48 AM

Himari: *All right, then, Kev, time to turn on your charm. We can't have Hulga checking any security feeds, nothing, if I'm going to get in to Mr. Gladkins.*

Kevin: *Right … can't let all those heroes stationed at the nukes down. Here goes … something. Now Himari, remember. Don't be jealous.*

Himari: *Um … right. I'll keep that in mind. T minus twelve, you guys.*

Kevin: Hi, Hulga. You might not remember me, but man, do I remember a face like that. *I mean, it looks almost green-ish.* How are you doing this fine morning?

Hulga: Hmph. Fine morning. Little early, if you ask me. What do you want?

5:49 AM
Kevin: Gosh, did they put you on the graveyard shift again? I'm so sorry. Liam was saying how underappreciated you were, and I couldn't agree more. For goodness sake, do they even provide good dental insurance, or do you have to handle that on your own?

Hulga: Ha! You know what? No dental. It's ridiculous. Only insurance is if I get stabbed by a hero or something. As if that's the only bad thing that could happen to a person.

Kevin: Oh, I hear you. Hulga, this could be from a completely unbiased third-party perspective, but I have the nagging feeling that you don't get to express your frustrations about work all that often.

5:50 AM
Hulga: Ha. You don't exactly complain to Mr. Gladkins. Listen, young man, stay away from SA work if you can. Probably get a better salary and benefits as a teacher, and that's saying a lot.

Kevin: No! I was going in for an interview today. Came so early because, you know, jitters. But are you telling me that this workplace is dissatisfying?

Hulga: Ah, it sounds great when you get here. "Opportunity for advancement" and "a potential role in world domination." Exciting stuff, you know? But here I am, stuck at a desk all day, every day, just taking calls, watching security monitors, answering emails.

> **Kevin:** *Yikes, security monitors. Hope all's going well, Himari.*
> Wow, so thrilling. Man are you steering me in the right direction. Are you saying I should just leave and not even show up to the interview? Would they kill me for that?

5:51 AM
Hulga: Well, kid, I'll tell you what I told my nephew. You seem like a very nice young man — wouldn't be telling many people, but I think I've taken a liking to you. So listen here. They're gonna nuke most of the United States today. So, if you can, pack a bag and head to Canada. Oh, but don't tell anyone I told you. I'm not supposed to know. I just saw the notes on Mr. Gladkins' desk when I was cleaning his secret lair. I just hate to see someone so young get blown to smithereens.

> **Kevin:** Wow. So difficult to process this information I'm hearing for the very first time.

> **Kevin:** I guess I'll take your advice and book it out of here. Seems rather silly they'd assign an interview on the first day of the apocalypse, but ain't that corporate life?

> **Kevin:** You know, Hulga, I'd hate for you to be here too, during the nuke-pocalypse. You're young. You're beautiful. You don't deserve to die.

5:52 AM

Hulga: *Sniff.* Aw. Young man, I don't think anyone's said anything that nice to me in thirty years. I guess it doesn't really matter. Someone has to man the front desk while the important people hide in bunkers.

> **Kevin:** You know, Hulga, I can't believe I'm saying this, but I'd rather you live and sacrifice myself for something noble. I can man the desk. I bet that Gladkins won't even notice, the jerk. Bet he doesn't even know the names of his employees.

Hulga: *Sniff. Sniff.* He doesn't. He called me Charlene the other day. That's not even close to Hulga.

> **Kevin:** Now, don't take that silliness from that boss. If he intends to nuke this place, then gosh darn it, you won't let him have your last day on earth. You show him!

Hulga: You know what? You're right!

5:53 AM
Unknown Source: *SMASH!*

Hulga: Haha! Take that, Gladkins! Buy yourself a new computer with all that money you don't give me.

> **Kevin:** *Dear Lord, what have I unleashed?*

Hulga: You like stroganoff, young man? I make excellent end-of-the-world stroganoff.

> **Kevin:** You know, as far as final meals go, that sounds good. *Not quite tacos, but beggars can't be, well, beggars.* Okay, Hulga, I'll take you up on that stroganoff.

Hulga: Ooh, I'm so glad you came by today. Come on, I live down the road a ways. We can have a nice stroll to work up our appetites. What's your name, young man? Never mind, it doesn't matter. I'm just going to call you Kevin. I've always wanted a son named Kevin.

5:54 AM
Kevin: *Well that's convenient. I don't know if I've always wanted a mom named Hulga.* Wow. I'm speechless.

Himari: *Kevin, I'm in, you wonderful schmooze. Hey, can you ask her where that secret lair is? Gladkins isn't in his office.*

Kevin: *I'll try, but she looks like she wants to hug me. And let me tell you, it makes a Liam hug look far more inviting.* Hulga, I really want to stick it to Gladkins for you. Since it's my first and last day on the job. Is there any way I can trash his desk in his secret lair? I really want to mess everything up, throw papers like confetti, but I am so bad at directions. That's part of the reason I came to you. He wanted to have the interview down there, but forgot to send me a map.

5:55 AM
Hulga: Sounds like him, making me do all the work. O-ho-ho, I like the way you think. Well, if you take a left after the front desk, there's a wall coated in electrical charges. There's a little button on the side. If you push it, the electricity turns off and you'll find a nice big door. Security code is 1234. Haha! He uses that code for everything.

Kevin: Okay, it's a bit complicated, but hopefully I can remember those four numbers. Might have to write them down.

Kevin: Now fly, Hulga. Off into the sunrise that comes

during this ungodly hour. And eat stroganoff like no one is watching!

Hulga: I will, young Kevin! I will! And if you survive, come on down, and I'll make sure there's plenty for you.

> **Himari:** *Okay, that was adorable. Kev, if we live, you have to go have stroganoff with Hulga.*

5:56 AM
Kevin: *Ha. Ha. Now, if you excuse me, I have a lot of emails to answer and files to organize.*

> **V:** *Ugh, wish she hadn't destroyed the computer. Could have emailed the district leaders to postpone the attack. T minus four, y'all. Get ready to wreak some havoc at every SA base in the country.*

Himari: *All right, past the zappy-wall, one two three four ... we're in.* Oh! Hi, Mr. Gladkins. Fancy meeting you here.

> **Dad:** Hima—girl I don't know, what are you doing here?

5:57 AM
Gladkins: Get her, boys.

> **Himari:** Oh, hello, big burly men. Oh, a gun. Very nice. Um, sorry, gonna have to stab you ... and you ...

Unknown Source: *BANG!*

> **Himari:** Ooh, this gun is nice.

Kevin: *You are so attractive right now.*

Unknown Source: *BANG BANG BANG*

Himari: That's easier than stabbing people. All right, Mr. Glad-kins, hands up and back away from the ominous big red button!

5:58 AM
Gladkins: Hahaha. Stupid girl. Even if I don't press this button and activate all the nukes at once, each nuke can be activated individually! The United States will fall. Nukes to Washington, New York, Chicago — Bentonville, Arkansas —

Himari: Wait, what? Bentonville, Arkansas? Why?

Gladkins: The headquarters of Walmart, of course.

Kevin: *I wonder if his tragic backstory involved Walmart. Not sure why. Maybe he didn't get something on sale.*

Himari: Oooh, interesting trivia for the day. Um, anyway, back away from the big red button.

Gladkins: Heh heh heh. It doesn't matter, girl. No one can stop the individual nukes. They all have orders to fire by ... dang it, what time was it? Just don't shoot me while I press the intercom button. Hulga, what time are the nukes supposed to be fired?

5:59 AM
Kevin: *Dang it, I'm so bad at phones. How does this work? There are, like, ten buttons blinking.*

Gladkins: Huh. She must be on her five-minute breakfast break. Anyway, they will all be fired!

Himari: That's what you think! Got a TV in here, Mr. Happykins?

Gladkins: Oh. Well, yes, I do actually. Don't really know how to work the remote ... Juan does that.

Himari: *Good Lord.* Okay, well, here. I'll show you how to use it. *Counting down to universal attack, everyone. Ten, nine, eight, seven, six, five, four, three, two, one—GET THOSE SA NUKES!*

VORTIE AND CORTIE
JUNE 17

6:00 AM

V: *It's showtime. Never attacked a villain headquarters on a butt scooter before, but you do what you gotta do when your leg's not working. Wheeeeeeeeeee! Faster, Caleb! Wheeeeeeeeeee!*

> **Cortex:** *I think you're handling the gravity of our situation really well. Also, when did you get that butt scooter? Was that when you sneaked out of the fourth Harry Potter movie to "look at the sunset alone"? Wow, those guys with guns at the front don't look happy.*

V: *It's okay, give me a big push. I'll take out their ankles while you distract them.*

> **Cortex:** *Distract them how? I'm not Kevin. I can't charm them and ask about dental insurance.* Hey, fellas, you have great dental insurance! *See? Now they're all confused.*

V: *All I needed.* Wheeee! Goodbye, Achilles tendons! *Ooh, Caleb, stab that dude.*

6:01 AM

Cortex: *Well, that was an awkward stab. He's not dead, but I think he's thinking his job doesn't pay enough to retaliate.*

V: Run while you can, suckers! It's the edge of the apocalypse, and I may be on a butt scooter, but I'm out for blood! Wheeeeee! Onward, down the tunnel!

Cortex: I am both concerned and very much in love with you at the same time. Wow, it's dark down here.

V: Another round of angry people running at us. Push me! You got top, I got bottom. Heehee, kneecaps!

Cortex: You get all the fun parts. Sorry, yeah that shoulder doesn't look so … you might want to get ice for that. *Great, now I sound like Liam. Ugh, there's like twenty of them.*

V: Could have used some backup out here, but the only hero around that I know is Cactus Boy, and he doesn't get up early for anything.

6:02 AM

Cortex: Yeah, this is pretty weird. *Duck!* Because Kevin said all the other places had at least five recruits. *Weird dude with a septum ring on your right.* But maybe they heard about your airports and decided not to come.

V: *Okay, you can't judge the Phoenix airport based on the Tucson airport's food selection.* Ooooh, you wore shorts, my friend. That was a bad idea. I can see your nice kneecaps so clearly. Bye bye!

Cortex: You're so extra.

Cortex: Okay, that was the last one. V. V, leave the poor guy's kneecaps alone.

6:03 AM
V: I can't take just one as a souvenir?

> **Cortex:** I'm not even going to comment. Let's push you away from the poor bleeding guy and deeper into the tunnel. Let me know if you see something that looks like a nuke that could blow up a portion of the United States.

V: Okay. I can come back later for one if we don't die. Those were some really nice kneecaps.

> **Cortex:** So Peace Corps, huh?

V: Helping people and messing with Shadow Assassins who think I'm obsessed with kneecaps are not mutually exclusive. Oh, look, that's gotta be the nuke, right?

> **Cortex:** Well, they painted a bunch of smileys on it. Ah. I get it. Gladkins. Wowsers, that thing's huge.

6:04 AM
V: And not guarded? Sweet. Let's dismantle this baby.

> **Juan:** Ah, look who it is. My favorite super couple.

Cortex: *Ugh, probably should've waited for the police when he was unconscious back at the house, but the ambulance arrived first.* Awww, we're your favorite?

> **Juan:** If you think you're dismantling this nuke, you're sadly mistaken. I have orders to send it off promptly at 3:24 AM on a nice little trip to the White House.

V: *Oh, that's not too bad, then. Should we let this one go?*

Cortex: Guess it sucks to suck. It's already been 3 AM, my dude. *Oh, wait, right. I forgot about the time change in Arizona. Whoops.*

Juan: Oooookay, well, those of us who can tell time are going to continue monologuing, all right? You can't get through me to this nuke. You know why?

6:05 AM
V: *What's he holding up?*

Juan: This little baby is a remote to activate the nuke. You take one step forward, and I'll set it off prematurely.

Cortex: *Don't suppose he'd be down for a dance-off?*

V: *I've seen him Riverdance. You'd lose.*

Cortex: *When did you see him Riverdance? Okay, sorry. There's a nuke and I shouldn't ask how you know about people's dancing habits. What should we do?*

V: *I don't know, stall him until Kev and Himari can do something? We'd better tell them getting Gladkins away from that mass-destruct button isn't enough. They're going to have to find a way to remotely shut down the whole grid.*

TACO + BURRITO (AND ... THE OTHERS)

JUNE 17

6:05 AM
Himari: There, so that's how you change the channel.

Kevin: *Himari, I know this isn't an emergency, but some supervisor wants coffee, and I have a feeling the bean water isn't going to suffice.*

Cortex: *Glad to see I caught you guys at a clearly stressful time. Himari, we have a problem.*

Himari: *Clearly. Nukes blowing up the country.* Okay, so now we're going to change the channel to your security feeds of the other SA district headquarters. Oh! Look at that. A bunch of heroes, villains, sidekicks, and henchmen taking over.

Gladkins: What? Well, ha! It doesn't matter! I can press the button HERE! Bwahahahaha!

6:06 AM
Himari: I'm ... holding a gun to your head. But okay. *What's up, bro?*

Cortex: *So you remember Juan, right?*

Kevin: *I'm going to see if they'll do tea.*

Himari: *Good call, Kev. Ah, yeah, Juan, the man I hate with a burning passion? What about him?*

Cortex: *So he's apparently holding a remote to activate our nuke in Zona, and yeah. We're kind of at an impasse. Basically, we flinch and he sets it off. Classic Juan move.*

Cortex: *He's starting to get suspicious why we aren't saying anything. V's trying stand-up comedy, but I don't think it's working.*

6:07 AM
V: Why did the chicken cross the road? Because it greatly desired a quick death with an explosive amount of feathers. Ba-dum-tsh! Eh?

Himari: *Omg. But Caleb, all I know to do is keep him away from this button. But ... maybe he has a remote way to shut OFF all the nukes too?*

Kevin: *Bad news. There are no raw sugars in the break room. They'll have to make do with Splenda. Also, wasn't that the whole point of me recruiting people? Because each of the nuke sites needed people there to shut them down?*

Himari: *Yes, it was. If there's a way to shut them down remotely, Glad-kins definitely hasn't programmed it. I'd ... have to do it really, really fast. Omg.* Listen here, Gladkins. I need to know your code to get into your control panel ... wait, never mind. Don't move. One two three four. Neat. Oh, nice desktop.

Gladkins: Argh! How do you have such legendary hacking skills?

6:08 AM

Himari: *How do you have such incredibly horrible password security?* Okay, typing with one hand while holding a gun in the other is a little annoying, but don't worry, I can still shoot you the second you move. All right, here we are. The nuke launch sequence. And that passcode ... was created by Kosuke Takahashi.

Dad: And I didn't tell him. Ha!

Gladkins: I've never had someone so resistant to torture before.

Himari: Great. Good job, Da—er, Kosuke.

Cortex: *Yikes. Guys, V's comedy ain't getting any better. She's resorted to mime.*

6:09 AM

Himari: Okay, Mr. Guy I Don't Know. You've gotta let me know the passcode so I can get in.

Dad: Right. Um. Well. Here's the thing ...

Dad: I didn't tell him because I can't remember it.

Kevin: *Never have I been so proud and so disappointed. Kind of like the supervisors when I gave them their tea.*

Himari: Omg. Dad. How?

Dad: Well, at least it couldn't be tortured out of me, huh? Heh heh ... Um, we can try a couple. First try LuxIsAwesome<3, that's capital L, capital I, capital A, and a little emoji heart.

6:10 AM
Himari: *I am so ashamed.*

VORTIE AND CORTIE

JUNE 17

6:10 AM

Cortex: *Please never do theater. Also, Juan looks really annoyed. He might just press that button whether we step toward him or not.*

V: *You're right, you're right. Okay, new tactic.* Juan, I think it's time to have a serious chat about our feelings. *I'm channeling Liam.*

    Cortex: *Because Juan LOVES Liam.*

Juan: I'm really tempted to just push this button and have it over with so I can move on to killing you.

    V: See, that's not very nice. Let's talk about those feelings. Why are you so angry? Maybe you just need to let it out. You know, in single combat or something?

6:11 AM

Juan: Ha! Are you challenging me to single combat? While riding a … what is that, anyway? Haven't seen those since the elementary school playground.

Cortex: *Wait, he's seriously taking you up on combat?*

V: *Do not underestimate a villain's honor. He NEEDS to defeat me. Watch this.* What? You too scared to fight me? Wow. So big and tough when you're holding a nuke button, but after all these years, you can't even take me on a butt scooter.

Juan: Not true! I simply ... have better things to do right now.

V: Pfft. Like what? It's not even time to set off the nuke yet. You just know that no matter what, I will ALWAYS be better than you.

Cortex: *V, I don't like this. Let me fight him, and you go take care of the nuke. Can't have you do this while you're injured.*

V: *Hey, it's okay. You don't always have to be the hero. Let me give it a shot for once.*

6:12 AM
Cortex: ...

Cortex: *Okay.*

Cortex: *Go get him, you weirdo who is obsessed with kneecaps.*

Juan: That's it. Come at me.

V: Hahaha, you think you're gonna win? You really think you're some-Juan? Hahaha. *Okay, he set down the button. Go get it. Sneaky sneaky.*

Juan: DON'T MAKE FUN OF MY NAME!

V: Oh yeah? You Juan-t a piece of this?

6:13 AM

Cortex: *Yikes, that was a really close swipe to V's throat. Gotta get to the remote. V? I know it's hard on the scooter, but can you get his back to it? He keeps watching me and you. Or maybe go with the bashing-his-head route. That seems to work sometimes.*

> **V:** *Can't reach his head, but I can get his kneecaps.*

Unknown Source: *slice*

> **Cortex:** *Okay, great. His attention's drawn away. Now to sneak up to the remote.*

V: Haha! You are now wearing shorts! Aww, is that a Little Pony tattoo? Is that why you always wear pants?

> **Juan:** I'll get you for that! And your little butt scooter, too!

6:14 AM

Cortex: *Nearly there. Wow, how does Himari do this pickpocket stuff? I have to keep making sure he's not watching. Why'd he drop it so far away?*

> **V:** *Babe. Juan has EXQUISITE kneecaps. This is going to be fun.*

Cortex: *Glad you're enjoying yourself. Okay, leaning down. Knees cracking. That's not good. And got it.*

> **Juan:** Auuugghhhh! What is WRONG with you, you little kneecap-loving pervert!

V: I got one! Oh, Juan, it's so lame when you just lie there bleeding.

Juan: Auuuuugghhh!

6:15 AM
V: Oh, by the way, Juan, look what Caleb has! I'm so proud of you, babe!

Caleb: Yeah, much as I hate Juan and the fact he betrayed you to the SA and they brainwashed you into a mindless killer, I can understand why Himari didn't like hearing that other man's screams. Maybe we should talk about this weird obsession.

V: *Oh, don't worry, this is just a rock I found. It's just funny watching Juan scream as if he actually lost a kneecap when he really only has a little cut on his knee.* Heeheeheeheehee.

Caleb: *All righty. Guess it's all up to them back in Pennsylvania. Let's hope Dad remembers …*

TACO + BURRITO (AND ... THE OTHERS)

JUNE 17

6:15 AM

Himari: Fifteen wrong answers. I'm going to get locked out soon.

> **Dad:** Okay, um, let's see. Maybe it was that one nickname I used to call you when you were little ... what was it ... ?

Kevin: *Hey, guys.*

> **Himari:** *Little busy right now, Kev.* Okay, which one, Dad? You called me a lot of weird things.

Kevin: *Yo, Taco. I want to talk-o.*

> **V:** Kevin, no one cares about tea and coffee right now.

6:16 AM
Kevin: Alberta.

> **Dad:** Gosh, I can't remember. Something science-y, I think?

Kevin: OHMYGOSH GUYS IT'S "ALBERTA" AND NOW I'M YELLING IN THE MIDDLE OF THE LOBBY AND SOME WOMAN DEFINITELY JUST TUCKED HER BRIEFCASE CLOSER AND SCUTTLED AWAY. YEAH, I SAW THAT, HELEN.

    Himari: Oh! Kevin, you're a genius. Dad. Was it Alberta? Like "Albert-a Einstein"?

Kevin: *Even though she's smarter than Einstein. I keep telling her that.*

    Dad: Ohhh, you know what, yeah, try that.

6:17 AM
Himari: It worked, I'm in. Kevin, how did you even remember that? I think Dad has called me that in front of you, like, once.

    Kevin: Sure, I forget most stuff, but I remember everything about you. I have since day one.

Himari: Aww, Kev. I don't even know what to say. Okay, going to see if I can—hey, what are you—no!

    Kevin: What's that noise? It sounds like a siren.

Unknown Source: Launch Sequence Activated.

    Gladkins: Bwahahahaha! Thanks for logging me in! Nothing you can do now! Shoot me if you want, but nothing takes back pushing the big red button!

Unknown Source: Counting down. Ten.

    Himari: *Omg, omg, I have to undo this.*

Unknown Source: Eight.

Himari: *Omg, there's so much code. How can I do this in ten seconds? Omg.*

Unknown Source: Five.

Himari: *Okay, going back through. Dad always puts that one phrase in the code ... Aha!*

Unknown Source: Two.

Himari: *Back, back, reverse, send* — DONE!

Unknown Source: Launch canceled. Disabling missiles.

Himari: Okay, I'm going to shut down the grid entirely. How is everyone doing?

6:18 AM
Cortex: Kevin, heard from all the individual launch sites?

Kevin: Just waiting on Bentonville. I guess they have a spotty connection.

V: So they've ALL been successful? (Besides Arkansas, anyway.) That's some insane heroism.

Kevin: Yeah, but from what I can tell, quite a few people were taken out in the process. I've been trying to keep it to myself, distracting y'all with the tea stuff, but many places only have one or two heroes and villains left. We lost a lot of good people today.

V: … Oh. Well. I guess … there were some true heroes today. Some old-fashioned, brave-hearted, real heroes.

Kevin: Just heard back from Arkansas.

6:19 AM
Kevin: They shot him, but he managed to kill off the last SA guy before he slumped to the ground. Losing a lot of blood and can't see straight. Too far away from an ambulance or hospital.

Kevin: V, says he knows you. Name's Slicer. I'm not getting any more responses. Which obviously means he's probably fine.

V: Oh my gosh. S-slicer. He … he ended up being a hero in the end after all. I knew you could do it, buddy.

Cortex: He always was one. I mean, he did save me. I'm sorry, V.

V: *Sniffle.* It's fine. I'm just proud of him. Proud of us all.

V: Hey, Himari, how's it going?

Himari: Churning out some real whack code here, boss. No one's going to be able to set up a launch sequence for these missiles anytime soon. Hear that, Gladkins? That's right. Go sit in the corner like a good boy until the police come for you.

Cortex: Speaking of, we should probably wait around for them to take some-Juan away too. Glad V keeps threatening to "cut off" his other kneecap. He's been sticking to the ground.

6:20 AM
V: *Heehee, it's really funny. He's literally squealing.*

Kevin: And not in a manly way. Liam says the Indy nuke's all taken care of and wants to know if you guys want to meet him for tacos tomorrow to celebrate a teamwork bonding experience well done. Says he'll get to work on the serum as soon as he makes amends with Billy for storming out on him like a sad little hare.

Himari: Never thought I'd say this, but I'm looking forward to some tacos with Liam and my best friend-os. Over and out, you guys. Way to save the world before normal people wake up in the morning.

EVENING TALK SHOW TRANSCRIPT

Ted: Wow, those are some amazing videos from what's come to be called "The Rise of the Heroes." Sounds like a movie title.

Paul: Sure does. Heroes, villains, sidekicks, and henchmen all banded together this morning to make a coordinated attack on all the Shadow Assassin bases in the country to take out thirty-two nuclear bombs with destinations all over the United States.

Roger: And an unknown duo took down the Shadow Assassin headquarters itself, which apparently was in Pennsylvania this whole time. Who would have thought?

Joe: That's right, Roger. Glad to have you back, buddy. That was some real bad food poisoning. Speaking of back, sounds like Kosuke Takahashi is back too. TakahashiCorp has yet to release a statement, but it appears he's safe and sound, rescued from SA HQ.

Paul: Sure thing. Apparently the police have been looking over all these headquarters, and there's some pretty scary stuff there. Don't think the SA will be able to come back from this for a long, long time. Not without their state-of-the-art torture chambers.

Ted: And let's not forget those handwritten records of every member of the Shadow Assassins in the office of a Mr. Gladkins. That guy apparently does not do well with technology.

Roger: Well, Ted, our hats are off to all of the heroes, villains, sidekicks, and henchmen who gave their lives to keep us from being blown off the face of the earth.

Joe: You will be remembered. Better make a toast to that, eh, boys? I got some nice beer for us.

Roger: We'll be making toasts here ... until after the break.

GROUP CHAT
AUGUST 8

3:02 PM
Cortex: Got here as soon as I could. You said it was an emergency? Turned on the group chat in case V needs to come to our rescue. She's looped in but in the middle of a charity event back home. Should be done any minute now.

> **Liam:** If by emergency, you mean I haven't given you a good ole hug for the past two months, then come on in here.

Cortex: You did not just make me drive down to Indy for a hug, did you, Liam?

Cortex: Also, I like what you did with the place. Turning it into a coffee shop and all. What are you planning on doing with the rest of the cabins?

> **Liam:** Figured we could offer folks a home who need one. And give them a job at the shop. Billy was talking about expanding it into a bakery. We have plenty of space to do a lot of good.

3:03 PM
Cortex: Well, I'm sure you'll get plenty of customers. Also, if you're looking to hire, Kevin's starting to worry about the whole theater-major thing at Ball State. Maybe you could turn one of those cabins into a stage or something.

> **Liam:** Maybe that will make up for the whole stabbing him in the face, you know?

Cortex: Yes. Oh, yes, nice hug. Okay, Liam, emergency?

> **Liam:** Sure thing. Follow me downstairs.

3:04 PM
Liam: Watch the last step. We built some of the steps a little longer than others to trap burglars, but honestly, I'd just feel bad if some poor fella broke his leg, burglar or not.

Cortex: How very Victorian of you. Wowser, this looks just like Himari's room, but with more tubes of liquid than robotics pieces.

> **Liam:** Yeah, thought I'd put that college education to use, you know? Now, I know I told y'all it would be a few months to get the serum right —

Cortex: You have the serum?

3:05 PM
Liam: I wanted to make sure it wouldn't cause any random mutations, had to get the graphic designer to create a nice label for the bottle — don't even get me started on how lazy some get with the vectors, my friend. Took some time to finally collaborate on something, but he didn't put no one hundred ten percent in.

Cortex: Liam.

> **Liam:** But a little less than two months later, voila. I wanted you to have the first vial. Don't worry, I have the formula written on my computer. I'm planning on replicating and mass-producing this next week.

> **Liam:** We should have everyone's powers back to them in no time. Might get some side effects like some nausea and ability to make more reckless decisions, but shouldn't last too long.

3:06 PM
Cortex: Wow, umm, thanks, Liam.

> **Liam:** What's wrong, friend-o? You got a little glaze in your eyes right there.

Cortex: It's ... sweat. Liam, I can't tell you how much I've wanted this. Ever since you took away my powers, I wanted to get them back.

> **Liam:** I think I'm hearing a "but" coming. Don't worry. Little Liam can take it.

Cortex: I've been thinking about something for two months. Maybe you can answer it.

> **Liam:** Sure thing. I can answer anything, except for physics questions. Some folks seem to get their sciences mixed up.

3:07 PM
Cortex: Gladkins. I figure since you were buddy-buddy with everyone at SA, you might have better insights about him.

Cortex: I mean, you had good motivation to stab me with serum. No really, you did. No need to get misty-eyed, man. But I don't understand him. He wanted to nuke the United States, but we don't know why except that he's evil.

Cortex: I thought maybe you could provide some answers.

Liam: The only tougher nut to crack than Hulga was Gladkins, but from what I can tell in my research on him, he started off like a normal guy, same as you and me.

Cortex: *Same as me, got it.*

Liam: And after losing a job, a wife, a kid … things spiraled out of control. He was what Mama liked to call an All-In-One Human. A control freak. Mama had weird idioms.

Liam: Life done him wrong, so he decided to do it wrong right back. Not saying it was all that polite or anything, but the more control he tried to have, the less he seemed to gain. It was like he was clenching his fist around the water in the lake. Until it slowly trickled out.

3:08 PM
Cortex: *Got it. Lost his mind.*

Liam: That answer your question?

Cortex: …

Cortex: Liam, I can't accept this serum. If anything, the powers would make me tempted to jump back into hero work. The wrong kind of hero work. Can't tell you how long it took to shake off the media when they kept asking if Cortex would have a comeback. Half of them thought I faked the power-loss thing for publicity.

Liam: Yeah, that does sound a teensy bit familiar. Dad couldn't get the media away from him, even after he claimed he "retired." People don't know what to do when their favorite heroes turn in their capes.

3:09 PM
Cortex: *Yeeeeeah, definitely wasn't disappointed at ALL when I found out my number-one hero turned up washed-up at my mom's party.*

Cortex: Before I get to Dimension's point, I think I want to do something more with my life. Starting with helping you with the graphic design on these bottles. Seriously, dude, why'd you pick some rando?

> **Liam:** Felt bad. He left a business card in a coffee shop, and I like to help small businesses. Well, send me what you got. No vectors, please.

Cortex: Wouldn't think of it. Haha.

> **Liam:** And Cortex … ?

Cortex: Yeah?

> 3:10 PM
> **Liam:** Just take it for the road. In case you have to use it.

Cortex: Oh, Liam, I don't kno—

> **Liam:** If anything, it can give you some inspiration on what NOT to do when designing a label for a super important serum.

Cortex: I guess I'll let it inspire me, haha. Thanks, Liam.

Liam: …

Liam: You —you initiated that hug?

3:11 PM
Cortex: Well, sure. You're my friend-o, aren't you?

Liam: Don't cry, don't cry, don't cry. Yeah. Yeah, I guess
I am.

PRIVATE MESSAGE

AUGUST 11

8:49 AM

Himari: Hello, nobody. It's your good pal Himari. Figured Kevin has a "manly diary" using my tech, so I might as well make a little entry myself.

Himari: Speaking of my tech. Dad has agreed to let me have the SA nukes to play with. I have some great ideas for turning those former SA headquarters into nuclear power sites. They've got a lot of the infrastructure already there, and most of them are in remote locations. Besides, I think there are a lot of former secretaries, henchmen, and sidekicks who might be looking for a job.

8:50 AM

Himari: I don't think Dad's totally over the whole arms-dealing mission of TakahashiCorp, but at least he's letting me take some of it in my own direction. At least for now, TakahashiCorp is focusing on defensive weapons. No more nukes rolling off the line.

Himari: Anyway, figured I'd log on here because nobody's really home. V dragged Caleb along to help with a kids' event they have going on at one of the local charities. She's started really liking kids. I think it's freaking my brother out a little. But it's better than her original Peace Corps plan, so he should be thankful.

8:51 AM
Himari: I'm so proud of V. She even started going to a counselor and is working on taking out her insecurity and aggression through exercise and yoga instead of, you know, killing people. That poor counselor. I can't imagine the sort of things V says all casually. "Oh, yeah, so that one time when they had me rip out that guy's spleen — "

Himari: Oof. Hope that counselor is being paid a whole lot better than Hulga.

8:52 AM
Himari: Speaking of Hulga, Kevin went to visit her for the day. He goes every once in a while and she makes stroganoff. Enough to take some home too. It's pretty good. Maybe I'll go with him sometime. He says she's picked up a job as a lunch lady and likes it a lot better than the SA.

Himari: So ... Kevin. I think my brother has finally gotten over giving him death glares every time he even speaks to me. So that's good.

Himari: I'm really going to miss him when I go back to school.

8:53 AM
Himari: Here's the thing about Kevin. I've always been surrounded by a bunch of really smart, really talented people. But I never really felt secure. I felt like I was kind of on my own to figure stuff out.

Himari: But when Kevin's around, I feel like I don't have to worry so much. Perform so much. He doesn't really care what Himari he sees, whether it's Super-Tech Himari or Taco-Falling-Apart Himari. And he always seems to know just what to say to cheer me up.

8:54 AM

Himari: We had our usual Taco Tuesday date tonight. You'd think I'd get sick of Mexican by now, but that's the great thing about Mexican food. So much variety, so many spices. It's always delicious. You just can't go wrong.

Himari: Kind of like Kevin. I never know what weirdness he's going to come up with next, but whatever it is, I'm looking forward to it.

Himari: I love my burrito. And you can tell him I said so, non-manly diary.

SIDEKICK SUPPORT GROUP FORUM

TOPIC: QUITTING BEING A SIDEKICK AND DATING A HOT HENCHMAN

Kevin: I'm not exactly looking for answers to this thread, unless they're somewhere along the lines of, "Gosh, I sure wish I could be Kevin," but figured there's nothing hotter to a girlfriend than finding out her boyfriend posted on Meta-Match after they made their relationship official.

But let me tell you about this girl. Because she doesn't think she's something, but she really is. I can't get all the words right, so I'll try to put it in some Kevin-isms.

She makes the spotlights on stage dim in comparison. Most beautiful brown eyes you've ever seen and can somehow rock both pink and black hair.

She's like a perfect stage manager. Always in the background, but man, would everything fall apart without her. I wish she could have center stage for once. She deserves it.

She's beautiful and smart, something that doesn't seem to compute in that brain of hers.

And somehow she sees something in me.

Folks, I can't put into words how she makes me feel. I'd give up the stage, I'd give up my jokes (gasp, horror), and I'd give up being a sidekick to spend a moment with her.

Although you won't see me quitting the stage anytime soon (landed a lead role in Next to Normal; come to Marion if you happen to be bored this fall), and she cannot, alas, stifle my humor, we both decided I could put an end to my sidekick days. She wants to quit being a henchman too.

After all, we can be better villains and heroes when we put the masks away.

With my hero down for the count, and my inability to grind coffee beans, I think I need to set my sights on something else as graduation approaches next year. Something tells me I'd love to do something with theater in the local area, but a certain former SA member has ideas about opening a coffee shop called "Billy's Baristas."

If he can show me the ropes, he said he might have a mighty nice job available for a friend-o.

Says we can bring my improv theater troupe from my school to put on some performances and do open mic nights. Despite what my hero's girlfriend says, this ex-SA dude says I have a nice voice. Plus he mentioned turning one of his old cabins into a theater space for the community. Maybe all those theater history classes I skipped will finally pay off.

Either way, I can't wait to see my henchwoman blossom. She has so many great ideas for inventions, and no doubt, will have a bazillion job offers as soon as she graduates. Maybe she'd be open to the idea of a stay-at-home dad. She did mention wanting to turn her dad's company into a state-of-the-art place working on clean nuclear energy and helpful inventions.

Instead of exploding stuff. I think that's a pretty good direction for the company to go.

Guess I won't be hopping on this app a whole lot anymore. I see why Cortex dropped it. As much fun as I have reading these threads, I think I lost something of myself in here. I think we all did. And now, one day at a time, we're piecing ourselves back together again.

In the meantime, I have my whole life ahead of me, and if many a celebratory taco meal goes well, a whole life ahead of me to share with the best sidekick someone could ask for.

No wait, a hero.

Do not miss

DEAR HADES

A Standalone in the Dear Hero Storyworld.

Coming Soon from L2L2 Publishing.

Until then, please enjoy this bonus scene!

BONUS: PRIVATE MESSAGE
SEPTEMBER 10

Liam changed chat name to "My New Greek God Friend-o"

6:47 PM
Liam: Hope you don't mind the chat name. My friend Billy was absolutely freaking out when he saw your moniker on Meta-Match.

Liam: He's a Percy Jackson fan and all that.

Liam: Unless Greek gods hate Percy Jackson. Do they find it appropriating? Should I go for something more up your alley? Like Medea or Oedipus? You're a brooding dude. You seem like you'd appreciate some good ole regicide.

6:48 PM
Liam: Anyway, I didn't even know they had Greek deities and stuff on there. Well, it's a major honor to meet you, sir.

> **Hades:** Right, yeah. The line between Greek gods and superheroes really isn't all that broad. Powers, egos, ridiculous outfits—we got 'em all.

Liam: True, I hear that Great Guy is an offspring of a deity ... shall I hazard a guess to which one?

Hades: Zeus. Who else would try to force themselves into every girl's DM? Like father like, well, demigod son.

6:49 PM
Liam: Thanks for reaching out to me in my forum "Guys Who Like Dead Stuff." Apparently, once you try to start chatting someone's ear off about taxidermy, they ghost you on this app. Even the villains. Some friend-os, huh?

Hades: Yes, yes. We both have a thing with dead things. Anyway, I was actually hoping you could help me out.

6:50 PM
Liam: Shoot. Helping a Greek deity who offered to autograph my taxidermy bunny? Why on earth would I say no?

Hades: I'm having a bit of relationship trouble ...

Liam: You? Your photos with Persephone, as my friend-o Kevin would say, are, in fact, "the bomb." You're like the epitome of a good relationship in Ancient Greek mythology.

Liam: Or do Greek gods not know what bombs are?

Liam: Okay, so imagine your colon after you've had a dubious taco ...

6:51 PM
Hades: I've been around for thousands of years, Liam. I know what bombs are.

Hades: Also, please never offer me a taco ever.

Hades: Anyway, it's not with Persephone. We're actually doing really great. But it's with ... the fam.

Liam: Ah.

Hades: Half of them think I kidnapped her ...

6:52 PM
Liam: Tell me you at least offered her some french toast. I got a real spankin' recipe with pralines for your next kidnappee if you want it.

Hades: And the other half see we're doing really well and want the same for themselves.

Hades: Um, I DIDN'T kidnap her. I thought I was clear on that in the taxidermy forum.

Liam: So that's a no to the recipe?

6:53 PM
Hades: I'm just not sure what to do. Seph and I only get to hang out a few months out of the year, and my family keeps invading the Underworld to answer one of the above questions. They pester me even AFTER she leaves. A lord of the underworld needs his privacy, you know?

Hades: So I'm reaching out to anyone who has possible ideas.

Hades: You mentioned being a "relationship expert."

6:54 PM
Liam: Shoot, I don't mean to brag, but I definitely brought my besties Kev and Mari together this past summer.

Liam: Death threats and kidnappings can do that to a couple, you know. ;)

Hades: Again, I didn't kidnap her.

Liam: But I can't take all the credit. Honestly, this whole Meta-Match app brought them together in the first place. But I will say stabbing people in the jugular and singing campfire songs does work its wonders.

6:55 PM
Hades: Wait a moment, you said Meta-Match brought them together?

Liam: I really think the campfire songs are what ultimately did it.

Hades: Like an app where people can meet and match?

6:56 PM
Liam: That seems to be the gist of the whole thing, yes. But I like to think of it as a haven for taxidermy enthusiasts.

Hades: Actually, that's not a half-bad idea. A place where people can pair up. That could help me with my issue of gods and heroes constantly asking me for dating advice.

Liam: Heroes too?

Hades: Yeah, well, most of them are dead. Most people I meet are dead anyway. But I guess they want to meet the love of their life in Tartarus because they spent too much of their lives stabbing people instead of writing love letters or something.

6:57 PM
Hades: But even the ALIVE ones are breaking down the gates of the Underworld and giving Cerberus a belly rub just to get to me and get my "take" on their love life.

Hades: But with an app like this ...

Liam: You could get a little more peace o' mind.

6:58 PM
Hades: Now for the relatives who won't stop asking me if I kidnapped Persephone ...

Liam: I mean, you could always make an "About Page" on the app and tell your story. That's what the founders of Meta-Match did.

Hades: They did?

Liam: Yeeeah, but no one else reads About Pages except for ole Liam over here. I like to make the app developers feel special and like their effort was worth it.

6:59 PM
Hades: Maybe I could make it mandatory to read before someone signed up for the app.

Liam: Forcing someone to read the prologue? Now that's cold, good sir.

Hades: Thank you, Liam, for your time. You've given me plenty to work off of.

Hades has left the chat

7:00 PM

Liam: Is that still a no to the french toast recipe?

7:03 PM

Liam: Aww, man. I never even got him to sign Mr. Hopper.

REVIEWS

Did you love this book? Please leave a review!

It helps our authors more than you can possibly know.

Thank you so much!

~The L2L2 Publishing Team

HOPE'S ACKNOWLEDGMENTS

First, to my Lord and Savior Jesus Christ. I can often feel like the sidekick in many stories. I feel left out, forgotten, and often like Kevin, I drop the ball. Thank you for being the hero in my life and trusting me with several missions, even when I can't even make coffee properly.

Of course, I cannot write this section without thanking Alyssa. She's hilarious and deals with my high-maintenance episodes of: I Can't Write for Beans, Please Let Me Quit Now. She refuses to let me drop out of the race, and I would have never written this sequel if not for her.

To Cyle and Tessa, my wonderful agents, who relentlessly push these weird projects I send their way. Thanks for taking a chance on such weird humans, and we absolutely cannot wait to see what comes of these stories years down the road.

To Michele, you were our hero. Not only did you fall in love with these stories, but you took them on when their home unexpectedly went under. We are so grateful for you, your encouragement, and for doing more projects with you.

This was such an out-of-the-box idea, we never thought we would find a home for it. But here we are with a loving home and a champion editor. So so so grateful for you.

ALYSSA'S
ACKNOWLEDGMENTS

And here we are, once more, at the end of a silly, zany novel.

First, hello Hope, I acknowledge you, you magnificent unicorn. I am so glad we could write this together. It's the most fun writing I've ever had. Thank you for all the doors you've held open for me in the writing world. I would never be here now without you.

Gotta say thank you to the OG hero, Jesus Christ. Thank you, Lord, for being with us through all our crazy. Your story is the ultimate story, and it inspires me every day.

And to my family, Mama, Daddy, Steph, Nana, Papa, "The Weird Family," Grandma and Grandpa, "the aunts," and all ten million of you rooting for me and sharing everything I post on social media and anxiously awaiting my next book—you all are the best.

To the Taylor University prowrites, you guys inspire us constantly.

To Megan Burkhart, whose idea for a Midwest hero/villain encounter sparked Liam, my personal favorite character in this book.

Cyle's Henchfolks, Tessa, Cyle, and the crew—Hope and I know how insane we are. Thank you for being willing to go along for the ride. Cyle, thank you for throwing wide the doors of the publishing industry to two timid professional writing students all those years ago. We hope to make you proud.

To Linda Taylor, who always believed in us, supported us, and taught us everything we know.

To my best friends/sisters Stephanie and Julianna, who have put up with my weird for longer than anyone. Julianna, we've come a long way from writing about our propeller-hat adventures on lined paper at the playground, and you never once suggested that maybe this whole author thing was a bad idea. Stephanie, I appreciate you actually reading my books. Even if I never succeeded in sharing my love of books with you, I hope I did share my love of you.

To Michele, who took us in and welcomed us to the L2L2 family — what would we do without you?

To the Pizza Squad, who always support their strange writer pals.

And to all the first responders around the world making a difference — you're the real superheroes.

ABOUT THE AUTHOR

HOPE BOLINGER

Hope Bolinger is a graduate of Taylor University's professional writing program and a former literary agent at C.Y.L.E. More than 1000 of her works have been featured in various publications ranging from HOOKED to Writer's Digest.

Some of her books include the Blaze trilogy (IlluminateYA), Roseville Romances (Mountain Brook Ink), and the Sparrow Duology to release in 2023.

She's a theater nerd, occasional runway model, is way too obsessed with superheroes, and may be caught in a red cloak, fairy wings, or a Belle costume in her downtown, for no reason.

Her favorite way to procrastinate is to connect with her readers on social media. Check out more about her at hopebolinger.com.

Hope loves to hear from her readers! Follow her on social media, check out her website, or drop her a line to let her know what you thought of Dear Henchman. *Happy reading!*

———

www.HopeBolinger.com
Facebook: @HopeBolinger
Twitter: @HopeBolinger
Instagram: @HopeKBolinger

ABOUT THE AUTHOR

ALYSSA ROAT

Alyssa Roat grew up in Tucson, Arizona, but her heart is in Great Britain, the inspiration for her YA contemporary fantasy *Wraithwood*. She is the managing editor at Mountain Brook Fire, a former literary agent at C.Y.L.E., and a freelance writer and editor. She holds a B.S. in professional writing from Taylor University.

She has also worked for Illuminate YA Publishing, Little Lamb Books, Zondervan Library, Sherpa Editing Services, and as the online editor and a staff writer for *The Echo News*.

Over 250 of her works have been featured in various publications, from newspapers, to national magazines, to anthologies.

Alyssa is also the author of the Wraithwood Trilogy (Mountain Brook Fire) and the co-author with Hope of the Roseville Romance series (Mountain Brook Ink).

Her name is a pun, which means you can learn more about her at alyssawrote.com or on Instagram, Twitter, and Facebook as @alyssawrote.

Alyssa loves to hear from her readers! Follow her on social media, check out her website, or drop her a line to let her know what you thought of Dear Henchman. *Happy reading!*

———

www.AlyssaWrote.com
Facebook: @AlyssaWrote
Twitter: @AlyssaWrote
Instagram: @AlyssaWrote

More from L2L2 Publishing

If you enjoyed this book, you may also enjoy:

LAURA L. ZIMMERMAN

Keen

BANSHEE SONG SERIES
BOOK ONE

Half-faerie Caoine has no control over the banshee lament she sings each night, predicting the death of others. A senior in a brand new high school, she expects the same response she's received at every other school: judgment from fellow students over her unusual eyes and unnaturally white skin and hair. However, for the first time in her life she finds friends. Real friends. Life spins out of control when her lament comes out during the day, those whose death she predicts die right in front of her, and a dark faerie known only as the Unseelie prince blames Caoine. Her curse is not supposed to work like that. In a race against time, Caoine must uncover the Unseelie prince's identity and stop a spell before it unleashes hell on earth, all while trying to control her banshee song and finding a place among her peers. Senior year just got real.

More from L2L2 Publishing

If you enjoyed this book, you may also enjoy:

Leah spends her days scrubbing floors, polishing silver, and meekly curtsying to nobility. Nothing distinguishes her from the other commoners serving at the palace, except her red hair. And her secret friendship with Rafe, the Crown Prince of Imperia. But Leah's safe, ordinary world begins to splinter. Rafe's parents announce his betrothal to a foreign princess, and she unearths a plot to overthrow the royal family. When she reports it without proof, her life shatters completely when the queen banishes her for treason. Harbored by an unusual group of nuns, Leah must secure Rafe's safety before it's too late. But her quest reveals a villain far more sinister than an ambitious nobleman with his eye on the throne. Can a common maidservant summon the courage to fight for her dearest friend?

More from L2L2 Publishing

If you enjoyed this book, you may also enjoy:

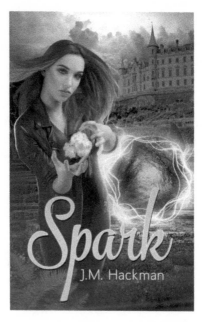

Brenna James wants three things for her sixteenth birthday: to find her history notes before the test, to have her mother return from her business trip, and to stop creating fire with her bare hands. Yeah, that's so not happening. Unfortunately. When Brenna learns her mother is missing in an alternate reality called Linneah, she travels through a portal to find her. Against her will. Who knew portals even existed? But Brenna's arrival in Linneah begins the fulfillment of an ancient prophecy, including a royal murder and the theft of Linneah's most powerful relic: the Sacred Veil. Hold up. Can everything just slow down for a sec? Left with no other choice, Brenna and her new friend Baldwin pursue the thief into the dangerous woods of Silvastamen. When they spy an army marching toward Linneah, Brenna is horrified. Can she find the veil, save her mother, and warn Linneah in time?

More from L2L2 Publishing

If you enjoyed this book, you may also enjoy:

Huntress Ro LeFèvre is offered a job to hunt a pest plaguing the Seven Seas. A siren has been sinking the king of Angleterre's ships, and in turn, vast amounts of his wealth. Fleeing heartbreak, Ro gladly accepts, but there's just one problem. The king will credit the Marquis de la Valère, and no other women are allowed on the voyage. Ro will just see about that. Hiring an all-female crew without the king's knowledge, Ro hopes they will follow her to the Caribbean, not take the gold and flee. But when Ro is plunged deep into the ocean by the siren she's being paid to kill, presented the sirens' side of the story at knife point, and pressed to join them or die, Ro must decide whether to complete her mission, join the sirens, or something in between. Before the sirens sink her ship.

WHERE WILL WE TAKE YOU NEXT?

Enjoy *Keen,*
Relish *Common,*
Discover *Spark,*
and Sink into *Silence the Siren.*

All at
www.love2readlove2writepublishing.com/bookstore
or your local or online retailer.

Happy Reading!
~The L2L2 Publishing Team

ABOUT L2L2 PUBLISHING

Love2ReadLove2Write Publishing, LLC is a small traditional press, dedicated to clean or Christian speculative fiction.

Speculative fiction includes any fantastical element, and usually falls in the genres or the many subgenres of Fantasy or Science Fiction.

We seek stunning tales masterfully told, and we strive to create an exquisite publishing experience for our authors and to produce quality fiction for our readers.

Dear Henchman is at the heart of what we publish: a riveting tale with speculative elements that will delight our readers.

Visit www.L2L2Publishing.com to view our submissions guidelines, find our other titles, or learn more about us.

And if you love our books, please leave a review!

Happy Reading!

~The L2L2 Publishing Team

Lightning Source UK Ltd.
Milton Keynes UK
UKHW010902161222
414026UK00001B/283